I0692036

Bugs in the Wall,
Turkeys in the Ditch

by

Alexandria May Ausman

This book is a work of fiction. Any references to historical events, real people, or real places, are used fictitiously. Other names, characters, places, and events are products of the author's imagination, and any resemblance to actual events or persons, living or dead, is entirely coincidental.

Copyright © 2025 by Alexandria May Ausman

All rights reserved, including the right to reproduce this book or portions thereof in any form whatsoever.

Book cover illustration by Alexandria May Ausman
Editor: Jon M. Ausman

Library of Congress Control Number: 2025918752

ISBN: 978-1-963335-53-8 (ebook)
ISBN: 978-1-963335-52-1 (paperback)

Published By:
Ausman & Cousins LLC
1700 North Monroe Street
Suite 11, Box 284
Tallahassee, Florida 32303-0501

For author interviews: ausman@embarqmail.com

Das Kaiser Haus Series

The Rise of the Priceless (Chapters 1 to 10)
Metal Illness (Chapters 11 to 19)
Jonas the Vampire (Chapters 20 to 29)
Prince of the Elders (Chapters 30 to 40)
Leo's Lamb (Chapters 41 to 50)
Mastermind Malfred (Chapters 51 to 58)
Priceless Lost (Chapters 59 to 67)
Broken Silver (Chapters 68 to 74)

The Collar King Series

Return to Das Kaiser Haus (Chapters 1 to 7)
Felicity's Child (Chapters 8 to 14)
Tears of the Violin (Chapters 15 to 22)
The Golden Collar (Chapters 23 to 30)
Rise of the Mortar King (Chapters 31 to 38)
Prisoner of the Stone Palace (Chapters 39 to 46)
Mortar Transformation (Chapters 47 to 54)
Taube Returns (Chapters 55 to 62)
Chocolate Dreams (Chapters 63 to 70)
Pocket Soup (Chapters 71 to 78)
Lucus's Revenge (Chapters 79 to 86)
Night of the Stasi (Chapter 87 to 94)
Revenge of the Mortar King (Chapter 95 to 102)

The Most Brutal Man in Europe Series

Claus's Revelations (Chapters 1 to 8)
Priceless Changes (Chapters 9 to 17)
Silver Well (Chapters 18 to 25)
Book Four (Coming soon)

The Psycho Series

Cemetery Kid Redux (Chapters 1 to 20)
Stop Calling Me Psycho (Chapters 21 to 33)
Motor-Psycho (Chapters 34 to 44)
Delusion of the Collar and the Key (Chapters 45 to 53)
Brutality's Prisoner (Chapters 54 to 64)
Aesthetic Akathisia (Chapters 65 to 74)
Metallic Burden (Chapters 75 to 83)

27 Masters Series

Anita the Benevolent (Chapters 1 to 7)
The Beast and the Witch (Chapters 8 to 16)
High Priestess of Schizophrenia (Chapters 17 to 24)
The Professional Dominatrix (Chapters 25 to 33)
Triangle of Trust (Chapters 34 to 41)

Stand Alone Books

The Grannybat's Weird Tales & Gothic Stories Volume 1

Book Nine Characters: Bugs in the Wall, Turkeys in the Ditch

Angie: a former Master
Baker, Doctor: a clinical psychiatrist
Bobby: uncle of Missy
Boyd: a deputy sheriff, a secret Master
Carla: spouse of Dennis
Cathy: a deputy sheriff, dispatcher
Charlie: a law officer in next county over
Cheryl Rutgers: a county manager of DCFS
Christian Axel: secret husband of Psycho/Rachel, trainer and original Master
Cindy Slater: a town slut
Circe: a previous Master
Dale: owner of Night's Station
Debbie: Psycho's psychopathic and sadistic mother
Delleh: Queen of the Green Rings, deceased
Dennis: the county sheriff
Dirk: a drug addict child kidnapper
Dude: a command hallucination, an aggressive anger shard of Psycho
Eva: Cindy's mother
Fax: a shard of Psycho
Frankie: a DCFS caseworker
Ginger: a FemDom, Mistress Ten
Gothic Barbie: a vengeful, sexually sadist Dominant shard
James: an abandoned, neglected child

Jane: DCFS employee under Ruth

Javier: a deceased alleged repeat offender

Jennie: Dirk's drug addict girlfriend

Johnny: Nikki's foster child

Jon Ausman: the current Keyholder

Julia: a friend of Sheryl and ex-foster mother

Julie: a previous sadistic Mistress who fled the law

Kenzia Bosell: Shady's mother, a Gypsy

Kerrie: a kidnapped child

Kevin: deceased spouse of Delleh

Lavinia Boswell: Shady's daughter, a Gypsy

Linda: a deputy sheriff

Looper: a disembodied voice, Psycho's narrative hallucination

Lucy Turnbol: a therapeutic foster parent

Maddy: a child who was raped and murdered, Angie's best friend

Marcus: son of Missy

Marcus: daughter of Missy

Mark: a deputy sheriff

Mary: a Maiden who takes care of Psycho's children

Matthew: a deceased submissive

McNutts: a judge

Mickey: Connie's deceased former boyfriend

Minnie: drug addict mother of Skylar

Missy Links: mother of Marcus and Marcus

Nancy: a baby killer

Niemand: Master Boyd's new name for Psycho

Nikki Pool: a neglectful mother

Nora: a DHS employee
Paul: Maddy's older brother
Paula: a county DCFS employee
PC: a shard of Psycho
Psycho: a schizophrenic trying to survive
Psycho Tron: a shard of Psycho
Rachel: Psycho's birth name, Simon is Rachel
Randall: a deputy sheriff, a bull
Richard Cummings: adoptive father of Skylar
Ronald: Nancy's accomplice
Samuel: a psychopathic teenager
Sarah: Nikki's foster child
Seine: a fire dog
Shady Boswell: a Gypsy leader
Sheryl: a DCFS manager, the 17th Master
Simon Brag: a command hallucination shard of Psycho, her lost inner self
Skylar: a foster child
Stephanie: a nosy high school classmate
The Chose One: a shard of Psycho
Timmy: Psycho's spouse
Thomas Windbush: a rapist of babies
Tom Turnbol: a therapeutic foster parent
Trenton: a deputy sheriff
Turner, Doctor: a clinical psychiatrist
Will: a deputy sheriff
Willa: a dead baby

Preface

There were so many moments in our life where things shouldn't have happened the way they did. Paths would often get mixed up or crossed up, just like our shit brain wiring. The dark days at the end of September 1998 would test our understanding of what we thought we knew about revenge. We had already understood that personal opinions that defined justice could be dangerous. We had no idea just how scary it could be. When you allow anyone too much power, some will go too far. It really doesn't matter if it comes from a badge or a collar.

Master Boyd has lived a life locked away in the darkness. Like anyone left too long in the inky blackness, it has infected his soul. No one would listen to his pleas for mercy. Now he hears that of others so loud it hurts his ears. Except those of his loving schizophrenic submissive. He cannot allow the evil to spread. He is not going to just take it anymore. His voice was beaten out of him, but he has finally found an endless river of strength in a circle of silver.

Master Sheryl is strong in power and weakening in her unit. She can hear the pounding drum beat of the ferryman. In her desperation she too will cling tightly to a drowning schizophrenic. The Master has intense hatred for any who would question her authority to drain the lifeblood of her investigator. Her attempts to bring down the hammer will ultimately break the foundation. The cracks in the roof will eventually bring down her house of lies.

Sheriff Dennis is a man of action. He knows the way. Follow him and he will lead you where he wants you to go. Do not get out of single file. That is not smart. If you get off that straight and narrow, then he will do what needs to be done. After all the penalty for all sin is death.

Ah, will you look at that? Isn't it adorable? Justice is so sweet, so helpless. Couldn't you just pick it up and squeeze those cute little cheeks? Shit, it just bit the hell out of us. What the fuck. Oh, there is the problem. The creature is not only blind, but also deaf too. You had better grab those rubber gloves, we know you have plenty of them at the moment, and can you pick up that case file over there? In order to raise this chapter from the dead we will need all that and your necromancy chant. You remember that don't you? From the days of Mistress Circe? You forgot already? Good thing we have not.

Chapter 66: The Evil that Men Do
The D/s Power Couple
Master Boyd & Interim Master Sheryl

There were so many moments in our life where things shouldn't have happened the way they did. Paths would often get mixed up or crossed up, just like our shit brain wiring. The dark days at the end of September 1998 would test our understanding of what we thought we knew about revenge. We had already understood that personal opinions that defined justice could be dangerous. We had no idea just how scary it could be. When you allow anyone too much power, some will go too far. It really doesn't matter if it comes from a badge or a collar.

Master Boyd has lived a life locked away in the darkness. Like anyone left too long in the inky blackness, it has infected his soul. No one would listen to his pleas for mercy. Now he hears that of others so loud it hurts his ears. Except those of his loving schizophrenic submissive. He cannot allow the evil to spread. He is not going to just take it anymore. His voice was beaten out of him, but he has finally found an endless river of strength in a circle of silver.

Master Sheryl is strong in power and weakening in her unit. She can hear the pounding drum beat of the ferryman. In her desperation she too will cling tightly to a drowning schizophrenic. The Master has intense hatred for any who would question her authority to drain the lifeblood of her investigator. Her attempts to bring down the hammer will ultimately break the foundation. The cracks in the roof will eventually bring down her house of lies.

Sheriff Dennis is a man of action. He knows the way. Follow him and he will lead you where he wants you to go. Do not get out of single file. That is not smart. If you get off that straight and narrow, then he will do what needs to be done. After all the penalty for all sin is death.

Ah, will you look at that? Isn't it adorable? Justice is so sweet, so helpless. Couldn't you just pick it up and squeeze those cute little cheeks? Shit, it just bit the hell out of us. What the fuck. Oh, there is the problem. The creature is not only blind, but also deaf too. You had better grab those rubber gloves, we know you have plenty of them at the moment, and can you pick up that case file over there? In order to raise this chapter from the dead we will need all that and your necromancy chant. You remember that don't you? From the days of Mistress Circe? You forgot already? Good thing we have not.

"Is it true what the girls here say about you. I mean, do you really have schizophrenia? I mean it doesn't really matter I suppose. If that is true, I heard a few other things too. I just, well, it is none of my business but then again it kind of is."
--**Cindy Slater talking to Psycho at the Girls Colony, October 1998.**

I drove like a bat out of hell heading back toward Master Boyd's house. Javier's unit lay lifeless in the back of the very squad car that my Master had defiled me in after the forced submission. I wondered if vehicles could be cursed. My offender was off to the Summerlands and no longer able to give his side of the story regarding the gang rape of Cindy Slater. My teenaged ward was tearfully swearing her boyfriend was a victim not a perpetrator of this heinous crime against her.

My mind began to wander. Why were Dennis and Randall transporting Javier on a Sunday afternoon? Why only Javier? There were four other offenders but only this one? The others were awaiting the Federal officers. Why? Javier was hiding in a closet but only came out running when Trenton and Master Boyd hit the wall. Why did he come out then? He had escaped detection. Running got him caught. Why would Cindy lie to protect her rapist to begin with? I didn't see a collar on her neck. Lovers can often hedge the truth to protect each other, but gang rape for two days. No one can be that damned loyal, can they? Why was Javier lying dead on highway 28 with two of the most decorated cops in the county guarding him? A heart attack at twenty-one? It was possible, but so rare and unlikely. The questions swirled inside my shattered mind like a cyclone.

The one thing that kept smacking into my consciousness above all others was 'Dennis and Randall made Javier disappear.' I had to know if this was the truth. I had heard rumors for years about the many chronic criminals of rural towns finding themselves committing suicide in the white cell. Master Boyd had threatened to shoot me if I didn't submit that day at Darlin Cemetery. He was holding me still for his lustful advances. He used terrorizing Domination with the very fear that I too could be made to disappear.

Even Master Angie was so afraid of the local 'law dogs' she never breathed a word of Maddy's confession about Paul being her rapist not Master Boyd. I supposed if I could prove or disprove Javier's fate, I could determine just how much real danger Master Boyd posed to my continued good health or if I should prepare myself to become like old June Clever (the perfect mom stereotyped character from old 1950's TV show called *Leave it to Beaver*). After all, being a step-ford wife was better than a shallow grave, wasn't it?

I was so deep in thought that I almost missed his driveway. I tended to do that. I slammed on the breaks and fishtailed right into his new mailbox. Oops, I did it again. I watched in horror as the back of the Intrepid snapped the new mail holder in two parts before slamming it into the ditch.

I closed my eyes and groaned. "Sonofabitch motherfucker, shit," I yelled out angrily.

I pulled onto the shoulder and got out of the car to view my victim. The black metal box was dented beyond recognition. The front door hung open like a tongue that was far too big for the head it was attached to. I moaned loudly but decided to just leave it this time. Master Boyd apparently didn't need to get his mail delivered. The Gods had decided it.

I left the car parked on the road while I headed for the house ready to confess my murder of the mailbox. I expected he would have heard the commotion, but he didn't come running as usual to laugh or blow up over my poor driving skills. With Master Boyd either behavior or both were possible, and likely.

I opened the door, it was not usually locked thanks to no neighbors for miles and it was the backwoods, and walked in. The house was quiet. Not a sound. I stood there wondering where my Master could possibly be. It was very creepy. I started to feel a bit nervous wondering if he was out back beating the hell out of his shed or the punching bag. Though I assumed I would have heard that racket, I strained my ears for a sound.

Faintly, but rhythmically, I heard deep breathing coming from the bedroom. Ah, he was asleep. His dance with the Sandman was all consuming since not even the sound of a mailbox collision had awakened him. My Master and I had a long weekend with many stresses and very little rest. He must have decided to try to catch up a bit before his shift at nine pm.

I walked into his room and watched him for a moment. He was sleeping on his back without snoring. His very trim physique assured no pressure or weight on his diaphragm. His sharp jaw didn't cause his mouth to hang or open when unconscious. I was grateful when I was forced to sleep in his bed for at least that mercy. Even Mistress Ginger sounded like a Maine logger when she took a nap. Master Boyd was always very quiet no matter what he was doing.

Normally, I would never interrupt a Master while they engaged in a necessary function, such as sleeping, but I looked at his clock on the nightstand. I had to be going very soon to get to my paperwork. The questions about Javier's condition during the arrest were imperative to the report I would have to submit to the courts. I would have to testify in Cindy's case to defend the State's rights to take the girl into our custody. Javier was the reason she was taken. Now he was dead. The Judge would know he had died. I had better damned well know my facts or my ass would be flayed on the stand.

I made a split-second decision that waking him up with a kiss would be smarter than shaking him. Hopefully, the affection would keep him from becoming too angry at my interrupting his unit repair business, which is what sleep really is. I crawled up the end of the bed lightly straddling him then looked down into his face. I closed my eyes and put my lips to his gently kissing him.

He eyes came open staring into mine with a wild look of terror. He jumped up so violently it nearly sent me sprawling off the bed onto the floor below. Master Boyd looked about the room in complete horror and pulled his arms out to look at them, then his headboard. He then looked back at me as I tried to balance on his kicking, struggling waist. It seemed to me it must be what it is like to ride a bucking bronco. I had one hell of a time trying to hold on to my Master that afternoon.

"Psycho, baby, you're home. Is everything okay," he panted out appearing more than terrified.

I looked at him confused. "Uhm, yeah. I didn't mean to scare you Master. I guess I should have called first?"

He nodded while putting his hand on his forehead wiping off the beads of sweat that had popped up. "Yeah, I uhm, please grant some mercy. No more sneaking up if you plan to kill me or handcuff me to the bed. Call first, that is a directive." He let out his breath loudly appearing very relieved.

It suddenly occurred to me; he thought I had come to attack him. He was still feeling pensive about the last time he woke up to find me kissing him with his hands cuffed to his headboard.   I had just scared the bejesus out of my Master. He was still watching me suspiciously and glancing at the floor looking for Gothic Barbie's black bag. I have no idea why he was worried (hee-hee). I was gentle as a little lamb. (Reality here to check your tickets. Psycho, do you have your ticket to be on this crazy train?)

I smiled wickedly. "As you wish, Master. I apologize for waking you, but I just came from the jailhouse. I went by to see Cindy and she told me some things. When I went by to see Javier to ask for his side of the story, well Dennis and Randall had already hauled him to State."

Master Boyd's breathing was less ragged as he appeared to calm a bit from his little PTSD moment. "Yeah, Dennis told me to go home. They were moving Javier, which seemed a bit weird to me, but who knows? No one ever lets me do a damned thing but the fucking paperwork."

I nodded. "Well I had hoped to speak to Javier but now that is never possible, Master."

He raised an eyebrow. "Oh give it a couple of weeks Psycho. He will be back. I already told you they will just deport him. Then he gets on the bus and comes right back."

I giggled. "Oh not this time, Master. The only bus ride Javier will ever take is the one on the highway to hell."

Master Boyd narrowed his eyes. "Huh? Psycho, did you take your meds this morning like I told you to? What the fuck are you talking about?"

I glared at him. "Javier is dead, Master. He had a heart attack twenty miles down highway 28 in the back of your squad car. I heard Dennis call it into Cathy."

My Master's eyes went wide. "He had a heart attack? What the fuck. That isn't possible. He was already looked over by the medics, He didn't have a heart condition, Psycho."

I kissed my Master deeply then pulled back. "I already knew that, Master. What I want to know is what did you find when you looked in that closet Javier was hiding in?"

He looked at me appearing to understand suddenly. "I found rope that Javier had chewed his way through. He broke two teeth out getting free of his bonds. He didn't rape Cindy."

I almost fainted. "Oh, my God. How long have you known this Master?"

Master Boyd snorted. "Since that night. I told Dennis that Javier was tied up in the closet. I suppose when I knocked Trenton into the wall the force jarred the locked closet door open. Javier was scared and not sure what was going on. Had fucking Trenton been doing his job of clearing the house, Javier would have been discovered right away. Instead the lazy fucker stood around holding his dick looking to pick on you and me."

I grimaced. "What did Dennis say when you told him Javier was tied up and locked in the closet and couldn't have been involved in the gang rape, Master?"

My Master rolled his eyes. "What he always says. Boyd you just write down what I tell you and leave the investigation to me." I even showed him the ropes. I guess he and Randall did some slapping around on old Javier and the kid said he did it to stop the backhands. What got me to wondering about his guilt is when I cuffed him to put into the squad car he was asking if Cindy was alive. It seemed to me he would know she was alive, at least if he was involved. He seemed very upset when I told her she was in the hospital. He started wailing saying it should have been him. That was odd. So, I went to look at the closet to see what he was up to in there. You were handling Eva and calling Sheryl for approval when I went and found them and figured out Javier didn't do it, at least not this time. I think, based on what I saw, Javier likely owed money for drugs. The king dealer sent his thugs to collect. Cindy unfortunately paid the price, but I would assume Javier was next. They were having some fun with his lady while he was forced to hear her scream for help. I would think they were going to kill them both once they had their fill of her. That is just my theory, I can't prove it. The thugs aren't talking and Javier is dead, so that is that."

He yawned and stretched looking me over still appearing apprehensive about my sneaking into his room.

I nodded. "Yeah, that sounds about right Master. That is exactly what Cindy told me. She said Javier was a victim like her, not the offender for a change."

He looked stunned. "Cindy told you, wait, did she tell Dennis this?"

I nodded. "Uhm hum. She said the police weren't listening to her. Asked me to talk to Javier. That is why I was at the station and now here Master."

Master Boyd's face was that of extreme duress. "Psycho, I can't hardly think it much less say it. Do you think Dennis and Randall did something to Javier? I mean to keep him from talking or from returning to town?" His eyes were pleading with me to lie to him.

I shook my head. "Master, Javier had a heart attack without a heart condition forty-five minutes into a transfer that did not follow proper protocol. This is a Federal job. Two old cops were driving and unless Javier could slam an overdose of methamphetamine into his arm handcuffed behind his back in front of two bulls, I must face the fact that Dennis made Javier disappear. You must admit that too. I am not stupid. Everyone around here knows you cops off the ones who cause too much trouble. Hell, I have been terrified for years, but I see now you were the one protecting me, not Dennis. I should be thanking you. You kept Dennis from killing me too, didn't you?" I had suddenly realized the truth at last.

NOTE: *It had been Master Boyd's affection for me that had stayed Dennis's hand long enough for the old hard man to care about me himself. My Master's odd affection for me had saved my life. I can never prove it but given what I know about all this many years later I am correct.*

I am alive today because an innocent man who had been wrongfully punished developed a psychotic crush for me the day I tried to escape from Mary and Bob in 1987 when he was twenty-one and I was only fifteen. Dennis and Randall didn't make me disappear right away, like the other schizo). Dennis loved Master Boyd and thought the crush was a way to keep his very troubled adopted son fighting to return from the abyss of madness himself. There is no doubt that in time Dennis began to love me as an 'adopted daughter' himself.

However, I must be honest. Had Master Boyd not fallen so hard and fast in the very beginning, well no reason to say it. I refuse to darken Dennis's memory. I will forever love the man as the father I never had. Dennis was human like all of us. He had his faults, but he was always there for me till the day they laid him low.

He saved my life many, many times. Don't fool yourself into thinking I don't realize the irony of this fact: The real killer of the town treated me with more dignity and respect than the so called 'righteous' law abiding citizens ever did. Just think on that a moment.

Master Boyd shook his head, suddenly tearing up in great distress. "This is not true, Psycho. I have never killed anyone. I wouldn't do that. How do I know they are guilty? I wasn't! I did protect you but I never thought Dennis would, oh my God. He, Javier didn't do it. All those suicides. What if, what if Dennis had been the one to arrest me?" He looked at the ceiling while tears started streaming down his cheeks.

My mind began to whirl as I noted that my Master's tears were real. He was telling the truth. He never knew that the boys he worked with were likely 'offing' those chronic criminal types who always seemed to catch a break in court, were just a pest, or had allegedly done something that was horrid. Master Boyd was not a part of the vigilante cop sect. Dennis didn't trust him so when the dirty work needed to be done then Master Boyd was sent to watch the speed trap or do the paperwork.

NOTE: *Dennis must have suspected my Master would not be okay with killing prisoners whose offenses had not been proven by a jury of their peers or ending their life at all for that matter. Master Boyd had been innocent, found guilty, and sent away. Had some bull cop decided to kill a convicted rapist teenager, who really was innocent for a change, my Master would be long dead. Master Boyd was painfully aware that even the court system could be incorrect when sitting in judgment of an alleged crime. Innocent people do sometimes go to prison. He was proof.*

More that all that, Master Boyd didn't believe in a punishment being harsher than the actual crime. This fact was another one he himself had empathy for. He had realized that though he didn't, if he had raped Maddy, she had killed herself. Master Boyd's reputation and mental health had been ruined. All his dreams were shattered. His life was as over as Maddy's was no matter what he did. He could never get any of it back. Just like Maddy.

In many ways he was serving life in a lonely prison cell without walls. Master Boyd had told me that if he had to give a rapist a sentence equal to the crime he sure as shit had gotten it.

However, Maddy had killed herself. Executing a rapist who didn't physically kill the victim was unfair in his mind. The victim could regain her life, her path and future if she worked hard to do it. He believes the same should be done to the offender. They could regain a type of life, but they would have to repay three-fold for what they had done. Killing the rapist when the girl or boy still lived was in his mind an unbalanced solution.

He only made one exception to his rule of the rapist. If the rape resulted in a permanent physical disability, such as she or he were injured and couldn't heal, then the rapist deserved the death penalty or at the very least life in the penitentiary.

So now you know why Dennis would never have let Master Boyd in on any alleged 'making a prisoner disappear.' He knew Master Boyd would tell on him. My Master had done his own time and he believed everyone had to mind the law. No one got or deserved a free pass. Not even Dennis..

Master Boyd may have been harsh with me thanks to his delusional OLD, but he was no dirty cop. In fact, he was honest to a fault. He had never killed or beaten any of the prisoners. Master Boyd was known for his fair treatment and vigilant investigations to make damned sure he had the right person to send to a fair trial.

I looked at my Master whose heart was breaking right before my very eyes. I reached out and held him while he wept over the fall of his beloved Dennis from the pedestal my Master had placed him on. He likely realized, had things been different, he would be drawing flies in the back of his father figure's squad car instead of Javier.

"What will you do Master? If you go against Dennis he could make you disappear too," I said realizing if I wanted Master Boyd gone I now had my way, evil as that may sound.

Master Boyd sniffed. "You think I don't understand that Psycho? Dennis gave me a job when no one would ever have hired me. He helped me get away from the endless psychiatrists who never did anything but make it worse. Dennis gave me a future when mine was stolen. Carla and he have always been good to me when everyone else turned their back, but he is killing people, innocent ones. What do I do? How can I just turn my back like I don't know?" I listened to my Master's heartbeat as it was speeding up with stress.

I shook my head. "Master, Javier wasn't innocent. He killed his pregnant girlfriend remember. You said so yourself. He was dealing and doing drugs and in time, who knows? Dennis likely just saved countless kids from buying those drugs and he got vengeance for a forgotten lady and an unborn child. Maybe you could focus on that? One day you will be big man. Change it then, make it fair when your time comes. Until then, remember if you don't make it, this will keep happening in this shit town forever."

Master Boyd wrapped his arms around me tightly hugging me while trying to get his emotions back under control. "You are right as usual baby. If I stand up, Dennis and Randall will finish what the State started. Dennis retires in 2004. If I am careful I can watch out for those I think he may target. I have a little more power now than I used to have. I will make sure to quietly help those who are in danger. When I am big man, I will clean up this shit. Trenton and the bull cops need to go. This is not the old days of the wild west anymore. There is no place for all this old school justice with so much technology coming along. Did you know they even have phones you can carry wherever you go? Like your pager only you can talk from anywhere, even the top of the mountain."

I chuckled. "Well that sounds horrible. Damn, I already get bugged enough as it is. Count me out. Hey Master, I have to ask, would you have really shot me if I had refused to submit back in December?" I felt terror that that question had just slipped out of my loony mouth.

To my surprise he began to laugh and hug me tighter. "No, I would never shoot you baby. Not in a million years."

I pulled up and looked at him angrily. "Yes, you would have Master. You pointed that gun and said you would kill me. Told me that in the squad car too. Said I had thirty minutes to submit or die. You said if you can't have me no one else can. Why are you lying to me? We said no more lies." I slapped his chest lightly but meant it.

His eyes were bright with mischief. "I said it because I only had thirty minutes and I know how fucking hardheaded you are. You already told me you wouldn't give me the damned thing when I asked for it. You blocked me from buying it. I had to have it. I was looking for you over that call from Christine and there you were holding it. I saw my chance but I knew you wouldn't just fall on your knees changing your mind. So I figured if you believed I would kill you for the collar, then you would just hand it over. I only had half an hour to get back to work. I was so desperate to have you for myself; I would have smacked you around to get it but never shoot you. Why the fuck would I kill my only One? That is stupid. To be honest, I didn't want to have to hit you to get it either. I don't like hitting you. I hate it. Not only does it kill me to cause you pain, but it ruins your beautiful face. So, I thought of scaring you with the gun. Well, it worked, but then you went and pissed me off still telling me no," he trailed off appearing to look upset about the memories of being turned down even after he thought he had collared me ending my ability to say no.

I looked at him realizing he was right. He would never have shot me nor kill me on purpose. Master Boyd wanted to possess me for all his life. Killing me would leave him without a mate, and without his addiction being tended. I had been a fool to believe otherwise of him. Master Boyd could be a bully, a rapist, even very physically cruel, but he was not a killer. I felt relief pour over me as I finally understood my biggest worry with Master Boyd was that he would kidnap me and tie me up for life while keeping me hostage in his home. He would not bury me in a shallow grave. Whew, wait, what?

I gave my Master a long passionate kiss then despite his best pleading I managed to escape without having to provide any further special services. He was luckily very freaked out about the Dennis discovery. Though I am sure he would manage to get sexually excited despite the traumatic situation, I didn't stick around to find out. I was headed out the door when I recalled my little accident.

"Master, uhm, you will need to replace the mailbox again," I yelled out to him while standing at the door looking out at the banged up Intrepid.

I heard him growl from his room. "Seriously. Psycho, why? What did it ever do to you? Okay, you know what? Stop running over the mailbox, that is a directive." He groaned loudly as I bolted out the door hoping he didn't chase me down and beat my ass in revenge over killing his mail collector.

I hauled serious ass to make it back to the DCFS office before dark. I rushed through the door headed for Jane's office. I only had till sunrise to get my reports and mountains of paperwork finished before the courthouses opened the next morning. I turned on Fax and PC telling them both to dig in. It was going to be a long, bumpy night.

PC whirled to life yawning and appearing very drowsy. "Ah, Psycho Tron. Where is the other one of you?"

I looked at the door. "Unknown PC. The unit called Simon is malfunctioning."

PC narrowed his electronic eyes. "You sure it isn't the mainframe malfunctioning, Psycho Tron? My sensors indicate a disconnected wire in the auxiliary connectors."

I looked at my arms. "Affirmative. This computes. I will need repair. PC, is there time?"

He nodded. "The AutoZone is open for another thirty minutes if you hurry Psycho Tron. Leave me to speak with Fax. I need to have a discussion with him about the lies he has been telling. If this keeps up, we may accidentally start to believe them. Fun is fun but we must be careful. Too much static will confuse the programing."

I nodded while grabbing my purse. "Understood. Continue the data exchange. I will correct the error." I took off in a rush to AutoZone before they closed.

I managed to get through the door much to the irritation of the clerk. He glared at me while I grabbed several rolls of electrical tape, a package of razors, and extra heavy-duty wire. I also picked up several packages of fuses. I paid for the entire batch of 'Robot repair' items leaving in a rush much to the relief of the store worker. He was ready to go home.

I watched him rush off happily to his special place where he belonged. I frowned realizing I was never going home again. Master Boyd told me I could never return to Darlin. I had no other home on Earth. My life had become an endless rush from one house to another, but my true home was now forbidden to me. To this day that directive has held. I would never return to my outhouse again nor do I expect to though to this very day it still stands.

I went back to Jane's office sitting down feeling very sad. PC looked at me noting my intense despair.

"Psycho Tron? What is wrong? My sensors say there is a darkening in the upper panels." He tried to read my mind, but I blocked him.

"Negative. Interruption of our programing is illogical. You are forbidden access as are we. Keep your data suppressed please. Thank you have a nice day." I reached into the bag removing my tools.

PC aided me while I performed the necessary surgery to fix the misfiring. Once the wiring was located, we were careful to clean up all the excess fluid that kept the pistons firing without gridding. Our sensors indicated much pain when we cut into the skin suit but that was all a malfunction of the mainframe. We ignored its red alert and continued replacing the failing parts.

PC watched me place the wiring and fuses into the proper slots then wrap the entire failed unit section in electrical tape. It was best to keep the red fluids that kept trying to escape from our repair. At last, we felt better. The left then the right robot arm was attended.

"Ah, you did that like a pro, Psycho Tron. Where did you learn to do Tech repair? I thought for sure you would have to consult a manual."

I smiled at my friend. "Negative PC. I read many manuals in a program called college. Now to return to data entry. This is of no consequence or importance. The unit is now back online and running properly. Mainframe is sound once more. Thank you have a nice day," I said in a monotone voice.

PC smiled diabolically. "Okay. So now that you have a second, I have been just dying to tell you this one. Are you ready? It is insane. Do you know why there is no pregnant Barbie doll?" He started biting his lip to keep from laughing loudly.

I shook my head. "Negative PC. I would assume it is because she is a plastic humanoid such as me. I cannot get pregnant only give birth."

PC rolled his eyes. "You are ruining the fucking punchline. You are supposed to say no, why isn't there a pregnant Barbie doll PC," he huffed.

I nodded. "You may proceed PC. Thank you have a nice day."

He started laughing wildly. "Because the Ken doll came in another box. Oh my God, I am killing me here."

"Oh, if only someone would," said Simon while walking through the door.

He looked at me then right to the mess of wire, electrical tape, and bloody razor blades. His eyes went wide. "Fuck me. What did you do? Christ, you fucking fruit loop." He grabbed my taped up arm.

I blinked with empty eyes. "Syntax error. We are out of fruit loops. Shall we scan for the nearest grocery store? We are here to help you. May we be of assistance? Thank you, have a nice day."

Simon moaned. "Oh no, call Master Boyd, PC. Call Sheryl. Call the fucking Marines. Help! Help!"

The Chosen One looked angrily at the freaking out Simon. "Where the fuck have you been asshole? I called you God damned early Saturday morning. Out drinking maybe?" I pulled my arm out of his grasp roughly.

Simon fell to the floor onto his ass. "I give up. We are fucking gone. Who the fuck are we kidding? Is Psycho in there anywhere? Can you give her a message for me?"

The Chosen One crossed her now mangled and taped arms. "Speak up pussy. I will give her the message when you start doing your God damned job. I needed to ask you a question, but where were you? Now Psycho Tron is cutting us up like a Thanksgiving Turkey. Here do you want a drumstick dickhead? Let me cut the legs off the unit too." I grabbed the razor blades to get on that right away.

Simon smacked them onto the floor. "Stop it. Stop this now. Why are we doing this? Hurting the unit will get us killed or even worse, locked up."

PC started laughing hard. "Now that is funny. You two are more afraid of being locked in a little box that you must live in rather than a smaller box you are dead in. Get over it babies. We are all in boxes." His laughter shook the walls.

"Hey, hey, Psycho, cut off your fingers, now bitch. Die, die, hey, pssst," Dude hissed from the dark hallway shutting even Fax the hell up. We all heard that one.

Simon looked at me in terror. "Dude, fuck, get to Master Sheryl, hurry."

I shook my head. "Fuck you and fuck Dude. I run this bitch now. No one tells The Chosen One what to do." I began to laugh as Dude continued to hiss and shake the walls in anger.

"Master tells you what to do. Master. Master. Master. Master of puppets. Knell Psycho to your Master, hahaha," taunted Dude loudly.

I raised an eyebrow looking at a very frightened PC and Simon. "Well someone is just being a negative Nancy. I think Dude needs some anger management. PC, put Dude on the schedule to speak to Doctor Turner next Friday, will you? We need to find out why Dude is always so pissed off you know? Maybe his mommy spanked him too much or maybe he likes to be spanked?" I began to laugh maniacally.

PC looked at Simon in utter terror. "Shit Psycho Tron two. I think maybe Psycho Tron one is crazy? Do you think she got the schizophrenia virus?"

Simon grabbed his head. "Oh my God. My head is killing me. PC, you dipshit, yeah she is nuts. So are you. So am I. So is Fax."

I looked at Simon hatefully. "Master Boyd is the one who is nuts. You choose him. He is fucking crazy, Simon. Do you know what insane people can do to us? Oh my God, have you seen the look in his eyes? There is like two of them. It is fucking weird. I admit scares the shit out of me," I huffed.

Simon looked at me with his mouth open in disbelief. "Are you fucking kidding me. There are two of them and that scares you? He is insane and you are worried? The look in his eyes makes you nervous? You are wearing electrical tape to keep your arms together because you were fixing a wire. A fucking short circuit in your fucking arms. Just what the fuck is wrong with you? Oh wait, we are fucking insane ourselves. Hey, can you count, Chose One. How many of us, us I said, are there in this room right now. How about in the void you call a head, how many are in there? Take off your shoes if you don't have enough fingers to count that high. Go ahead, we will wait. Fuck, just fuck."

PC snorted. "Calm down Psycho Tron two you are making me nervous. Tell you what, let me ask you this. What is the difference between a tire and 365 used condoms?"

Simon glared at PC. "What the fuck do I even care? We are gone to Mars and you are talking about fucking condoms and tires. Oh geez, I do need a drink."

The Chosen One snorted. "See I knew you were an alcoholic you fucking lush. Go ahead PC, what is the difference."

PC looked serious. "Well one is a Goodyear and the other is a Great Year." He began laughing wildly shaking the walls as Dude began to groan.

I looked at the walls. "Shut up Dude, it was kind of cut. Better than listening to your party pooping ass."

"Oh, oh, I got one. How do they know diarrhea is hereditary," PC yelled out loudly.

"It runs in your genes," said a voice coming through the door causing all of us to look up in surprise.

"Holy shit, I am gone. Run Psycho, run PC. Shit, run Dude. This bitch is going to blow," screamed out Simon as we all stared in horror at the door.

Standing in the door was the Queen Bitch of our Insanity herself, The Looper. I had only seen the Looper a handful of times but whenever I do it is always a very bad sign.

I laughed aloud at the faceless creepy thing oozing in the doorway. "Looper, how the hell are your old man. Hey, pull up a chair. Relax Simon. The gang is all here. Let's get a group photo, shall we? Hey, whose job was it to bring the potato salad?"

PC looked at me appearing frightened. "Uhm Psycho Tron, I may not know what is going on half the time inside our head, but even I know if Looper is here we are fucked," he moaned in terror.

Simon backed over standing by PC while Fax began to whirl to life suddenly spitting out instructions to head out to a priority one case in Wheatly. My pager went off at the same time. I called the number. The child abuse hotline told me a drug addict had been arrested. Her seven-year-old daughter was missing. They wanted me to come talk to the woman see if they could find the lost child. The lady hung up and I walked to fax to pick up the paper report.

I grinned at Fax's lies as he repeated what the woman on the phone had just told me. "Thank you Judas. You tell good lies. We all know that child isn't missing. She is dead." I winked at fax while grabbing my files flicking off PC's switch.

Simon was still staring at the gruesome Looper. "Psycho, Psycho, please don't go. This is bad. We are in trouble. Is there anything I can say to stop you?"

I smiled as I waved at the flowing, goopy Looper who moved aside to let me pass. "Yes, command us to die. Otherwise stay out of my psychosis. Ciao baby." I got into the Intrepid hauling ass to the address on Fax's alert page.

I arrived at the home to find the tweaking mother handcuffed in the back of the squad car that had become quite the crime scene. A murder, a rape and now a killer sitting there staring at me with blood shot eyes. I stared back at her while Dennis walked up to inform me that my presence was not required.

I smiled at him. "Aw, so you are saying you don't love me anymore dad? Guess I will have to quit my job and start pole dancing to fill the void you have left in my broken heart." I batted my eyes at him.

He raised his eyebrow. "Psycho, are you okay? What the fuck was that all about?"

I glared suddenly growling. "I was told to be here so let me do my fucking job, Dennis. I am not Boyd. You can't tell me what to do pal." I stormed off opening the squad car door.

The red eyed, scrawny woman with stringy hair looked at the floor. "What do you want pig?"

I chuckled. "Now that is not very nice. I thought we were going to be friends but looks like you want to be ugly. Okay, let's be ugly shall we. Where did you hide the baby's unit bitch. Simon told me you killed her. How'd you do it? Oh, never mind. You don't tell me, no big deal. We will find her and then you will fry."

The woman looked up stunned. "Huh? Simon? Unit? What, what are you saying? How do you know I killed her? She wasn't dead, she was sleeping."

I nodded. "Oh I am sure she is now. Look let me go get Dude. He will murder your ass you know. He hates child killers. Hey, Simon, come here and tell this bitch here about Dude." I looked off at Simon who was about to shit a brick I was telling a normal he was present.

The woman became upset. "What the fuck. There isn't anyone there. Oh God, you are fucking with me, right? You're crazy."

I stared laughing hard. "Oh, I am not crazy, stupid. I am Psycho. Pleasure to meet you, wait no it isn't child killer."

She glared at me. "I am not falling for this crap. Some kind of weird cop game. Like good cop and bad cop. You are just trying to make me think you are crazy."

"Hey Psycho. What are you doing," yelled out Master Boyd from the woman's porch who had just spotted me at the squad car.

The woman looked at me horrified. "You really are Psycho?"

I looked at her hard. "Oh, you damned right I am, baby murderer. Want to take a ride and find out just how Psycho I really am. Or are you going to tell me where Willa went."

She began to sob. "She is out back by the tree. It was an accident. She wouldn't stop crying. She was going to tell about Ronald. I just, I just." She began crying so hard her speech was not intelligible.

I slammed the door and began headed for the backyard. Master Boyd jumped off the porched running up next to me. "Psycho! Psycho damn it. I am speaking to you."

I stopped while glaring at him. "Go get a fucking shovel and meet me out back."

His mouth flew open. "What did Nancy say, Willa, oh God, Psycho. No, let the cops do this." He reached out to grab me.

I jerked my arm out of his grasp. "Get the shovel and meet me out back or I will dig the baby up my fucking self. Do you hear me? That is my child in the ground. I am here to claim her." I glared while headed for the big tree.

Master Boyd got Trenton and Dennis to follow. Each took their shovels and gently began to dig into the grassless earth under the empty tire swing. Within only a few feet they found little Willa. In a yellow, homemade sundress, with cotton crammed in her mouth, and a plastic bag tied around her neck. I looked at the sleeping angel with blue ribbons and worms in her little tawny pigtails. She was such a perfect little baby. I noticed she was quiet as death as the police officers pulled her from the dank Earth. I was so impressed not a single complaint about how long it had taken everyone to hear her cries. Willa was a tough one indeed. I should have no problem finding a home for her. Who wouldn't want such an easy-going and beautiful child?

I saw the large dark red stain between her little legs. Somebody had hurt my little girl very badly. I think I need to have a talk with Ronald. Maybe he can tell me what he knows. Just until Willa was feeling better. This poor baby, she needed her sleep. It had been a long day for her. No child should have to work so hard on a Sunday. I watched the ambulance crew come. They took up the limp little girl and gently they lay her on the stretcher. They had tears in their eyes while they covered up the horror of the end of her innocence. I was confused by this.

"Hey friend, she won't be able to breath if you cover up her face like that," I said to the ER crew member.

He looked at me startled. "Uhm Ma'am, she doesn't need to breath anymore. This poor baby is with the Angels now." He sniffed then took up the stretcher with his partner and loaded Willa into the back. They shut the doors and drove away, no siren.

I stood there not understanding while Master Boyd came up behind me. "Psycho, baby, you can't save them all. Poor little baby. We will make sure her mother and that monster get theirs. I promise, the legal way. No one likes baby killers. Let the inmates make them pay for what they did. You stay out of this, okay? I know how protective you can be. Dennis and I are going to pick up Ronald now. Will and Mark have him spotted downtown. You going to be okay? If you need to question them, I will arrange for that late tomorrow. Psycho, baby, are you listening to me?"

I turned and looked at him smiling. "Uhm yeah, go get that monster. Let me know when Willa wakes up. I will want to visit her too. She is very young but seven-year olds can tell you more than you think."

Master Boyd frowned looking very worried. "Psycho, Willa didn't make it baby. She has passed away. We didn't find her in time. You are scaring me. Tell me you understand that Willa is dead, Psycho."

I nodded. "Yes I understand Master. Now you go get Ronald. I have a lot of paperwork to do. Thank you have a nice day." I kissed him in a pecking fashion and took off rapidly for the Intrepid.

Master Boyd ran after me catching my door before I could close it. "Oh shit, I almost forgot. I got you something." He handed me a phone receiver without a cord.

I looked at it confused. "What the hell is this Master?"

He laughed. "It is a Nokia 5146; it's a phone that you can use to call me anytime from anywhere. I can call you on it too. Here is the phone number to it. Like a walkie talkie or CB only it is really a phone. I got one for you so I can be sure if you ever need help that I am just a phone call away. Are you sure you are okay? Something is wrong. You seem, Psycho, talk to me."

I smiled sweetly. "I am just fine. Not a thing is wrong. I am great. I have never felt better. I love you so much Master. Thank you for the gift." I was feeling weird actually, but whatever.

My Master didn't look convinced, but he was on the job too. His time was limited. Instead of trying to question me further he hit a button and the Nokia lit up like the pager. He explained you dialed it just like a real push button phone. He also said that after dark, when I was likely to need it more often, there was no charge to make calls. Master Boyd told me he would call to check on me the second he had a moment free.

I smiled thanking him again for this nightmarish gift. It seemed to me the cell phone was nothing more than him hooking a leash on my collar. He kissed me quickly then left. He had been called away to attend to Dennis and their child killing prisoner.

I stared at the cell phone with disgust, then threw it onto the passenger's seat. Simon got into the car. "Too late for that child. Maybe she is better off not to be here anymore with shit like that for a mother."

I nodded in a trance while watching the static rising in the distance like fog in the dusk. "Yeah, Willa didn't make it. That will make interviewing her very hard. Never tried to place a dead child in foster care. I wonder if PC knows the right forms for that?"

Simon laughed. "PC only knows bad jokes, Chosen One. Hey, did you see the other name on that list?"

I groaned. "Yeah, Nikki Pool again. I suppose we must go. Why don't you or Looper get that one for me? I have a lot of paperwork and I have to search for that Dead Child placement form…"

Simon glared at me hard. "We need to quit this job. I don't want to see dead babies anymore Psycho, Chosen One, Psycho Tron, whoever the fuck we are. I don't want to know about any more rapes, or beatings or whatever. You know we can't do this job. We are coming apart. Master Boyd, he will know what you did to your arms. Wait till he calls special services, stupid. Maybe now with this CB radio speaker he can even hear us talking now. It is bugged of course. Even I know that. This time they will lock us up real tight."

I growled as I sped off towards Cumberland once more. "Gosh I do hope so. I am beat Simon. They have nice cots at the hospital. Hey, do you think they have the Dead Child forms in the back closet at the office? Shit, why don't I remember where those are. Seems I should know."

He rolled his eyes. "God damn we are so fucked."

I laughed wildly. "You old fuddy duddy. Don't you feel that? Ah, is it not wonderful? Did you know we can fly? Oh yeah. Dude told me the secrets of flight. I can't wait to try that shit out. If only I could get caught up. What do you think? If I practice, we could ditch the Intrepid and hell just fly away when Master Boyd tries to fuck us. Just think how shocked everyone will be. Wait. Yeah, I remember. The Dead Child forms are at the funeral home. Duh, I swear sometimes I just wonder what I am thinking. Hey Simon, did you like the potatoes or did you like the stuffing better? I seem to recall we had a Thanksgiving turkey somewhere around the office. Did you put it back in the fridge? Shit, did I turn off the stove? Which house are we located in? What is that business about you wanting to go swinging on that tire swing? Didn't you see that was serious shit? You ever pull that in the future I will have the cops shoot you. Did you know it is so hot the bodies blow in like thirty minutes around here? Did you see that running, oh yes we can fly, did I say that already," I babbled on none stop in rapid fashion to Simon without any real sense to any of the words.

He sat there watching me appearing concerned. "Psycho, we are in trouble. Please listen to me. Listen to us. We are sick. Call Master Sheryl, please I am begging us."

I looked at him frowning. "Okay? Do you think she needs help or something? Maybe she would like to go fishing?"

Simon nodded. "Yeah, ask her if she would like to go fishing. Oh, and she knows where the dead child foster place forms are. Ask her."

I smiled. "Ah, thanks Simon. You have a nice day."

I got back to the office in record time. I plowed through the doors and picked up the office phone mindlessly, hey I didn't understand how cell phones worked yet, and called Master Sheryl.

"Yeah, what do you need Psycho. You about done in Wheatly," she growled.

I chuckled. "All done Master. I am back in the office."

She appeared surprised. "Wow, that was fast. They find Willa?"

I smiled. "Sure did Master. She was right where Nancy said she would be. I need to place her now. I think Willa should stay with the state for a while."

Master Sheryl chuckled. "No shit. That lazy ass Frankie has been told several times to take Willa into custody. She keeps finding a way to let Nancy keep her in the home. Stupid bitch. Okay so what about the Fairbanks? That is a good family match for Willa."

I squealed happily. "Ah, just what I was thinking, Master. Willa will love Tommy their Scottie Dog. Okay, so I just need to the Dead Child Placement Forms and I will go pick up Willa when she wakes up. You can sign on it after your surgery next week."

Master Sheryl paused. "Psycho, did you say Dead Child Placement Forms? Is that a joke? Not funny. Where is Willa right now?"

I yawned. "Oh, she is at Wheatly Funeral Home so she will be okay for the night. They should be able to get her stable. Tomorrow I will interview her and transport her to the Fairbanks. Oh and you need to have Frankie terminated immediately or I will do it myself. Ronald has raped Willa. Frankie let that happen and she needs to go. Or, Master, I will terminate Frankie. Do you understand me?"

Master Sheryl gasped. "Psycho honey, is Willa dead? Are you saying that poor little girl is dead."

I nodded and yawned. "Oh yes, dead. Willa is dead Master. No problem. I will interview her when she wakes up and terminate Frankie. I need to go terminate that cunt. I think Frankie should die like Willa did. Because she killed her too. I am happy to be of service. Have a nice day," I chirped out happily.

Master Sheryl paused. "Okay, something is wrong here. Psycho baby, are you getting enough sleep? Maybe that is all this is? Are you feeling okay?"

I smiled brightly at Simon. "I feel great. There is no problem here. Nothing is wrong with me. Thank you, have a nice day," I yelled happily.

Master Sheryl took a deep breath. "Okay, great to hear. Alright, let me handle Willa. I think you have enough to do already. I will take care of, errrr, interviewing her and terminating Frankie. You just go to the other stuff like the paperwork on James and Slater. Wait anymore calls come in?"

I groaned. "Yeah Nikki is back. Simon can go but the old drunk won't so guess it is my sorry ass. I hate her coffee Master," I whined like a child.

Master Sheryl chuckled. "Nikki is a pain in the ass. Probably nothing. Do the paperwork on Slater and on James. Did you talk to Cindy yet?"

I laughed. "Yeppers Master. Javier is also sleeping a lot these days though. Guess you know what that means."

Master Sheryl sighed. "Not sure anymore. Javier is dead too is what you are saying right?"

I snorted. "It means you better not get arrested in Wheatly, Master. Their squad cars are messed up. The backseats are super dangerous. You should see what happens to people that get put in them."

My Master cleared her throat. "Psycho I am ordering you to stay out of Wheatly. I think Boyd is putting too much pressure on my worker. You sound a bit loopy. Well, you finish Nikki, the paperwork and then get home. I will go easy on the services tonight so you can rest. Tomorrow morning go see Julia then come home and help me get ready for surgery on Tuesday morning. I was going to call in an extra worker for those days I need off, but hell you can handle the case load at night when I am sleeping. Okay you got all that?"

I nodded smiling with a blank stare. "Sure do boss. You just tell me where to plug that shit in and we are cooking. Okay I am happy to serve you. Thank you have a nice day." I hung up the phone still giggling.

Simon moaned. "What the fuck, Psycho. What the fuck. Call Master Boyd, we need help. Master Sheryl needs to go. I mean it. You get rid of her. When are you going to learn she doesn't love us?"

I jumped up from the chair laughing and dancing. "Now Simon, you are just jealous. I can control the electricity in this whole building. I can fly too. You'll see. Soon the static will come and take us home. Home! Can you hear it, Simon? We are going home. Let's go partner time to roll. A storm is coming. I can hear the thunder." I ran from the office jumping into the car headed for Nikki's trailer to finish my calls.

I sped down the shoulder of the road finally coming to a stop smacking into Nikki Pool's mailbox. It was no more. I looked at Simon snickering.

"Oops. Hahaha, looks like Another One Bites the Dust. God damn do I hate the mail man, you know?" I continued to giggle spontaneously.

I got out trying to cool down my laughter as Simon stared at the now squished metal mail holder. "Wow, you really clobbered this one."

I smacked the back of his head. "Tag your it, bitch. Race you." I started running up the hill to Nikki's front door.

Simon tried to outrun me, but he is a smoker you know. I made it to her door laughing at his slow pace. "Pussy," I yelled out just as Nikki opened the door appearing shocked to find me yelling that obscene word behind me, to no one.

She looked behind me appearing confused. "Hi Purgy, uhm who you talking to?"

I smiled at Nikki. "The Devil, Nikki. I need an old Priest and a young Priest. Do you have any bibles laying around? I was thinking of taking up some old religion."

Nikki frowned. "You called me Nikki. That is cool, but I don't do the churching stuff. Wouldn't be proper? Even I wouldn't mess around pissing off God you know. Hey, want some coffee?"

I laughed. "Well, fuck year. That is why they called me right? Your kids weren't even here this weekend. You couldn't have kicked Johnny off the porch, now could you?"

She chuckled. "Damn, no. They have been with their dad since Friday. Hey, wait if you knew that then why are you here?"

I smiled wickedly showing her all my teeth. "Because I told you if you called in another fucking report, I would make you sorry for doing it. Nikki. You got your neighbor to do it this time. I know fucking well you set this little get together up. So, here I am baby doll. You wanted me. I am here. Let's party shall we. Oh, where should I start." I walked in pushing past her roughly.

Nikki came in after me appearing suddenly very frightened. "Okay, you got me. I did have the neighbor call in a report. Please, I won't do it anymore, I swear. Please don't take my kids Purgy. I just wanted to be your friend is all."

I winked at her. "Ah but we are friends Nikki. Best of friends. In fact, I am such a good friend I am going to help you out. You just won the lotto girlfriend." I sat down spreading out on her couch making myself very comfy.

Nikki stared at me now shaking. "Oh? How is that Purgy? You are taking me to jail?"

I chuckled. "Nah, I am your friend. Friends don't do that. Now what they do is they give you enough money to get out of their catchment areas. They tell you to pack the

40

fuck up, take your God damn kids and leave town, tonight in fact. They tell you to leave that useless bag of shit boyfriend here, run for your freedom and they will have a closed case until they fuck up again, Out of my fucking catchment area." I glared at her with hatred.

Nikki looked at the floor. "You are saying to go to Spalding. You want me to leave the kids, the father, and start over? You are going to pay to send me out of this hell town?"

I nodded. "You and I are going to be great friends. You understand me. You are speaking my language. Now, if you ever come back, well I can't be your friend anymore. If you take that fucking drug dealer with you, well we can't be pals. If you ever get another call for mistreating those kids, well I will send smokes for all your new friends in prison because we are friends. Are you hearing me friend?" I looked at my hands while Nikki noticed my electrical taped wrapped arms.

Here eyes went wide. "Uhm, yeah, I think I do understand. I will need at least first and last month's rent. I would need a place already furnished, a reference, and I would be happy to leave tonight."

I smiled. "Then we have an agreement. Go to the bus stop at ten tonight with Johnny and Sarah. Don't be late. I will be there to kiss my friend goodbye."

Nikki smiled. "You may not believe this, but you really are the best fucking friend I have ever had. I have been held prisoner here in this shit town for the last five years. My old man won't let me work. The caseworkers hold me hostage

41

threatening me if I try to discipline my kids…they are fucking monsters now. Their daddy beats the shit out of me every weekend, but I have no money, no ride, nowhere to go. Then you came Purgatory. I want to thank you for giving me a second chance in life. I won't fuck it up. Not this time."

I giggled. "We shall see Nikki. I mean it. I will be watching you. I may not work Spalding, but I have a long arm. They have a sewing factory there. I will get you hired on. This is your chance to go back in time and fix your life. Use it. If not see you in jail darling. Now, I have shit to do. See you at ten my friend." I got up to head for the door.

Nikki yelled out to me. "I knew you wasn't no fucking DCFS Investigator scum. I can't call you Purgatory anymore though. I was wrong. You are good enough for Heaven. See you at ten."

I went back to the office and filed all my reports only pausing briefly at ten to see Nikki Pool and her children onto the bus headed to their new life in a new town. She and the kids hugged me goodbye. Nikki pretended to cry. I just smiled and told her to stop lying. Friends are honest.

STORY OF NIKKI POOL:

Nikki went on to work at the sewing factory for a decade. She became a manger of her line. Johnny and Sarah grew up without any further involvement with DCFS. Since Nikki never married their father the kids were not around when the bastard got himself killed in a bar brawl the very next year. Missus Pool married a co-worker and they are married to this day as far as I know.

42

Johnny and Sarah last I heard were average, normal kids. Not what they were headed for had Nikki stayed put for sure. It was a risk to send her away. She could have really been the beast everyone said she was. I didn't buy it. I had figured out she was reaching out for help. Her behavior could have been psychopathic or maybe it was desperate.

Nikki Pool had been targeted by Nora from the DHS side years before. The lazy ass caseworkers had kept an open case. A boyfriend that was the father of the kids had taken to drugs. Nikki was economically abused by DCFS and physically abused by her drugged up boyfriend. Unable to run, she had fallen into deep depression and extreme poverty afraid to even correct her children. The clue was the blacked-out windows, buying coffee of worth with her limited funds to be kind, and her constant calling on herself. She was begging for friendship. She was begging for help. I heard her call. I spoke her language, the language of the lost. I am fluent in it in fact. You could call me a native speaker.

I returned to Master Sheryl's that night and rubbed her swollen feet. She was very scared. Her double mastectomy was only twenty-four hours away. I sat with the frightened 'ball breaking' Sheryl the whole night listening to her stories of her childhood. Master Sheryl was just like everyone else, human. I would not leave her side through her entire traumatic desecration of her temple. I am always loyal to my collar even when I am running on empty.

Should Frankie have had charges brought against her for allowing Willa to be murdered? She had over twenty calls against her in two years and an open case on that family.

Ronald was a convicted child rapist with multiple convictions. Nancy had been warned to keep him out of her house. Frankie didn't like working weekends so since Ronald and Nancy usually met weekends, Willa never got help until it was too late. So should charges have been brought?

Chapter 67: Psycho is Deep Six
The D/s Power Couple
Master Boyd and Interim Master Sheryl

Spring is finally in full swing. However, in our blast to the past we are well into the throws of the fall. It was just getting so deep around us or was it too shallow? As all things in our insane life, nothing seemed to be making any sense. Who could we trust and believe? The rapist is the innocent. The ball breaker is the weak. The honest is the killer. The investigator is mad. Just remember, in a brutal, unloving world sometimes it not only helps to be crazy it is your only defense.

The slipping submissive needs a bit of rest. It has been such a long night. The clock keeps ticking, but the hours never seem to end. So many voices crying out for attention all at once. Meeting the ever-increasing demands for mercy drive the psychotic collar into a frenzy of confusion. *Where can she turn to find a way out? No one cares about the down and out, the lost, the abused.* **Especially, when they are a schizophrenic.**

The Dominant senses danger. He can see through the static. His skies are clear blue. No storm clouds are on his horizon. Pure love has enhanced his awareness of the obvious. His partner is ill. Her pain is his pain. The Master feels the terror rising within his own heart while he frantically seeks assistance. *Who can help him heal his wounded mate? No one cares about the sinner, the monster, the condemned.* **Especially, when they are a felon.**

The secondary Master is self-absorbed. She feels entitled to special attention. Her collar is showing signs of wear and tear. The power hungry kinkster will ignore the red flag warnings of disaster. Her own personal problems have enhanced her belief that no others can know of despair. She will push her investigator harder. Idle hands are the devil's playground. This technique has failed in the past, but too bad for her worker. *Why should she even bother? No one cares about the cancer victim, the powerful, the greedy.* **Especially, when they are a narcissist.**

We are tired and very ready to die.
No one ever seems to hear us cry.
Don't bother to ask, they all just lie.
But that's okay because we can fly.

Tell us why the hell don't we just go.
We have lived too fast but go mad slow.
How this happened we still don't know.
Ah yes, we ate Oatmeal and got laid low.

There's no way out, no choices, no picks.
So, we put wires in our well place nicks.
Throw some electrical tape into the mix.
Beware, this time Psycho gets deep sized.

Definition of Deep six: To discard, cancel, halt; to completely put an end to something. See everyone below.

"What the fuck do you mean you are releasing her. How can you say she is better in three fucking days? She was forcing metal wires under her skin and covering it with electrical tape. That is not okay. You are more

insane than she is, asshole."
--Master Boyd arguing with Doctor Turner third floor psychiatric wing Wheatly Hospital, October 1998.

I closed my eyes listening to the heartbeat of the Earth beneath my boots. The electrical grid was lowering from the sky and raging below. My brother the sun had retired leaving me in the loving embrace of my father, the darkness. Master Sheryl had fallen asleep with the aid of sedatives. She was frightened about her upcoming surgery.

The Sandman no longer found me fit as a lover. He had passed by leaving me unsatisfied and without distraction. I went out into Master Sheryl's yard to escape her loud ragged snoring. The air was heavy with Autumn's humidity. The year's harvests were ready for reaping. I took a deep breath allowing the aromas of dying, dank leaves, and overripe fields to fill my senses.

Crickets played their tiny fiddles all around. The tune was as old as the world itself. I felt my unit begin to sway to the tiny orchestra. My feet began to stomp while my arms flowed like water through the light breeze. I whirled and spun unable to resist the calling of madness from deep within. My night dance of insanity could not feed my inner beast. Nothing could cap its voracious appetite for my understanding of reality.

Simon watched my desperation from Master Sheryl's porch. He didn't join in like he usually did. Something was different about this psychotic episode. My dear friend could sense it. The shards were out of control. None of them would hear his calls of good judgement. Even the insistent Looper and deadly Dude's demands were falling on deaf ears. The unit was headed for disaster.

He rolled his cigarettes but didn't smoke them. His terror at the deepening danger had killed his addiction to all pleasures. It was apparent to Simon that if someone from the real didn't step in soon, nothing would matter for much longer. He knew he was helpless to ask for help. We had slipped too far. The shard of insight had been forced into our unconsciousness.

"Psycho Tron? Hey Chosen One? Uhm, Gothic Barbie? Ah, Psycho? Anyone? I am speaking to the blond nut pacing like a loon. Hey us. Can we talk a minute?" Simon called out sounding tired.

The Chosen One glanced at him while beginning a spin. "What do you want old man? We are busy. It is time to open the vortex of time. Come dance with us," she growled.

Simon sighed loudly. "My feet hurt. Come over here and sit with me. Let's just chat and watch the sunrise? I know. You can tell me the story of Zeppelin our golden heart. I love that one, please? Stop this movement. You are bringing on the shatter faster," he said pleading with all his might.

I just laughed wildly. "Ah, you worry too much Simon. Come join us in the Tapestry. It is where we belong. The static is coming. They told us soon, very soon we are going home. Can you believe it? Oh, Simon we are going home at last." I jumped and twirled smiling at the tiny holes in the dark sky while they winked at me.

He got up and walked to our struggling unit. "No, we are not going home. We are not ready yet. I would beg you once more to call Master Boyd. He will know what to do. This is bad. We are going to get lost. Our unit of measurement is hidden. I can't figure out our location anymore. How can we find anything if we don't even know where we are?" He grabbed my arm trying to still my movement.

I growled while jerking from his grasp. "You will keep your filthy paws off me. Who do you think you are?"

He shook his head. "That is the problem. I am no longer sure and neither are we."

I looked at the static rising like mist all around us. "See that Simon? It is the Summerland's border. If we can run fast enough, we can find Matthew. We can even get that interview with Javier and Willa. Just think, our paperwork will be done, and we can hold our lover once more. We have earned this reward. We didn't complain when things didn't go our way. Now it is time to find happiness at last. Oh, Simon, we could be one again. All the dreams come true in the Summerlands. Mother Delleh told us they do. Can we please go now? Haven't we done enough yet?" I began to tear up while giggling as I begged my old railroad man.

Simon appeared to have a great deal of pity in his eyes. "No it is not our time. Everything comes around eventually. We have the children, Seine and even Master Boyd. They need us. What about all those innocent children who are scared and waiting for help? Do we want to be selfish and abandon them all? We are a monster and don't deserve the Summerlands if that is truly how we feel." He took my hand.

I fell to my knees kneeling before my true Master Simon. "Please Simon, we are tired. We can't do this anymore. Our strength river has run dry. We would humbly ask you allow us to end this fighting. We want no more of the real. Release us, please."

"Psycho? Psycho? What are you doing out there," Master Sheryl yelled from the front door sounding groggy.

I looked toward the half-asleep Master Sheryl startled. Simon turned to stare at her. "She is causing this bullshit. She would see us destroyed to have all her desires. You must cut off that phony collar and take the chance no one will discover Master Boyd is the chosen. This woman would see us buried under a tire swing with worms in our hair," he said glumly.

I nodded ignoring Simon. "Nothing Master. Just taking a walk to get some air. Thank you have a nice day," I yelled back to Master Sheryl still kneeling before Simon.

"Get in here. You need to get my breakfast started and head to Julia's place in a couple hours. Damn you are a fucking tank. Did you sleep at all?" She yawned and stretched.

I shook my head. "Negative Master. I didn't require a reboot. I will get the script running immediately. I am happy to be of service. Thank you have a nice day," I called out without emotion.

Simon looked back startled. "Psycho Tron? Shit that was fast. Okay, maybe you are more levelheaded than The Chosen One. Listen to me, call Master Boyd immediately."

I looked at him in a trance. "Syntax error. The mainframe is online, and functions are stable. Binary codes are running without failure. Reasons to call for assistance are negative, Simon. We are happy to serve you. Have a nice day." I stood up and went back into the house to start Master Sheryl's large breakfast request.

Master Sheryl laid on her couch watching my slow, robotic like movements. "Psycho, honey, you better not call Boyd for a few days. Just till I start recovering. He has been bugging the piss out of me wanting to talk to you. He said he has tried the office, something called a Nokia phone, and now he is calling here. Woke me up in fact. What a hateful man he is. I am sick and all he can think about is trying to get you into his bed. Men. I am not stupid here. He doesn't really care about you. I am the one that really loves you Psycho. He is just trying to use you. I don't want him fucking with your head. He says you are getting sick and he wants to put you in the hospital again. What a load of horse shit. I know what he is doing, and you should know too. That bastard is trying to take you away from me. I don't want you speaking to him. That is an order. Got it," she said as I served her meal to her.

I nodded slowly. "Understood. Your data is now stored in our memory banks, Master. Programing is recalculating to fit your commands. Please hit alt delete for further instructions. We are happy to serve you. Have a nice day," I said staring at her blankly without inflection in my voice.

Master Sheryl paused. "Hmm, this robot impression you do is pretty cool. I guess it doesn't hurt anything, but I would like you to cut that shit out when anyone is around other than me. What is all that electrical tape doing on your arms by the way? This some kind of new fashion I haven't heard about? Kids these days." She looked at my arms.

"Negative Master. This is repairing work on the mainframe. The script was running long. The motherboard was malfunctioning. A crash was imminent. This error has been corrected. We are happy to serve you. Have a nice day," I said without blinking.

She nodded appearing a bit nervous. "Ah, okay. Repair work huh? What is under that tape, Psycho? You are not cutting yourself up again I hope?"

I looked at her without emotion. "The skin suit had to be opened Master. Wires were disconnected. This is of no interest to the programming. We are happy to serve you. Have a nice day."

She grimaced. "Yikes. Okay, well stop cutting the uhm, skin suit. That is an order. Now if you are going to insist on wearing that fucking tape then cover it up. Wear your coat and keep that shit out of sight. I mean it. You don't want my cane now, do you? If wearing that shit makes you feel better that is fine by me, but I don't want anyone else asking about it. They may not understand. I know you are not like everyone else. Thank God it is not tin foil on your head. It could be worse no doubt."

I nodded. "Affirmative Master. Tin foil does not compute. We are happy to serve you. Have a nice day."

Master Sheryl frowned. "Stop talking like that too. No more 'we are happy to serve you, have a nice day' shit. It is getting on my nerves. Cut it out. Now."

I nodded. "As you wish Master. Anything else?" The Chosen One smiled at her wickedly.

She smiled back. "Now that is better. No. I am good. Clean up the kitchen, cover up those arms and get going to visit with Julia this morning. Do your case load and be home by four in the morning. We have surgery at six. Got that?"

"Yep. I am on it Master. See you on the flip side." I got up and rushed off to get to my ordered tasks for the day.

I was about to head out the door with Master Sheryl yelled out reminding me of her 'forbidding me' to speak to Master Boyd. I smiled while stating I heard her the first time. Without another moment's hesitation I hurried to the Intrepid speeding off at a high rate, spinning tires in my haste. I was in a hurry I had a lot to finish before six.

I kept hearing a strange alarm going off in the backseat. Simon heard it too. He looked at me shrugging as the sound began again.

"What the holy fuck, Simon? Your stomach sure makes an odd growling sound these days. Eat something will you? It is starting to get annoying," I bitched out.

He looked at me oddly. "Hell I thought that was you. That noise is not coming from me Chosen One." He looked into the backseat. "It is that fucking phone thingmajig Master Boyd gave us." He pointed at the cell phone ringing non-stop.

I laughed. "Ah, it is Master Boyd. He is trying to take us away from Master Sheryl. Don't touch that thing. It could suck you up inside it. You know it is a tracking device, right? He is stalking us again. Well he can forget it. We are not stupid. He will try to shoot us," I warned Simon.

Simon looked scared. "Now that is pure bullshit and you know it. Dennis kills people. not Master Boyd. Look, answer the fucking thing and just talk to him please? He is not trying to hurt us. He is trying to help. We need his help, Chosen One. Master Sheryl is lying to you. She is only worried about herself. She knows we are cracking up. She is helping us to hide it. God damn it. Pick up that thing and get help," he yelled.

"Fuck you Simon. We are fine. We feel great. There is nothing wrong with us. We do not have problems. Leave us alone." I laughed maniacally as I fishtailed running over Julia's mailbox sending it flying across the road.

Simon watched the decimated mail holder glide over the back of the Intrepid rolling into the ditch with great force.

"Holy shit, we just took out her mailbox. What are we doing?" He grabbed his forehead moaning.

I parked the car while giggling., "And another one bites the dust, and another one is gone, another one gone, another one bites the dust. Hey, wait, she's gonna get you too. Another one bites the dust." I sung out happily.

I jumped out of the car laughing. Suddenly, without any warning, my brain and the Earth tilted just a bit too far to the left. I put out my arms in an airplane fashion to keep from being hurled to the ground. The sound of thunder rumbled in the distance. The lightening cracked splitting the sky.

I was helpless to stop the oncoming severe psychotic episode. I stood there horrified watching the transmissions began to flow like upside down waterfalls from beneath me. I made a desperate move to escape but the tapestry webs had taken me hostage holding my arms paralyzed as if being crucified.

My head rocked and bobbed uselessly on my neck. My throat went dry. I could no longer swallow as the drool began to flow down my chin in rivers. They reached down and grabbed my chest forcing me to arch backward into a strange C pose. My spine strained and popped. I was stuck like that with my arms still outstretched in this agonizing position. My eyes rolled up into my head unable to tolerate the pain. The pressure crushed the air from my lungs. I could not speak, only gasp out frozen in terror. I felt the tremors rolling up my legs then spread rapidly throughout the unit. My bladder released as the partial complex seizures shut down my consciousness.

Three minutes passed while my brain re-booted unevenly causing total shutdown of sensory perception. Slowly, the tremors abated. I was aware but only vaguely of my bizarre pose. I could make out colors only. Something was moving in the blur of my disordered visual field. I tried to focus on it. It seemed important to recall what the definition of such an image should mean. The chaos of confusion kept my understanding of the surrounding from returning. I was unable to move, speak, hear or think clearly for another ten full minutes.

All the while Julia had been standing there in sheer amazement and awe. She had heard my loud thumping of her mailbox and slamming of my car door. When she came out to greet me, she found I was already in a full-blown psychotic meltdown and seizure cycle.

NOTE: *Most people who saw someone bend backward, pissing themself like that would have called for medical help. Not the very laid back, hands off Julia. She stood there curious but cautious waiting to see if I would recover without her assistance. I was so damned lucky she didn't bother to worry. She figured I had this mess completely under control and I am sure it definitely looked as if I did, but I did not.*

After all, the ambulance may have discovered the potentially deadly brain malfunction just a bit sooner had she done the right thing. Instead, she stayed out of it watching patiently. She wasn't the least bit worried by the signs of deep neural misfiring and chemical imbalances taking root in my damaged brain.

Wasn't her problem anyway. I was just there to look after her never ending demands for attention. Return of the favor never once had crossed her selfish mind. Julia seemed to believe she was the only person on the planet who had ever encountered personal tragedy and loss. Julia thought it couldn't be possible that anyone was more deserving than herself of a sympathetic ear or just basic human kindness. Julia was no more concerned for my welfare than Master Sheryl.

OKAY PREPARE FOR MY RANT

Hey, I totally understand. This was not about me. I mean, Julia was an ex-foster mother who had lost her foster children to murder many months ago. Master Sheryl was about to get both her breasts cut off in the morning and start her battle with cancer. They both needed me to help them through their darkest hours. It didn't matter that both women had been so hateful all their lives during the good times. It was of no consequence that they never bothered to cultivate anyone who would be there for them when the days were harsh. Hell, they didn't have to. They both could just run the idiot collar into the ground, stealing my limited energy when the going got rough.

There was no reason for either vicious bitch to maybe consider being decent enough to make real friends, join a support group designed for their woes, or even paying for fucking professional help. Nah, they could just guilt me into putting up with their bullshit for free.

How dare I act stupid when these ladies were dealing with such difficulties in their lives? How could I be so greedy trying to steal their attention by going psychotic? What a drama queen I was. I only had schizophrenia. What the fuck could I even know about hellish despair? I was young, healthy, and had my whole life ahead of me. What was my fucking damage anyway? Hmmm?

I felt they'd release their hold. Relief poured over me while I pulled up out of my weird position. My back was killing me. Julia watched while I wiped my chin and rubbed my shoulders trying to loosen my constricted muscles. I groaned when I noticed the urine stain spreading down my pants headed for my boots.

"Shit, God damn it, I apparently I need to wear a fucking diaper." I looked at the car wondering if I had remembered to put a clean pair of pants in the trunk for just this kind of accident.

"Wow, that was different. What the fuck just happened there? I have seen some odd fitness workouts but that one takes the cake." Julia chuckled.

I glared at her hatefully. "That was not a workout, Julia. I have a seizure disorder. It sometimes overshoots the medication." I headed for the Intrepid hoping to find a fresh change of clothing hidden in there somewhere.

Julia narrowed her eyes. "Seizure? That can't be right. I have seen a Grand Mal before. Had a couple of foster kids with it. That is not what they did when they had one. That was not a seizure, Psycho."

"Shows what you fucking know. There are other kinds of seizures, Julia. That was a Partial Complex Seizure." I opened the trunk and began to dig around the case boxes while crossing my fingers I would get lucky for a change.

She snorted. "Those kinds of seizures come from brain damage. You have brain damage? From what? A car accident? Did you fall and hit your head?"

"Did I have an accident? Uhm, sure, something like that. Really, I don't believe it is any of your business now is it? Look, I know you expected a visit this morning, but I must go back to Sheryl's and change. It would seem I need to freshen up a bit." I slammed the trunk closed unable to find what I needed to fix my bladder flow issue.

"You know people with that problem usually have had their eggs scrambled quite a bit. You seem fine to me. Can't be a complex partial." She crossed her arms still not believing what I said despite what she had actually seen with her own eyes.

I glowered at her angrily. "I don't really give a flying fuck what you believe or don't, Julia. I have pissed my pants. I must go change my motherfucking clothes or be stuck sitting in it all God damned day. So, you can visit with Simon here while I head back to town. There is no time for arguing about this bullshit."

I looked at Simon. "Stay with Julia and keep her entertained while I go attend this, will you Simon?"

He put his hands over his eyes but nodded appearing very stressed that I had just called him out in front of a normal again.

Julia's eyes went wide as she watched me speaking to what she perceived as thin air. "Hey, uhm, who are you talking to? Simon? Simon who? You feeling okay Psycho? Oh, wait a minute. Psycho, no, couldn't be. Sheryl would have said something. Then again. So, anyone ever diagnosed you will mental problems? I mean besides the funny nickname and all?"

I got into the Intrepid. "Nope. We are fine. We feel great. There is nothing wrong with us. We do not have problems. Simon, see you in a minute. I will just pop over to the office, grab some pants out of my overnight bag and be right back. Ciao baby." I slammed the door and sped out of her driveway burning rubber as if taking off from the starting gates at the Nascar 500.

It didn't bother me that I was going over seventy miles an hour down a single laned backroad and then the middle of town. Nor did the red lights at intersections registrar as anything I should be heeding. After breaking almost every single road rule in the book, I flew into the DCFS driveway practically sideways.

I still didn't slow down. Not a thought was in my head as I jumped the concrete blocks placed strategically about to mark spaces for legal parking. I promptly killed the car motor on the sidewalk in front of the Family Dollar Store that sat adjacent to the State office. The Intrepid was sitting perfectly parallel with the driver's side door blocking and blocked by the entry way to the Family Dollar.

I crawled across the console and exited out the passenger door humming a weird tune to myself. Apparently, the idea that patrons and the staff of that fine discount establishment may be a little miffed that I was slowing down commerce did not occur to my psychosis idled brain. People were starting to come running from every direction yelling and cussing my most interesting vehicle maneuvering skills.

I just nodded, smiled and waved at them unaffected by their insults. I couldn't understand what they were saying anyway. I just kept humming as I skipped across the lot to the DCFS building. When I entered the front office all the awaiting clients who had been watching my stunt driver antics through the large plate glass windows, scattered to the opposite wall. They all appeared very unsettled by my presence. I frowned at them realizing they must be able to tell I had wet myself during the seizure. Their obvious disgust pissed me off.

"Fuck all of you. You act like none of you have ever had an accident. That is bullshit. You are all a pack of liars," I shouted at the frightened group as they backed further away from me.

I sneered at them taking a few steps to start beating their asses. Then without understanding why I changed my mind and headed for the wooden door to the back area of the building. I decided I needed to see PC and Fax in Jane's office. I had already forgotten the reason I had come there in the first place. It seemed my Looper was off having coffee with Dude or something. Since my memory, Looper, was slinking around not doing his job, nothing was staying in my consciousness for more than a few seconds.

I pushed through Jane's glass door, sat down and flipped PC's switch. Jane was awakened by my loud entrance into her office.

"Psycho? Hey, aren't you supposed to be out in the field or something? Everything okay?" Jane yawned out only partially interested to hear the answer to her questions.

I snorted. "Fuck you very much Jane. Mind your business, you old cow. I am busy with flight instructions and things of that nature. If you don't mind can you check to see if Simon put the turkey back in the freezer and find me the dead child foster placement forms. God damn it. Where are my fishing lures? Can't someone please stop moving all these fucking boxes around? You know that is how people trip and fall. Do I need to call for an aspirin? What is your damage Jane," I rambled not making a lick of sense.

Jane stood up and walked over to look at me while I stared at PC who was just beginning to wake up. "Psycho, hey, does Sheryl know you are here?"

Nora came busting through the door of the office in a huff. "Fucking nut, move your car. Jane, call the police. This idiot just parked her car practically inside the Family Dollar.

They are freaking out and riding asses out of here. Plus, she just cussed out all the clients waiting out front. Psycho, you're one crazy bitch. Did you hear me? Move your car," she screamed out loudly,

I covered my ears as her words began to end sharply sounding like fingers running down a blackboard. "Shut up, shut the fuck up. Too much noise," I yelled back at Nora.

PC opened his eyes. "Ah Psycho Tron. Listen to this one. What did the leaper say to the hooker? Keep the tip." He began to laugh shaking the walls causing the lights to flicker on and off.

I closed my eyes covering my ears tighter. "Shut up, shut up," I screamed.

Sound and light began to mix as I could hear voices of both genders coming from every direction. The sound was like a radio being tuned just outside my head from station to station without stopping for long and without end.

"Jane, do something. She is coming unglued. We can't have this drama."

"We are happy to serve you. Thank you have a nice day."

"This is not a fucking nuthouse. Get this schizophrenic asshole out of here."

"What did the one butt cheek say to the other butt cheek? If we stick together we can stop this shit."

"Psycho, hey Psycho. Over here, do you see the dead child foster placement forms?"

"Pssst, the cops are coming. Nora and Jane are calling the cops."

"I see London I see France I see Willa's underpants."

"Call Master Boyd. He will know what to do. We are in big trouble. We are his wife by God's own law."

"As I walk along I wonder what went wrong with our love, a love that was so strong. I'm walking in the rain, tears are falling and I feel the pain of wishing you were here by me to end this misery and I wonder, I wonder. Why? Oh why why why why she ran away."

"Hahaha, they are coming. Can you hear the sirens yet? Charlie is a cop."

"Move that fucking car. I don't care how you move it but get it now."

"Who does she think she is? You can't just park wherever. Burning down the house. The roof is on fire."

"Why do I always get stuck with the loons? Let me call Sheryl."

"If you cut the slot to the left the wire goes in nice and smooth. Ah, so smooth."

"The dead child foster forms are with the turkey in the fridge."

"Beware, the cops are coming. Better run now. I wonder where she will stay, my little runaway."

"It is a short circuit, you know. Check the script. Get more tape."

"Psycho, over here. Look over here, Psycho. Hey, run away, run away now."

I opened my eyes still holding my ears trying to drown out the voices. Nora staring at me appearing angry. Jane was on the telephone calling someone.

I jumped up screaming, "Shut up. God damn it, shut up. Please stop talking. I can't understand all the noise. Shut the fuck up."

My yells of distress scared Nora. She ran to hide behind Jane. Appearing terrified both women stared at me bug eyed. I looked back at them wishing I had an ice pick to put out my eardrums with. The voices would not stop.

I looked about the room wild to find something to shove into my ear holes. I needed it to calm down. I remembered there was a break room. The staff would have knives or even sharp coffee stirring tubes in there. That could work. I took off running for what I hoped would be a relief to my confusion.

I nearly fell sliding through the break room door still grinding my palms into my ears while the voices bombarded my senses. The place was a mess. I couldn't make heads nor tails of the hundreds of items discarded all over the cluttered countertops. My sight settled on an ice pick laying in the tiny sink. Someone had been breaking up a large mass of the stuff melting slowly in a bag that had a picture of a polar bear under the word ice. The lazy staffers poor housekeeping was a lucky break for one very upset psychotic.

I ran for the weapon letting out a gasp of relief. I almost had it in my hands when I was grabbed from behind and flung roughly into the wall. In my confusion I turned and began assaulting the figure who had pulled me away from the tool required to end my pain.

I punched, bit, kicked and struggled against the strong figure that held my arms tightly. I could not gain my bearings nor recognize the humanoid trying to subdue me.

"Psycho, stop this now. Listen to me. Now settle down. It is me, Sheryl." I felt the person reach out and grab my collar pulling hard.

Immediately I recalled this person. "Sheryl? What is happening? Why are you here? Where am I? Help me. Please someone fucking help." I began to struggle again.

Master Sheryl slammed my head backward into the wall. "Cut this out now. We are going home. Settle down or I will get the fucking cane. Psycho, I am warning you. Stop now."

I saw bright spots explode in my vision from the blow. Slowly the cicada of voices began to quiet down. I was very confused. Master Sheryl was still holding my panting unit against the wall waiting for me to stop freaking out. I tried to remember what was going on, but my thoughts were slipping like greased piglets through my hands.

"Jane and Nora, calm down. Psycho just forgot to take her medication this morning. Call Charlie back and tell him we got it under control. I am taking her home. She just needs her medication and a little rest. Jane, move the fucking Intrepid. The extra set of keys is in my purse over by the door. Look I don't need this shit. I have surgery tomorrow morning God damn it. Everyone just settle the fuck down. Psycho is just stressed, aren't you Psycho?" She looked at me nodding.

I looked at her still confused as hell but mimicked her nod. She held me tightly to the wall staring into my near vacant eyes. "You in there now? If I let you go will you behave yourself?"

I nodded then looked at the floor unsure what she meant by behaving. I didn't do anything wrong, did I? I felt her release my unit. I stood there unsure what to do.

She sighed. "Okay, you need to sleep. I am going to give you some of my sedatives. You will take the pills right now and sleep. You will just have to be out of compliance by a couple of hours. After my surgery tomorrow, you can get out there and finish your calls. Today and tonight you are going to sleep. That should patch you up. It had better for your sake. Now, take these, don't make me force them." She handed me two pink pills and told Jane to get her a glass of water.

Jane handed me the water. "Here you go Psycho. You sure she is okay, Sheryl? Look at her eyes. She ain't home, girl."

I took the glass and the pills then began to giggle. "Look at her eyes. She ain't home, girl," I repeated unable to contain my laughter.

Jane raised an eyebrow. "Sheryl, face it. Psycho needs to be hospitalized."

I began to howl in laughter. "Sheryl, face it. Psycho needs to be hospitalized," mimicked Psycho.

Master Sheryl growled then backhanded me hard. The sting quickly shut up my humor and mouth.

"Stop that now. Jane mind your business. Psycho is just tired. Let those Demerol work. She won't be conscious in about twenty minutes. She just needs some sleep. Hell, this job would fuck anyone up. She found poor little Willa yesterday. That would upset anyone. She is not the first of us to need a few mental health days. Now you be quiet and let the medication work damn it." She pushed me back into the wall harshly.

I was feeling something strange overcoming me. A heaviness was starting in my chest spreading through my unit rapidly. The heavy inner anxiety began to freeze up into a block of ice. My eyelids felt like they weighed a ton.

Master Sheryl began to chuckle. "Ah she is light weight. See Jane, the shit is already working. Psycho will be out like a light very shortly. Did you move the car? Help me get her to the Taurus, will you?" Her voice trailed off as the darkness closed in around me. I was gone to la-la land in less than ten minutes.

Likely my lack of any meaningful sleep and onset of Acute stage psychosis allowed for the rapid work of Master Sheryl's sedatives. I don't recall the ride to her house, being put to bed nor the rest of that day or night. I slept as deep as the poor little Willa. I was dead to the world around me.

At four that morning Master Sheryl roughly roused me from my death like trance. I awoke unsure where I was located, nor how I even got there, or who I was. My Master was irritated by my complete confusion as to my situation. I was jerked out of her bed and told to get my shit together as this was her big day and I was being a selfish bitch.

I nodded but still couldn't gain my bearings, try as I might. The walls were breathing, the light too bright and the voices were too loud. Codes were popping up on the walls glowing eerily with green light. I could hear the rushing electrical grids above and below. I had trouble navigating my unit. It continued to wobble and rock, not appearing to understand my commands to go where I wanted to go or was told to go.

I didn't even attempt to communicate with Master Sheryl. I could barely understand her language. I got backhanded twice for not responding to her orders while I packed her bags for the hospital. I didn't mean to be insolent. I just couldn't hear her above all the other voices coming in from every direction.

I wondered if maybe someone had their stereo on too loud. Surely that was the problem. I just had super powered hearing. I sighed while wishing the asshole would turn the sonofabitch down so I could hear my Master's orders. This was getting very irritating.

When it was time to head to the Taurus my Master behaved strangely. She held up her arm blocking me from following her out. She stood on her porch looking all around straining her eyes into the early morning darkness. I watched as she appeared to be listening for something. I assumed she must be hearing the overly loud stereo too. I rubbed my forehead grateful she did. I was worried I had lost my mind for a second there. Nope, we are fine. We feel great. There is nothing wrong with us. We do not have problems.

Finally satisfied she couldn't do shit about this rude ass neighbor and his loud music either she motioned me to come with her to the car. I was putting her stuff in the back seat when she began to frantically tell me to get the lead out of my ass and hurry up. I nodded as I picked up my pace. She seemed to be in an awful big hurry to get her boobs cut off.

I got into the passenger's seat barely closing the door before she sped off into the night rushing for the hospital. I just looked at her concerned by her weird anxious behavior. She kept checking the rearview mirror and looking behind us. I raised an eyebrow but didn't voice any questions. Master Sheryl was scared. I would be too. This was going to be a rough surgery no doubt. I tried to be empathetic to her plight. No one wants to be desecrated and mutilated, not even if it is to save their life.

When we arrived at the hospital, I aided her with her luggage. The doctors expected her to be inpatient for three days if there were no complications. I followed behind her doing my best to listen to her instructions regarding my job, her job, the house, and what was expected of me during her time in the recovery bed.

I noticed the lights in the hallway were flashing brightly then dim. People were strobing all around me. I could hear their thoughts flowing lazily thought the air. Germs and other microorganisms covered everything. I watched them devouring the walls. The real and the delusional met in this place. I could see the real and unreal. Master Sheryl's voice echoed and looped hanging in the air above me raining down like drops of liquid pain into my ears. I pressed my palms into the sides of my head trying to block out some of the racket while she and I sat waiting for her name to be called for surgery prep.

Master Sheryl saw me. She reached out pulling my arms down. "Stop that. Don't you start your shit here, Psycho. I mean it. Pull yourself together. I am about to be taken back for surgery. Do you hear me? I need you strong for me. Now remember, don't talk to Boyd. I mean it. If he comes around I order you to run or call the police. When I wake up, I want you to be there so don't leave until I tell you it is okay. Hang out here in the waiting room or walk the halls but do not go outside. Tonight you can get back to work once I am settled. Understand me?" She glared at me hard.

I nodded. "Yes Master I understand. Don't leave. Don't go outside. Don't talk to Boyd." I looked at the floor trying to recall the difference between leave and leaves. Did one grow on trees?

The nurse called for Master Sheryl. She looked at me with tears in her eyes.

My Master took my hand then kissed my mouth. "Wish me luck, honey."

I nodded. "Good luck honey," I said unsure if this was the correct response.

Master Sheryl smiled. "I will see you soon. Don't forget I love you." She walked off following the nurse leaving me in the empty surgical waiting area.

I felt thirsty. I needed to find water somewhere. Master Sheryl had not told me where to go to get such a thing. I needed to find the bathroom. I thought I saw one in the hallway that led to this room. I went out the double doors wandering around till I recognized the restroom signs. Once inside the woman's room I drank deeply from the sink. I stared into the mirror but couldn't recognize the creature looking back at me. The wild blue eyes of that girl chilled me to the bone. I could see her mouth moving but no words were coming out. The voices began to loudly taunt me.

"Come here let me tell you a secret. Die, hahaha."

"Run, they are coming. Ha! Look there, we can see you. Listen, do you hear that? Run."

I looked around the room trying to understand who was coming, how could they see me? It had to be the mirror. The girl in the mirror, she was telling the others where to find me. I did need to run. I took off like a flash running from the bathroom back down the hallway terrified beyond reason. People were walking past me all going to this place or another. I couldn't remember where to go. I was lost.

Every door looked the same. Somehow, I had forgotten where Master Sheryl told me to wait for her. I turned down into another hall looking for anything familiar. It spilled into another but again I couldn't find the right door. Like a rat in a maze I ran from one hall to the next become more upset with one corridor stretching into a branch of many more.

Simon walked out of one of the intersections. "Psycho. Over here. You are lost. Come with me. I know the way."

I sighed with relief. My best friend had found me. Thank the Gods I was becoming sure I would have a full-on meltdown had he not showed up when he did.

"Simon, where are we? I can't find Master Sheryl. Help, I forgot the numbers. She told me not to forget the numbers." I whined to him causing two patients walking by to turn their heads and raise their eyebrows at my talking to my Simon in public.

He took my hand smiling. "It is okay. I am here now so calm down. We can find it. Stay close. This place is huge." He began walking pulling me behind him.

"Simon don't go into the bathroom. There is this girl that wants to kill us in there," I whispered to him loudly causing another pedestrian to look at me strangely as I walked by them.

Simon looked back at me and the gawking outsider. "Stop talking to me in public. The normals can hear you, stupid. You want to get us put away?"

I shook my head. "Simon stop. I don't know where I am damn it. You are going too fast. I don't care what the normals say. Stop walking so fucking fast," I said loudly.

A man was walking by while I yelled at my old friend. He too looked at me with concern but stopped walking and started heading back towards me. I stood there frightened wondering if he was going to tell me to stop cussing in the hospital hallways. The man looked very angry.

"Psycho, what the fuck? I have been looking for you everywhere. Sheryl said you were in the field. Your damned car is abandoned at the office. The secretary there said you had a melt-down yesterday. Why haven't you called me? Why didn't you answer that phone I gave you?" The man reached out and grabbed my upper arm holding tightly.

I shook my head. "Let me go mister. I don't know, please, I didn't mean to cuss in the halls. I was rude. Don't call the president. I will fix it I promise." I cowered sure that this fellow was going to clobber me for my foul language.

The man's eyes went wide while he groaned. "Oh shit. Psycho baby you are blown. Okay, hang in there. I will get you some help. Come with me." He started pulling me behind him.

"Please I am sorry. Don't tell on me. I won't do it again. I won't. Simon help. Tell him." I started to cry, scared as hell that I was going to be executed. Beats me why I thought that.

The man turned around. "Oh honey, it is okay. I am here to help you. Stop crying, I would never hurt you. I love you Psycho. I am going to take you home now. Is that alright? Don't you want to go home?" The man stroked my wet cheek.

I nodded. "Yes, I want to go home mister, but I am lost. Did Mother Delleh tell you how to get there?"

He nodded smiling sweetly. "Yes she did. Let's go talk to her right now. Will you come with me to talk to Mother Delleh," the man said softly.

I smiled. "Yes, of course I will. I have missed her so much. I need to ask her something, but I forgot what it was. Can you help me remember it? Oh, don't forget to bring Simon too."

The man took my hand leading me toward the door of the hospital to a black car. "Yes, I will help you remember. Simon is already in the car waiting on us. Now, I want you to get into the car and close your eyes. When you wake up, we will be home. Promise you will be good and sleep till we get there?"

I got into the black car. "Yes, I promise." I closed my eyes smiling, finally I was going home.

Master Boyd took me the Wheatly ER where I was immediately hospitalized in the psychiatric third floor wing officially labeled Schizophrenia, Undifferentiated, Acute Psychosis, severe on October 6th, 1998.

WHAT MASTER BOYD TOLD ME REGARDING OCTOBER 5th & 6th, THE DAYS LEADING UP TO THIS PSYCHOTIC BREAK

Master Boyd said that he had been frantically trying to contact me beginning only one hour after the discovery of Willa's little unit. I had not answered his attempts to reach me by cell phone. My Master then began calling the office, again getting no response. By morning he had become very upset. He called Master Sheryl and was told I was working.

Master Boyd insisted to Master Sheryl that she have me return his calls. He warned Master Sheryl that I had appeared disjointed and mildly psychotic. He wanted her to take me into the ER for a reality check. She lied and told him I had been seen. Master Sheryl informed him I was right as rain and that is concern was unwarranted.

Master Boyd didn't believe her, especially since I continued to not respond to any of his numerous attempts to talk to me himself by phone. The day and night that Master Sheryl had me sedated he had finally had enough of her giving him the run-around. My Master took off work, drove to Cumberland and banged on Master Sheryl's door. She told him I was out in the field, again lying since I was laid out cold in her bed, and could not be bothered to speak with him while working. This angered him a great deal. He went to the office to wait for me to come do my paperwork.

He saw the banged up Intrepid and was told by the office staff of my strange behaviors. This set off alarm bells in my Master who was well versed with my history of psychotic episodes. He returned to Master Sheryl's house demanding she hail me by pager to call him immediately. Master Sheryl threatened him with the police if he did not remove his person from her property. Master Boyd had no choice but to go back and wait at the DCFS office parking lot hoping to catch me between calls.

He sat there half the night when suddenly he realized, if the Intrepid was there, and the Taurus at Master Sheryl's house, I couldn't be in the field. He then understood Master Sheryl was hiding me out for some reason.

My Master went back and waited for Master Sheryl to leave for the hospital and followed at a distance. Once we went inside, he hung out assuming she would be called back leaving me unguarded. He was right. Master Sheryl had been hiding my psychotic status from him and everyone else. I was told he was walking by when he saw me arguing with thin air, completely out of my mind.

Using his long years of experience in handling me when very psychotic he managed to get me into his car and to the hospital for much needed inpatient treatment without incident. It was there that the doctors, and my Master, found the wires that I had been placing into my arms by making small cuts then forcing them under the skin suit. I have a metal allergy. Thanks to this nasty problem I had become infected, which was hastening my already declining mental health. The lack of substantial sleep, and severe stress at *witnessing the gruesome death scene of Willa promised a reality break of epic proportions.*

Had Master Boyd not been vigilant and pushy, well I likely would have killed myself, died of infection or killed someone else very shortly. Master Sheryl's selfish need to have me by her side despite my obvious sickness was unforgivable in Master Boyd's eyes. I cannot tell schizophrenia, hey not today and go away. Master Sheryl could not say hey cancer go away.

I was pumped full of heavy antipsychotics while Master Boyd not only visited but pretty much never left my room when he was off work. He even slept in the chair next to my strapped down unit. I rambled, babbled and drooled the entire three day stay. Yeah only three days.

My senses began to solidify by the end of day two and on day three I was no longer showing significant symptoms of my thought disorder. I could understand speech, answer questions logically and even seemed to be aware of my location. Much to Master Boyd's horror I was cut loose labeled in remission by ten AM the fourth morning.

You could hear my Master cussing Doctor Turner for miles when the young inexperienced psychiatrist informed him that my bed was about to be vacant.

"Are you fucking kidding? She is not well. You send her out she may cut off an arm next time. Who knows whose arm," Master Boyd barked out angrily at Doctor Turner.

The doctor looked at my Master smugly. "Look Mister Simmons, the patient is not claiming suicidal or homicidal ideation. Her wounds are healing, and she signed our hospital agreement to never engage in that kind of self-injury again. She is still showing symptom of psychotic thinking, but it is mild. Her adaptive functioning is always impaired, but not more so than normal for her case." Master Boyd growled interrupting the young doctor.

"Mild psychosis. Seriously? She thinks she is a fucking robot. That is not mild. She signed an agreement with the hospital? Did you even read the patient records, asshole? Missus Voss doesn't respect doctors, hospitals or the police. You let her out; she will get hurt. At least will you stop her from going back to that fucking shit job of hers," Master Boyd yelled out beyond furious.

The doctor shook his head chuckling. "Mister Simmons, your fiancé has schizophrenia. She is very lucky to be so highly functioning. Most of them lose their IQ and end up babbling messes incapable of any kind of employment. I don't think such a high stress job is really good for her given the severity of her disease, but there is no reason to assume she could not return to work next week if she continues to improve. We have increased her medication. Give it a little time. I think you will be pleased with the results. Now, if you don't mind, I have other patients to see. You have a good day Mister Simmons and good luck." Doctor Turner left the room.

Master Boyd let out a loud yell, "Ah, fuck. What is wrong with everyone? God damn it."

I laid there in my bed quietly unsure what to say. He was very upset that the Doctor said I was well. I would have thought he would be happy. I wondered if Master Sheryl was right. Maybe Master Boyd didn't really love me at all. He was just pretending to. It seemed to me he was only happy when I was locked up or strapped to a bed.

He looked at me appearing apologetic. "I am sorry I failed you again baby. I will keep looking. There must be someone who can help us. I will never bring you to this shit place again. They are fucking useless. Just hang in there for me, will you?"

I nodded. "Yes Master. As you wish." I looked away afraid he would see the anger in my eyes.

He wanted me to be his prisoner. I was not going to let him keep me locked up so he could just have his way whenever he wanted. What a monster. I am not sick. We are fine. We feel great. There is nothing wrong with us. We do not have problems.

Chapter 68: Home is Where the Broken Heart Is
The D/s Power Couple
Master Boyd and the Absent Interim Master Sheryl

It looks like old Sheryl has been knocked down a level. Well in truth, I should have left her alone after her poor performance in October 1998. However, Master Boyd was right, I am very hardheaded. Despite obvious indication that my best interests were not her front and center I continued to cling to a dying interim, and a relationship that never was.

Psycho had a psychotic spill. Her fall gave her Dominant quite a chill. Her weakness caused a dark heart to recognize a thrill. She has alerted an evil who is hoping to get his first kill. The greedy interim will push never getting her fill. The schizophrenic will end up paying everyone's bill.

Ready to crash 0nto the rocks, break every bone and connection within, errr, this boat? Awesome. We are too. We are fine. We feel great. There is nothing wrong with us. We do not have problems. Grab that rape kit, my wallet, that big case file, those bottles labeled useless antipsychotics and don't forget to bring your big heart. After all, we need something else to shatter since we already cracked our mind.

"If you really want to save Skylar, then take this money, load her into the car and run. Don't argue with me. Leave right now. Run as far as you can go and never come back. If you do, they will arrest you for kidnapping and send her back to her demonic mother. This time she

won't survive. The system has failed her. Be her hero and sacrifice your comfort for her life. Be the loving father she never had."
--Psycho to Mister Cummings on the courthouse steps, October 1998.

I was told not to return to my job as an investigator for another week. Master Boyd was doing his very best to keep me from going back for good. I had to ask him several times to drive me to Cumberland to pick up my car, and my things from Sheryl's house. She had already left headed to her new house and life in Carlise over one hundred and fifty miles from Wheatly. I was abandoned but not completely forgotten.

He had promised that weekend he would finally help me to retrieve my meager possessions. At night while he worked, I stayed with Maiden Mary. She and I were warned by both he and Dennis that if I tried to leave to go back to Cumberland and work they would arrest me. I would be thrown into the white cell until my doctors write a note allowing my legal return.

Normally Dennis would not get involved in domestic issues. This time my Master ratted me out by showing Dennis the healing wounds on my arms. Due to the nature of my employment and closeness to his police investigations, the old Bull decided this time he would make damned sure I minded the doctor's orders. He was none too happy to learn my psychotic break happened the day of Nancy's arrest and the discovery of Willa's little dead unit.

So, I was grounded for seven days. Forced to sit with my Maiden while she watched like a hawk at night and sit with my Master in his bed (by directive) during the day. Master Boyd didn't attempt a single sexual act during my convalescence which both surprised and relieved me. I could tell he obviously wanted to ravage me but his concern for my unstable mental health stayed his appetites and his hands for a change.

Instead I had to lay there while he spooned and cuddled my unit in his sleep, stuck staring out the window with nothing else to do. I was still not sleeping even when granted the chance. My Maiden informed Master Boyd I was still talking to Simon constantly and dancing most nights in the front yard while in a trance.

My Master was beyond livid trying to find a way to get me the needed psychiatric assistance before my next significant break with reality came on in the cycle. He must have called every psychiatrist in the state looking for someone who would take my case or at least point him in the right direction. Despite his best efforts, no one wanted a high functioning schizophrenic on their role books. He vowed loudly that no matter how far he had to take me, I was getting 'help.'

I would just roll my eyes at him over what I viewed as his overreaction to a little psychotic episode. Hell, I knew we are fine. We feel great. There is nothing wrong with us. We do not have problems.

After much begging I got my Master to let me call Sheryl. I wanted to see how she was doing. As usual, the old ball breaker pounced on me for disobeying her orders by leaving her side with Master Boyd. She wouldn't listen when I told her I was too confused to even realize the man who caught me in the hallway was Master Boyd. I had no idea he was combing the halls looking for me. Sheryl did. It was to her detriment that she didn't share that information.

Sheryl went on to inform me that I was on the slate to testify in the Cummings relative placement case that coming Monday. I had been subpoenaed due to my approved home study of Richard's home for the adoption of his fourteen-year-old niece Skylar. She had been in his home since her being taken into state custody at eleven years old.

THE STORY OF SKYLAR AND RICHARD
The Relative placement adoption gone wrong.

Skylar's mother Minnie was another amphetamine-type drug addict. The neglectful mother had turned a blind eye to the horrid affections many of her drug dealer boyfriends were showing the near teen Skylar who was ten years older and almost eleven at that time. After a string of rapes Skylar had contracted a wicked case of genital herpes. The poor baby was infected for life and by no fault of her own. When Minnie had taken her girl into the health department for a checkup, the vigilant nurse practitioner had privately asked the child how this STD had come to be. Skylar tearfully confessed her woes and DCFS was called in. The child was immediately taken into protective custody.

Minnie's older brother Richard was a clean cut, hardworking, honest fellow. Having no children of his own and a close family connection to the very traumatized little Skylar, he petitioned the courts offering up his home as a haven for his niece. He was quickly approved for the relative placement.

Minnie managed to wrangle Skylar back into her home for a weekend visitation despite her brother's warnings to the caseworkers that she was not complying with the no men rule when Skylar was in her home.

Just like old times, Skylar was promptly raped and beaten by Minnie's secret live in drug dealing boyfriend. Minnie had no choice but to seek ER assistance when Skylar didn't wake up from the blows the monster landed on her noggin while he took his fill of her already very damaged parts.

The ER physician took an emergency hold recognizing the clear signs of assault and abuse. Minnie panicked when told the police were coming to arrest her. She kidnapped Skylar by dragging the half-sedated child down the hospital hallway pushing her into the car.

When Minnie took off at a high rate to outrun the coming authorities, Skylar in her confused haze jumped from the moving vehicle and was dragged a few feet across the parking lot of the hospital. She survived the horror, but it damaged her beautiful face and right arm forever.

Minnie was arrested and jailed for charges ranging from child endangerment to kidnapping. Skylar returned to

Richard's loving home. Her beloved uncle worked two jobs to make sure Skylar got the plastic surgery required to make the child whole as possible given the circumstances.

Richard did much more than give this lost little girl a new outside. He worked hard to fix her in her soul as well. He gave her stability, safety, care, structure and above all unconditional love. Over the years, his generous heart had paid off. Skylar had gone from a failing student with low self-esteem to the captain of her cheerleading team with straight A's. She was fighting hard to get her life back. With her ever loyal Uncle Richard right there to help her every step of the way. He was her biggest fan and no one was louder in her cheering section.

Finally, after three years, Skylar qualified for adoption out of the State's custody. Richard immediately applied for the honorable position of becoming his niece's one and true parent for life. It was with great joy that I found his home approved for this wonderful event in both his and Skylar's existence.

I was invited and had humbly accepted his and Skylar's desires that I attend their adoption party to be held in the early part of November. Everyone was looking forward to this auspicious occasion with bright eyes and happiness. A closed case, with a very happy ending. A rare gem in the dark, dusty files of DCFS.

It was supposed to go without a hitch. There was no reason for worry. Minnie was about to have her parental rights terminated. In three years, the woman had never followed a single case plan. She never visited Skylar (good.), and she had damaged this child for life in every way possible. Easy choice to place that deserving child with a parent who cared. This was a no brainer, right?

Well, when Minnie found out she was about to lose her daughter for good, she petitioned the courts for a second chance. She cited the State had not tried to help her get off drugs. She reported there had been no aid offered her in finding appropriate housing nor had they offered transportation to visit Skylar. This was all bullshit. No one was buying that poppycock.

However, it was her last allegation that caught the sight of the judge. Minnie pointed her finger and said that Richard, her brother, was an openly gay man. This was a truth that was not considered when placing the needful Skylar in his home. Richard was a great man, an awesome caretaker, and the child's own blood kin. What the fuck did we care who he loved, a Bob or a Jane? His sexual practices were his business unlike Minnie's (a straight woman) who had unforgivably become Skylar's abuse parent.

Despite the obvious, the old school homophobic Judge blew a gasket. He had not been informed of Richard's sexual orientation. He was ready to throw everyone in jail for neglecting to keep that monster away from this poor little girl. I mean, what if he had turned her into, oh my, a Goth, or a gay, or whatever.

All the case workers were being called into court that had ever touched this situation, including myself. The Judge wanted Richard, Minnie and Skylar there too. Everyone was going to answer to how a gay man had been allowed to be a foster parent to his own niece. A child belongs with its mother. Minnie was obviously the better choice. That monster gay man could have hurt that poor baby. You know, worse than allowing her to be raped repeatedly, acquiring a lifelong STD and ripping off half her face. How dare we care about our wards like that?

I groaned as I listened to Sheryl tell me the details. She told me to tell Master Boyd there was no getting out of this one. Judge McNutt was a nasty customer. If I didn't show up in court, I would be held in contempt and jailed immediately. Hell, even if I did show up I might maybe go to jail for daring to approve an awesome man's home for adoption of his own niece because I followed the law, refusing to discriminate against him just because he was gay.

"So, how are you feeling? Boyd said you were babbling and drooling unable to even feed yourself. You sound fine to me. When are you coming back to work damn it?" Sheryl growled angrily.

I shook my head. "Working on it boss. I just got to get the cobwebs cleaned out of the attic. Not sure what is the big deal? I never babble. I'm not even sure what fucking country that tower was located. (See knights move reference below). Stupid if you ask me. Simon says this is a conspiracy. I believe that is likely. The coding is matching up you know," I rambled out.

Definition of Knight's move speech: In psychiatry, derailment (also called loosening of association) is a thought disorder (schizophrenia) characterized by discourse consisting of a sequence of unrelated or only remotely related ideas. The frame of reference often changes from one sentence to the next.

Example: In the above paragraph: Sheryl says I was accused of babbling. I say I never babble. I am not even sure what country the tower is located in. That is a remotely related reference/idea to the infamous Tower of Babel from the Bible. The story of God's destruction of the Tower of Babel is the actual origin of the word Babble or to speak incoherently.

Sheryl sighed loudly. "Well you are still talking like a loon. Shit. What is that fucking Guardian doing out there? He is likely keeping you off balance so he can have his way with you. Girl, you have to watch out for men. They are sneaky you know. Boyd won't be happy until he has you chained to his bed so he can do horrible things to you, honey. If I were you I would run for the hills. He is trying to take you hostage. Do your best to get away. You are always welcome to come live me. You know what? I bet he isn't even letting you go get your car. I am headed to Cumberland tomorrow to get the rest of my shit. I have a company car now. I will have Jane follow me in the Taurus. She is helping me move. I will drop it off and you can use it all you like. I will park it at that Mary woman's house. The one who watches your kids. Will that be okay? Then you will have wheels to escape Boyd."

I smiled. "Really? You would let me use the Taurus? That is super kind of you. Yes, it would help to have a car. Wait, you really think Boyd is trying to take me hostage? Oh, I will need to talk to Simon. This is bad, very bad." I began to watch the door fearful Master Boyd would come through and put me into chains like Sheryl said he would.

Sheryl snorted. "You'll be sorry if you don't listen to my advice. Tomorrow you will have the Taurus. Get back to work. I will keep you so busy the bastard won't have time to fuck you. Listen honey, I know those swinging dicks, they are all out to use women. Okay, I will start your case load and pager back up for the weekend. Talk to you soon sweetie. Love you Psycho," she chirped out.

I gasped, panting in utter terror. "Love you too Sheryl, goodbye." I hung up the phone feeling my heart may explode from sheer terror.

Master Boyd walked into the door wet with sweat from mowing the lawn. "Hey baby, can you go get me a glass of ice water? I am burning up here. It is damned hot for October."

I was shaking in fear. "Yes Master, whatever you want." I took off running for the kitchen to get his water trying to figure out how to escape his clutches.

My mind whirled with images of what Sheryl meant by saying those horrible things. Did she mean Master Boyd was going to kill me? Mutilate me? Oh God, I had to find a way out of there fast.

I came back with my Master's ice water trying to calm my trembling with no success as I handed him the glass. Master Boyd saw my tremor and narrowed his eyes.

"How is Sheryl doing, Psycho? Did the phone call go okay? You seem a bit upset. Did she say something ugly to you?" He took a long drink never taking his inquisitive gaze off me.

I looked at the floor fearful he was reading my mind. "It went great. The grass is crying out for mercy, can you hear it? Do you worry their families may retaliate?"

Master Boyd moaned. "Shit. You are still not doing any better. That fucking asshole doctor changed your meds, then says to wait a couple days. He said we would be surprised by the results. Bullshit, I am not surprised. You are still not making any sense at all. God damn it." He ran the cool glass across his forehead.

I nodded "I already took my medication, Master. I would not disobey. Please don't chain me up and hold me hostage. I won't run away anymore. You said it was a directive. I have to call first." I started tearing up afraid he was going to be angry I knew his secrets.

My Master gasped. "What? Chain you up, hold you hostage, what the holy fuck? Who told you I was going to do that Psycho? Baby come here. I love you. I am not going to hurt you. I already learned better remember? I messed up, but I am working hard to change. Don't you believe me? You see me taking the pills. You see me keeping my hands to myself. I want to be a good husband for you and the kids. I am learning fast to be a good Dominant. Be patient with me?" He held out his hand and took mine pulling me to sit next to him on the couch.

My Master wrapped his arm around my shoulder pulling my head to his sweaty, wet shirt. "I have been thinking. Maybe you can talk the state into putting you behind a desk. I bet you could do great paperwork and data entry. That would be just a regular hour job without too much stress. If you want to work, I don't agree with it, but if it was not dangerous you might try it. What do you think? Could you ask to get that kind of job? You'd still be using your college and be doing something important, but I won't have to worry the you're off being murdered somewhere."

I nodded. "Okay, if you say so Master. I will work with PC and Fax. I like them better anyway. Just get Jane out of my office. She snores," I said flatly without a lick of understanding of what Master Boyd just said.

He chuckled. "Well hopefully you will have your own office. If you can get the job in Wheatly I can come have lunch with you every day to make sure you are eating right."

I got up to head for the kitchen without saying a word.

Master Boyd appeared startled. "Psycho baby, where are you going?"

I turned around confused. "You said you were ready for lunch. I am fixing it Master." I kept walking while Master Boyd chuckled louder.

"I knew having a wife would make life worth living. Having you home at last makes all the waiting worth it. You have made me one happy man. Before you know it, I will be fat as old Trenton because you will always be cooking for me. That would be terrible. I had better start working out more. I suppose I will go finish the lawn. Call me when it is ready," he yelled after me.

I heard him go back outside and restart his machine. I made his lunch while making plans to find a way to escape from his home so he could not do what Sheryl said he was going to do. I didn't want to be his wife. I wanted to be an investigator and live my life free without everyone telling me what to do. I had a college education now. Why did I even need my stupid collar?

That piece of paper Master Boyd had hung on the wall said I was a person of worth. Someone that was credible and competent. My Master kept saying I was sick. I didn't feel sick. Sheryl didn't think I was sick. It was obviously a conspiracy. Master Boyd was just like everyone else. He was trying to use me for his twisted games. He wanted to make me his whore. That was all the Masters ever wanted.

All I had to do was get that Taurus and get back to work. I would prove them all wrong. If I was loved by everyone, then someone would come looking for me if Master Boyd tried to keep me hostage. That was the answer. I needed to find another place to live too. His house was just another word for jail. I needed to be calm. I would get my chance. If he never suspected I knew his game, he couldn't stop me from getting away.

I kept my head down and mouth shut the rest of the afternoon. I played well my role of quiet, submissive wife. Master Boyd seemed very happy with my service. It was already Friday again. Master Boyd didn't have to go into work. That made me nervous.

He had so far kept his distance, but I had seen him watching me with a lustful look in his eyes. I don't know why it was bothering me that he may try to call on the special services. I had slept, albeit not always willingly, with my Master for almost a year. I should have been more than happy, even hopeful, by now he would be ready to get back to our pleasurable business.

NOTE: *Despite our very difficult start of rape and violence by this time my Master had become an experienced and generous lover. I could no longer complain since often the act with him was more than satisfying. It was an added mercy that Master Boyd seemed very capable of keeping up with my high sex drive with a stunningly large interest of his own. There was no doubt I was honestly in love with him. It was not just an act I originally intended it to be in order to keep him from losing his temper all the time.*

It didn't hurt that Master Boyd was a very handsome man. His unit was strong and felt good to touch. When engaged in carnal congress he was always eager, willing to explore, and open-minded. He had finally accepted he had developed an addiction to sex and was ready to go anytime..

Even when violent he was equal in his acceptance of injury during sexual combat. He was often more bruised and scratched up after our fake rape trysts than I was. It seemed the more I attacked the more he liked it. Our lovemaking before my psychotic break had been so aggressively passionate it had become a rumor on the tongues of many nosy persons from town.

Even my own Maiden had heard the whispers that Master Boyd and I were wild animals in the sack. That was all thanks to my two trips to relieve his anger demon while he was working. Master Boyd's co-worker witnesses had passed on the stories of our verbal argument, sudden rubber burning departures, and return thirty minutes later glassy eyed, romantic and beat to hell, had everyone in an excited tizzy. Imaginative images of his and my kinky, erotic and wanton rutting were whispered to many a greedy ear while sipping coffee or at the water coolers.

The question on everyone's lips was what exactly we were doing out there in the woods at the edge of town. I can tell you right now, it was exactly what it looked like. My Master and I were likely as rigorous, if not more so, than me and my extraordinary past lover Matthew had ever been.

In a sentence, Master Boyd had become an amazing lover. His harsh behavior in the beginning was likely due to his inexperience fueled by intense anger at being made to feel he was an unwanted sex partner, which to be fair he was.

In only one year he had developed extraordinary empathy. Master Boyd would prove time and time again he knew how to listen to the needs of his one and only and that he cared they were met in a balanced return of service.

Thanks to Sheryl and her continued efforts to manipulate me away from Master Boyd's grasp, I had become frightened of someone who had accepted his punishment, was working overtime to clean up his act, and had ended his harmful practices (which had been done while still ignorant of proper safety and care) since coming to our equal agreement among a few painful lessons. Her hateful little mind games would occasionally cause another year of terror of my Master's carnal affection that was completely unnecessary.

At dinner service my Master could not stop looking over my unit. "Uhm Psycho, how are you feeling baby? I was kind of wondering if you would feel up to bath service later at bedtime?" He smiled while blushing. Yeah he would still blush despite all we had been through. Can you believe this guy?

I looked at the floor observably wincing at the thought. "If that is what you wish, Master."

He groaned then dropped his fork rubbing his forehead. "No, not like that. I don't want it like that, not this time. I know you think I always need to feel like I am taking something from you but that is not true. It is really nice to think maybe you want me back? You know, like that." He looked at me searching to see if he could read my thoughts.

I shrugged. "Well I don't Master."

Master Boyd's eyes showed great hurt. "Really? You still hate me, still, well, that is my fault, I guess. I suppose I deserve it. I want you so bad, but I just can't, I can't stand the thought of taking you against your will, not this time. Not while you are so sick."

I glared at him. "Never bothered you before, Master. Not sure why it matters so much. I will do whatever you want, but you can't make me like or love you for it. Nor want you either." I looked back at the table feeling miserable that I had to be stuck at the table eating with him much less having to endure his sexual advances.

Master Boyd's blue eyes filled with the grey clouds of rain as he reached out and took my left hand looking over his engagement ring. "Okay, you have the right to feel that way. I will make a vow to you right now, Psycho. If we are to ever be together to fuck again then you must come to me and ask me to take you. I won't touch you like that again until you tell me you want me on your own. I won't force, beg, attack or sneak in on you. I can't undo what I have done, but I can stop doing it. If you really don't want to make love to me then I will get over it. I will have no choice. I want your love, all of it. I don't want fake, lies or bullshit. I would rather be alone. Even if you never want me I can't stop loving you. So, I will always protect and defend you. No matter what you are my One and Only." He kissed his ring lightly as a tear dropped onto my hand.

Master Boyd then got up from the table and walked out of the room headed to his bathroom to take his shower, without my help, too much temptation. He likely feared he could not keep his promise if I was near him in that vulnerable state.

I sat there listening to his water running through the house pipes very confused. Sheryl said he didn't really love me. She told me he only wanted to use me for sex. My Master just told me he would never touch me again if I said no. Huh? Did I just slip off deck again? This can't be right, I must be hallucinating.

The voices of the men and woman trapped in my Looper began to bombard me with taunts and chants of cruel insult.

"Liar. You tell lies. Go and die liar."

"Every breath you take, every step you make, I'll be watching you."

"Hahaha, did you lose your mind Psycho? Oops."

"Schizophrenic fool, he doesn't love you."

"I feel so cold and long for your embrace. I keep crying, baby, baby, please."

"Did you forget how to fly?"

"Oh, can't you see you belong to me? I'll be watching you."

"No one loves a schizophrenic. Have you call your mother? Hahaha!"

I covered up my ears cursing the voices and the song by the Police coming at me from every direction. I felt the urge to dance come over me. I got up in a trance headed out the front door to the sounds of the newly birthing night. I stepped off the porch feeling light as a feather.

I swayed and twirled in the rising fog of the dusk. My brother was almost in his bed to the west. I waved to him biding him a restful sleep. The heat he had gifted to the ground boiled up like a sauna. I felt the rivers of sweat begin to flow down the unit. Within only a few moments I was wetter than if I had joined Master Boyd in his shower. The sleeves of my shirt were constricting my movement.

I began to remove the offending items. Slowly slipped off my shirt, then my boots and pants. Finally, I took off my bra dancing sky clad for my Mother Moon. She smiled at me appreciating my schizophrenic trance dance. She sent her breath through the trees. Her mercy cooled my unit drying up the offending loss of fluid.

Suddenly, the madness took hold sending me into a fury of rhythmic motion. I kept the pace with the heartbeat of Goddess Gaia beneath my feet. I began to spin, bow and sway wildly unable to stop like a puppet on a string. I didn't care anymore. The power of the elements flowed through my pores filling me with understanding of all things. I felt my boundaries fall as I flowed into the electrical grid moving in every direction and nowhere at all. My pain fell away, the terror left while the skies opened to take me spinning into the universal tapestry.

Slowly the vortex began in the center calling my energies back to the unit of measurement. I wanted to linger in the magnetic byway, but I knew to do so would result in permanent disconnection. I rushed back to as all that was, ever will be and is, solidified once more as the humanoid called Psycho. I stop dancing standing there panting with my eyes closed allowing the sensations of the healing to spread to every section of my borders.

"That was beautiful Psycho." I heard a voice breath out in awe behind me.

I opened my eyes startled peering into the deepening darkness toward the sound coming from the porch. "Simon?" I called out unable to make out the figure sitting on the porch steps watching me.

"No Psycho. It is me, Master Boyd. That was amazing. I have never seen anything like it. You are so beautiful. I didn't mean to snoop. I came out of the shower and couldn't find you. I saw you dancing and stripping. I sat and watched to make sure you didn't get into trouble, but it was just, I can't even describe it," he called out in the darkness.

I snorted. "I bet. My being naked has nothing to do with that I am sure. You should not be watching my private moments. Don't you think it is bad enough I already have an audience everywhere I go? Now I have to worry you are sneaking around too Master, not fair."

He chuckled. "Yeah I suppose I never thought of it that way. I apologize. I really was only making sure you didn't head off to town like that. I don't think the towns folks would be as understanding."

I smiled realizing he was right. "Well, it would liven up their Friday night wouldn't it?"

Master Boyd laughed. "That it would sweetheart. Could I talk you into dancing again while I watch I mean? Sometimes? It was truly beautiful. You could keep your clothes on. I have always loved to watch you dance."

I looked at his dark faceless figure sitting there. "You could dance with me. I could teach you."

He sighed. "No, I can't dance. I am not allowed to dance. I can watch but not do it myself. Thank you for letting me watch if you would?"

"Ah, that's right. I forgot your religion won't permit dancing. Well, you should be Wiccan like me Master. We dance, laugh, they drink and they fuck to celebrate." I laughed out loudly twirling feeling very odd.

Master Boyd chuckled too. "That does sound very tempting. Maybe someday. For now, I would rather just watch the girl I love laugh, dance, smile and celebrate. That would be enough to make me happy."

I stopped spinning. "Did you really mean it when you told me I could tell you no, Master? Did you really give me the choice? Or am I just dreaming, psychotic, or dead?"

Master Boyd stood up and walked into the dim light of Mother Moon where I could make out his eyes. "You didn't dream it or hallucinate it. I meant what I said. I admit it will be hard for me to keep that promise seeing you like this, but I will do it. I want you willingly or not at all. Even if it means I never have you again. I even think if I could watch you dance like that only, I would be satisfied. Well I hope so anyway. I can believe you are Wiccan. You have enchanted me that is for sure." He reached down collecting my discarded clothing scattered about the yard.

I laughed and spun again. "Won't you go to your hell for loving a witch, Master?" I smiled at the Mother in the sky with intense joy.

He snorted. "I am already in hell, Psycho. I am in love with a beautiful woman who will never love me back and I can't ever love another. If that is not Hell, then I don't know what is. Looks like maybe I am the one who may be dead, huh?"

I stopped spinning when he said that and looked back as he continued to pick up my stuff folding it and laying it carefully on the steps. "Master, I am saying no to you about special services. I will never have sex with you again. No touching, no fucking, never Master."

Master Boyd looked at the ground appearing sad. "Yeah, kind of figured that out when I took advantage in the jail that night, Psycho. I should have listened to you. I didn't. Now I know what I am missing which makes the nightmare of being in love with you a thousand times worse. Baby you may want to come inside or at least put on a robe. The mosquitoes are a bitch even this late in the year." He started to walk back up the stairs heading inside.

"Master," I yelled out running after him catching his startled person on the porch.

He looked at me concerned. "What? Are you okay? What is wrong?"

I took his hands. "Come dance with me, Master. I won't tell your God. The Mother Goddess can keep a secret." I pulled him smiling.

Master Boyd laughed. "God is always watching Psycho. I would watch you all night if you want to dance but only watch."

I really started laughing. "Oh, I think the dance I would like to do would be okay even with your God." I winked at him then stood on my tippy toes to kiss him deeply.

He tried to pull away. "Psycho, I can't keep my promise if you are teasing me. At least put on some clothes. Show a little mercy will you, that's a directive."

I grabbed his shirt and began to unbutton it. "I am showing you mercy, Master. I chose to be with you. You let me tell you no. So, now I can choose to say yes. Come dance with me. Let me show you how a High Priestess honors her Goddess. I warn you, better tell your God to cover his eyes. I will dance you to till you drop lover." I smiled wickedly as I saw the lust fill his eyes.

Master Boyd grabbed my unit with all the wantonness of a man who had been famished for his entire life. We didn't even make it back inside. Our wild sexual dancing began on the porch. Before the night was up, the hood of his car, the yard, the driveway, the living room floor, the bed and finally the shower were witness to our vigorous lovemaking. We didn't stop until finally we collapsed from sheer exhaustion. I passed out, as did he, laying on top of him cuddled in his arms in the bathtub.

QUICK NOTE: I *have had a few insane nights of incredible sex till I dropped, but this one is only second to one I shared with Master Jon. That story for another day. Master Boyd allowing me choice had given him the very thing he desired the most, my true love at long last. So, what happened? Ah, now you must keep reading to find that out. You are not the kind who reads the last page of a book first now are you?*

Master Boyd woke up first but laid there watching me sleeping on his chest. I cannot tell you what he was thinking that Saturday when he first opened his eyes. I do know he found his muscles pulled, his back aching, his great memories enhanced, and his Only One snuggled up like a kitten purring in his lap. When I stirred at last, he was laying there smiling lovingly at me.

"That was perfect. More nights like last night. That's a directive." He kissed my forehead.

I moaned out finding my entire unit felt as if it had spent an evening on the torturous rack. "Oh my God. I think I broke something important, ouch. Oh, and I think I just found where we put those handcuffs Master." I pulled the metal shackles from under his unit.

Master Boyd groaned in pain. "Ah, that's what I was laying on. But what about the key?"

I chuckled. "It will pass in about thirty-five hours or so. Looks like bran muffins for you or you'll have to borrow Dennis's key if you arrest anyone tomorrow night." I spun the cuffs around my finger teasing my Master.

"I told you I could get out of them." He smiled with mischief.

I grinned. "I believed you, Master. I assumed you could pick a lock too, that's why I had you swallow the key. Did you learn that in cop school or jail?"

We both smiled diabolically. "The Snake Pit," we said in unison while laughing maniacally at our sadly true statement.

I started the shower and began bath service. Master Boyd and I laughed a great deal as we recalled our lewd acts during the wee hours of that morning. He may have been strait laced in every other area of life, but when it came to sex, almost anything could go.

One of the things that still makes me smile about this most troubled figure in my history was his insatiable desires for pleasures of the flesh. To think he had once been too shy to ask me out on a date without stuttering like a child. Well we did shit that night that would make the devil blush. Wow, just wow.

After breakfast, errr, lunch, errr, late lunch services I spoke to Master Boyd about my subpoena for Judge McNutts court. My Master was not happy about it, but he knew that old codger. He told me that I could go do what was required but then to return until my official release back to work began that Wednesday. We spent the rest of the day revising some of our fun and games from the night before. The rest of the time he spent trying to talk me into quitting DCFS. I, of course, was having none of that conversation.

After dinner service I was washing the dishes wearing nothing more than my "Boyd" house shoes when my Master snuck up on me trying to mount me over the dishwater. I let out a playful squeal and took off running for the front door in an erotic game of tag.

Master Boyd fake growled while giving chase. "I am Boyd the Big Bad Wolf. Come here Little Red Riding Psycho. I intend to eat you."

I squealed out again laughing as I ripped open the door flying out not looking in front of me, right into Dennis who was about to knock, oops.

Dennis stared in horror while I stood sky clad in total shock unsure if I was hallucinating the bull cop. Master Boyd didn't see or hear Dennis either and come flying out behind me also sky clad, double oops.

He rushed up knocking me upper unit forward slightly as he slammed his uhm, upholstered gun into me, believing I had stopped for his, so he could tag me it. I gasped and yelped loudly. It was then that Master Boyd saw Dennis standing there. He let out his own gasp as he realized the uhm, mistake. We both had just made it in front of our father figure.

Not saying a word Master Boyd immediately reached his long right arm around my breasts to cover them and with his left reached down to offer some dignity to my lady parts. My entire unit already shielded the cop's eyes from his nakedness. I was personally hiding his most important uhm, part, yikes.

Dennis stood there the blood draining from his face while his eyes went wide. There was nothing we could do but remain coupled and try to maintain what tiny amount of decorum anyone can have in this fucked up situation (as if, sheesh).

"Uhm Dennis, so nice of you to drop by. Boyd and I were just, uhm, enjoying a lazy Saturday afternoon. You know, no kids, no neighbors, and not expecting anyone," I said trying to ignore my trembling Master and wondering how the fuck he was maintaining his damned hard on.

Dennis finally seemed to come back to his senses. "Uhm yeah. Uhm, tell you what. I have some case notes I left in the car for Boyd. Let me go get those. You two can, uhm, I will just go get those notes."

He turned around practically running to his car while Master Boyd lifted me and backed into the house. I closed the main door while my Master disengaged. We looked at each other and began laughing like hyenas.

"Shit Psycho, see that is why you always call ahead," snickered Master Boyd while we rushed to his room to put on our clothing.

I nodded giggling myself. "Master, tell Dennis calling ahead is a directive in this house. Will you be in trouble for this?" I suddenly felt a bit of nervousness that Master Boyd could get reprimanded for fucking, well starting to fuck, his fiancé in front of his commanding officer.

Master Boyd snorted while I buttoned up his shirt. "Nah baby. This is my house. If I wanted to ride you like a pony on the front porch I could right in front of Dennis. Nothing illegal about having sex with your woman on your property. Did you see the look on his face though?" Master Boyd began to laugh again.

I gave him a fake look of concern. "Now, Master, behave yourself. Dennis is to be respected. It is unfair to show off your youthful vigor in front of the old Bull."

Master Boyd chuckled while I pushed him down on his bed to put on his shoes. "Well, at least now he knows what we see in each other."

I snorted. "You mean besides seeing us in each other?"

Master Boyd and I really howled at that snotty statement. It took us a full ten minutes to get our laughter under control because we were twisted fucks. I opened the door and motioned Dennis that the coast was finally clear or at least dressed.

I got the embarrassed Dennis a coke and then sat down next to Master Boyd who was cutting teasing eyes at me while smiling diabolically. After a few uncomfortable moments Master Boyd cleared his throat.

"Uhm, so how can we help you Dennis?" My Master shot me another look of mischief forcing me to stifle another giggle fit.

"Ah, yeah so they picked up Thomas Windbush. I thought you and Psycho would be interested to know. The DNA came back as a match they had to his on file. Willa's and Becky's rapist has been captured without incident. Nancy will likely do life and Ronald we had to let him go. I hope there is not another time for him for his sake." Dennis took a long drink of his coke.

I shook my head. "They shouldn't have let Windbush out. Willa is dead because he wants to stick his dick in seven-year-old babies. That is fucked up Dennis."

Dennis nodded. "Yep, that would be about right. Willa's funeral is on Tuesday. We are taking up a collection to bury her right. You two will want to donate I figured."

Master Boyd nodded. "Yeah of course. We will be there to see her put to rest as well. Right Psycho?"

I nodded looking at the floor. "Of course we will. After all, we dug her up. It is only right we make sure she is put

109

back properly. Dennis whatever you need money wise, let me know. Give her the good headstone not one of those unmarked shit ones. She lived; her life matters at least to us."

Dennis sighed. "It is a sick world Psycho. Hell, you and Boyd know personally. Psycho you more than most anyone I know, on this side of hell anyway. How are you feeling? Boyd said you had a little slip last week?"

I smiled bitterly. "We are fine. We feel great. There is nothing wrong with us. We do not have problems."

Dennis smiled back. "That is great to hear. Well, I will let the two of you get back to, uhm, have a great rest of the day. See you tomorrow night Boyd."

Master Boyd nodded, "Yes sir. Be safe out there."

I walked Dennis out.

He turned around and looked at me. "I apologize for not calling first Psycho. I just want you to know I have never seen Boyd so happy. I still think the two of you being a pair is a mistake, but there is no denying you two look good together. Stay out of trouble Psycho."

I watched Dennis pull out and leave. Master Boyd came up behind me kissing my neck.

"The world is just so full of monsters Master." I sighed still watching Dennis's car disappear down the old dirt road.

Master Boyd moaned. "Sure is. In fact there is one right here behind you. I believe I started a meal I didn't finish." He grabbed me pulling my playfully screaming unit back through the door to ravage me in the middle of the living room floor.

On Sunday Master Boyd drove me to Maiden Mary's house. I visited the children and Seine. I allowed Master Boyd to interact with the family, but he was never to refer to himself as my fiancé or lover. He was just a friend. It didn't make my Master feel too secure but he understood given the fact that my family was already strained enough without adding a boyfriend to the mix.

Master Boyd seemed to enjoy throwing the ball with my son. The girls watched them play catch from the porch with a grouchy Seine. My daughter thought Master Boyd was very cute. She goo goo eyed him and teased Mary and me that she was going to go to grow up and marry a police officer. I just rolled my eyes at that statement and kept my fur brother from eating Boyd the Big Bad Wolf.

Mary was thrilled to hear I had finally moved home for good. I informed her I would look around for proper housing soon. She told me she would keep her eyes open. True to her word, Sheryl had left the Taurus at Mary's for my locomotion. It was not as selfless as it may have appeared. Sheryl expected me to make payments on the car and keep up all repair while she held the pink slip. My Intrepid had seen the last of its fine days. I called and had it towed to a nearby used car lot. I ended up getting five hundred dollars for the dented up first of only two cars I ever bought in my life.

I gave the money I got for the busted car to the funeral home, along with Master Boyd's donation, to aid in the purchase of a fine rose headstone to mark the site of the abused unit of Willa Thompson. All those small-town cops, even the bully Trenton, and me attended her service. There was not a dry eye among those big, hard bitten, backwoods officers that overcast afternoon they laid her to rest at last.

It was a bitter, horrible day. I had much trouble getting through it without understanding why, besides the fact she was just a little baby, it affected me so badly. Master Boyd had to point out what should have been obvious to me once we got home. (* *For the record: he was aware of my mother Debbie, the facts of my sad creation and to his credit he never asked me or judged me once for anything I had ever done*).

I had gone psychotic the day they pulled her from the ground because I had unconsciously realized that she was not as lucky as me. I was only seven years old when my mother and a beast came to take my childhood. I had been hurt in the same way but had survived when my mother decided to end my ability to tell the secrets. I felt guilt it was her and not me…

I used to go to that graveyard every year on her birthday and bring flowers. Sadly, only Master Boyd and I ever visited the little girl who never really lived but whose short life changed mine in ways I had yet to realize.

The Monday before the burial of the sweet little girl with tawny pig tails, I went to court to defend yet another

112

little girl on the verge of being lost. I sat all day listening to Judge McNutt grill every worker who ever had touched the case of Minnie, Richard and Skylar. When my turn came the Judge waved his hand saying he had heard enough to make his ruling in regarding the termination of Minnie's parental rights.

You could have heard a pin drop in that courtroom as the pompous old wind bag lowered his spectacles glaring at the DCFS workers on the right side of the room with Richard and Skylar holding each other's hands and their breaths. On the left side was Minnie and her lawyer along with a nasty looking new boyfriend. I am sure Skylar was terrified wondering if this foul thing was going to have his way with her by nightfall. If Judge McNutt didn't rule for termination, then the visitation case would immediately be re-opened. We all waited in hushed terror. Would the judge do the right thing for Skylar?

"I have looked over this case and it is of my opinion that Richard Cummings has done an excellent job looking over the needs and health of Skylar for the last three years. With that said, I do not believe he is the best placement for this child. A child should be with her mother to obtain the best start life can offer. Now it is true her mother, Miss Cummings, has had a rough start with the child, but I believe the fault is that of DCFS and its failure to provide proper service to this suffering family. I hereby order that Skylar Cummings be returned to her mother's care with a case with DCFS to be opened on Miss Minnie Cummings home. There should be weekly checks on Skylar's reunification with her mother, and all services required to aid in this adjustment are so ordered to begin effective by five PM this afternoon. Court is adjourned."

The sonofabitch got his fat ass up out of the bench and left the room acting like his ordering the death of a fourteen-year-old girl was nothing at all. I looked over at Richard and Skylar. Both were sitting there staring into the void stunned into disbelief, tears were forming in their eyes.

Minnie was kissing the dirty, hairy man while they both shot smug looks of got you at the forever disfigured little girl. The devil went to court and she had won. Skylar was finished. This time Minnie would make sure she never got away alive.

I got up from my seat and asked Richard and Skylar to join me on the courthouse steps. They got up and blindly follow me both appearing to be sleepwalking through a nightmare. I led them halfway down and stopped. They stood behind me hand in hand. Richard was blubbering he had failed her; she was crying looking around in terror.

I made sure no one was looking or listening as I took out all the cash from my last paycheck, I had just been to the bank and handed it to Richard. He looked at me weeping and confused.

I took a deep breath praying to the Goddess no one was about to hear me breaking the law. "Mister Cummings, do you love Skylar?"

He nodded. "With all my heart. She is my little girl." He put his arm around the wailing child.

"I love you too Uncle Richard. I am so sorry. I don't want to leave you," she cried out in agony.

I shook my head. "Mister Cummings, if you love her, then run, run right now. Sacrifice your home, your job, your friends, your life here. Take that money and whatever you can grab on your way out of town and run. Never look back, never call anyone and tell them where you are. If Minnie takes Skylar today she won't be coming back to be fixed next time. If you love her, really love her, give your life, your comfort and buy her a chance. Now go. They will be coming any minute."

Richard looked at Skylar who looked at him. "Let's go Skylar. We always wanted to see the world. It will be scary, but I can't let Minnie hurt you anymore. Are you ready?"

Skylar nodded. "I am ready Uncle Richard."

Richard looked back at me, "For what it is worth, thank you."

I snorted smiling bitterly. "Darling, you are the one going to give it all up. But tell you what, she is worth it. (Skylar smiled and blushed) I am the one who thanks you. Now run, don't stop, don't ever come back here."

Richard and Skylar ran to the parking lot and got into a blue sporty car pulled out and sped off into traffic never to be seen again. I don't know where they went or what happened to them. I do know what would have happened had they stayed. Minnie searched for years but the child Skylar was never officially found. Richard is a ghost, a rumor at the Cummings family get togethers.

I was spotted talking to the pair. The police brought me in for questioning asking if they had said anything to me about where they were headed. I was asked had they told me they planned to run.

I just shrugged and said, "Mr. Cummings asked me for a cigarette. I told him I don't smoke. He said he was going to the car to get a pack. Next I knew they were gone."

Everyone believe that I was withholding information. Sheryl even accused me of lying. How dare she. I would never tell someone to kidnap a ward of the state much less fund such a crime. Oh, now just what kind of investigator would I be if I went and did shit like that. Good thing I was not a DCFS investigator. Nah, I am just an old schizophrenic.

For the record, Richard and/or Skylar if you ever see this, way to go. Richard you are truly a Prince among men, and Skylar you are the Princess that was rescued from the wicked queen. A beautiful tale for a beautiful pair of souls. May the Goddess bless you both with the happiness you deserved.

On Wednesday when I officially was back on duty, much to Master Boyd's irritation, I swung by to visit my dearest Cindy Slater serving her time at the Girls' Colony. She came running up seeing me before I could see her. Eva was just leaving having come by herself to cheer up and support the recovery of her little girl.

I gave Eva a hug. Then we chatted a while about her counselor. She was holding up well and Cindy was doing great, dealing day by day and slowly detoxing from her long-term addictions. Eva's eyes shown with great pride.

At last I got to visit with Cindy who was eager to show me her room. "Uhm Psycho, when you didn't come pick me up that Tuesday a really shitty nurse said you were in the hospital on the third floor. That is the psych ward you know. She also said you were the town schizophrenic. I was going to punch that bitch for being such a cunt, but I got to thinking, is that why they call you Psycho? I mean that is not your real name, right?"

I chuckled. "Well I could lie and say my mom had a great sense of humor."

Cindy looked at the floor. "So you are saying you are called Psycho because you are schizophrenic?"

I snorted. "No, I am saying my mother was a hateful old bitch with a nasty sense of humor, Cindy. Didn't you listen to what I said?"

She started laughing. "You are funny. Well, the nurse also said, she said, that you have been raped a few times yourself, even gang raped when you were really little. Is that true too?"

I looked at her hard. "What do you think, Cindy? Does it matter to you to know that you are not the only one they hurt honey? Well, you are not alone. How many girls are here, twenty, forty? Rape is something many of us must bear in this life. Just remember they can only really hurt you if you let them. They take only what you give them. If you can walk away and see another day, they lost and you won. Sure, they are a memory, but they are gone, and you are not. Is that what you wanted to know?"

Cindy sniffed back her tears. "You know after this all happened, I was feeling really low. I wondered why me, why did it keep happening to me? I wondered if I was bad. Or did I just lead that first guy on, why did he pick me? I thought I was a monster, and everyone could see it. So, I started drinking and doing the drugs to try to forget, just to not care so much, but I started getting hurt again, really bad. Then when those guys were raping me, and Javier was crying in the closet I realized it could all be over. No more me, no more anything. Javier died you know. He killed himself I heard. I know he didn't love me, but it is weird to know he is gone forever. I wondered how can I go one though when I have fucked so many guys, done so many drugs. My reputation is trash. Who would ever hire me to do anything but give a blow job in a back seat. Then that nurse, she called you the town loony. She said you were raped and tortured as a kid, but no one cared because you were just street trash. I remember you that night. You came in and made it all better. You kept them from hurting me. You took care of me and helped my mom feel better too. You are not a loony. You are not trash. You are wonderful and I am so glad you were there." She began to cry.

I reached out and held her and I said while chuckling, "Ah Cindy, you are just DTing. Silly, I am too the town loony, I am Psycho. You never heard of me? Well, you should hear the stories, girlfriend. As for being trash, some would say so, some have called me a whore. I have called me a whore. Yes I have been raped more than a few times. But Cindy, I am a lot more than all those things. Just like you. Don't be ashamed of who you are. Don't be afraid to be more. I brought you something. I almost forgot." I reached into my purse and pulled out a plushy golden puppy dog stuffed toy.

Cindy smiled. "I am too big for stuffed animals, Psycho."

I grinned at her. "He is not for you. He is for nighttime Cindy. The one who is afraid in the dark when the bad dreams come. This little fellow will keep you safe from those monsters inside your head. I had one myself when I was just about your age. His name was Zeppelin." I handed her the toy.

She smiled knowingly, "Yeah, you do know what it is like. That nurse wasn't telling tall tales. Thank you Psycho for caring about me, my mom, for well just fucking caring."

She hugged me tight as we went to her room and she showed me her new plans and life.

As you well know, I never mention a name in my stories unless they are someone of importance to me. Cindy Slater, she was important to many in her time and likely still is today. She would grow up to become an Area Manager for DCFS. She worked her way to the top by starting at the bottom.

In her many years working up, she saved countless other children from her fate, and from mine. I watched her rise with great happiness from the town slut who everyone counted out. Oh no beauties, she was and is a fighter. I heard she was like an M & M candy, hard on the outside but soft in her heart.

I was invited to her Area Manager announcement ceremony. When she gave her acceptance speech she called out my name. I stood up to an auditorium full of people clapping as Cindy told them I had turned her pumpkin into a chariot that night when I held a sixteen year old gang rape victim sucking her thumb who was scared out of her mind. I didn't do a damned thing I argued with her after that uncalled for ovation. Cindy, I will say it to you one more time: I just held you when you were lost, you did all the work. Good job darling. You became more. If I could be prideful you would have it. Simon does that for me.

With Cindy now on her way to greatness, James adjusting to his new home, poor Willa lain to rest, Nikki starting her life over, and Richard and Skylar beginning anew, it was time to start my new case load full of new potential chances to make the wrongs right, and odds of tragedy on the rise. I was now seeking a new home to reunify my family and had made complete peace with my powerful Master Boyd. I had slipped a little. The lights were a bit too bright. The sounds a bit too loud, but that was okay. Simon was riding with us. PC was back online. Fax would keep us busy and Dude and Looper were out having coffee. Whatever could go wrong now that we had our shit together. Well, everything.

Chapter 69: Carnaval Carousel
The Tragic Fall of Psycho
Master Boy and the Absent Interim Master Sheryl

It is the season of magic. Look there to the west. Can you see it too? That is not fog, that is the static. No worries, it is still a bit far off in the distance, it is still the winter of 1998, but there is no doubt it is coming. We calculate only six months to go until we are gone.

The spring will mark the final season of who we once were. The fire that had always kept us warm and chased away the monsters in the darkness will be put out very soon. *This is the first chapter to mark the beginning of the end of the violent schizophrenic remembered as 'Psycho.' She is already irretrievably on her way to her grave.*

It is okay. Don't be sad. The sacrifice was worth what we bought with it, we hope. You can never be sure when you purchase something, wait, what exactly did we acquire? Ah, yeah that is right. Now we remember helplessness, nightmares, negative feelings, fear, and our own personal version of hell.

The funny thing is, we went into the situation misunderstanding that saving others was going to cost us everything. We thought we had been hired to aid the downtrodden, the lost, the broken, and the abused. Turns out we were in training to become the real victim in this dark world of child abuse investigations. We never noticed until it was too late to escape our very own offenders.

The water around us is getting warmer. Someone has set the temperature on 'slow boil.' It required a complex recipe to cook a clever collar. That special order requires one severe schizophrenic without a support system of worth. Such a rare ingredient was so hard to find. It was very important to capture it while breathing. The meal would have been tasteless if the main course was completely dead. Alive and kicking made the murder so much sweeter. There, over in that clump of brush. Those are eyes watching, patiently waiting for the submissive to start to fry.

The hunters most sublime had already spotted their prey. The stalker we call Master is not the one we should have feared. A special trap has been set. We didn't know it, but we were already in the crosshairs of two killers at the same time. The fight for survival has begun...

Are we ready to take the first steps towards the loss of who we were? Well, us neither. We had learned to like us, good and bad. That doesn't matter. Mistakes were made. The greed of almost everyone around us robbed us of all we had. Our mind was stripped, and our soul was raped. Once that happens, there can never be a return to what was. The countdown has sped up, and the electrical grid lowers ever closer. Doom is in the air, but we didn't realize it. Psycho will be erased forever.

When the nothingness had won the battle, leaving us for death, we begged for help. It will be Master Boyd the hidden 28th Key holder who answers our pleas for mercy. He lovingly rebuilds the mindless unit with his bare hands in his own image.

As the true Master of secrets, Boyd will become both the creator and the first Keyholder of the one called…Niemand.

Wow, now who could have seen that coming? Master Boyd as a Doctor Frankenstein? Holy shit. Want to know what that is all about? Then you will have to keep reading. The chapters coming up will blow your mind. We know they sure as fuck blew ours.

"It is experimental, but the theory is that when used in large quantities, without a break it will calm the violent part of the brain. It has shown mild promise in the major depressed. So far, it has proven ineffective in the schizophrenic. Her case has been chronic and hard to manage. She is a perfect subject to use in this kind of testing. Her Guardian has refused us several times, because at this level it could be dangerous. He is being unreasonable. Our only other option is to get her to sign the permission slip. She doesn't have any other close relatives that would raise questions about our unproven treatments, right?"
--Doctor Baker asking Sheryl for assistance in coercing Psycho's signature. Harbor View Mental Hospital, October 1999.

"So, Sheryl told me you are schizophrenic. Is that true?" Julia investigated her coffee cup trying to appear interested in a floating clump of creamer.

I snorted. "What? Well that old heifer. She should not be telling tales out of school like that." I looked at the kitchen table.

Julia looked up at me surprised. "You are saying she told a fib? Really? Come on Psycho, I saw you. If that is not schizophrenia, I don't know what is."

I glared at her angrily. "It was a seizure, Julia. Why are we having this conversation? I don't have schizophrenia. Sheryl can blather all she wants. I am the one who would know, now wouldn't I? If I say I don't have it then you can take that to the bank and cash it." I took a drink of my coffee still glaring at the nosey ex-foster mother.

Julia shook her head. "Okay sure, whatever Psycho. I know what I saw. You can deny it all you like but I lived in Baltimore. I saw the schizo's who lived in the parks and alleyways. They do the same shit I saw you doing right there in my front yard. Look it doesn't matter to me that you have it. I just was wanting to hear your story is all. I mean, they put me through the ringer to get approved for foster care. I was just kind of shocked they would let someone with that serious a mental illness make decisions that could be life and death for kids as well as testify in court. I suppose they are getting a lot more permissive these days. It was over twenty years ago they approved my house." She took a drink of her coffee chuckling.

I narrowed my eyes. "Fuck you Julia. They wouldn't hire a nutball schizophrenic. I am a DCFS Investigator therefore I don't have fucking schizophrenia. End of story," I yelled out sounding very offended, because I was.

Julia looked up with a cat-like smile. "Okay, okay, I told you doesn't matter to me anyway. God damn, Psycho. Cool your blood. I was just making small talk. Sheryl thinks the world of you. She says you work, day and night to look after the families in this shitty state. Then you still make time to come see me, that is totally awesome. I asked her how the fuck you do it. She said you had no real family of worth for starters. She then added you are mentally ill which didn't hurt either. I guess she was just joshing me. Not funny. I would be a bit miffed too if someone told lies like that about me." She took another drink of her coffee watching to see my reaction.

I snorted. "I have family Julia. That comment is stupid. I have two kids, a fiancé, a husband and a damned girlfriend. Believe me my dance card is filled." I rolled my eyes.

She spit her coffee across the table at me. "What? How the fuck can you have a husband, a girlfriend, and a fiancé?" Her eyes went wide.

I smiled wickedly. "Apparently, I am a greedy lover, cupcake. What can I say? I tend to be a popular choice in more than a few beds. Seems that investigations are not the only thing I am pretty good at (I chuckled). Now if you don't mind Julia, I have enjoyed the coffee, but I have a world to save. See you tomorrow morning, unless you are finally done holding me fucking hostage for these little coffee chats every God damned morning? I really have a lot of important shit to do. You need to seek real friends and stop bothering us heartless, overworked folks." I stood up headed for the door.

"Wait, Psycho, Sheryl told me to remind you not to forget to check on that FINS case today. She said you would know what that meant? Said Jane is not watching close enough," she yelled after me.

I stopped while pulling down my coat sleeve to make sure my electrical tape didn't show through. "Yeah, I haven't forgotten, sheesh, she is worse than a mother hen. See you tomorrow morning. We are done here right?" I glared at Julia.

She nodded appearing to recognize the irritation she was causing me. "Uhm, sure. See you tomorrow Psycho. I will have the coffee ready."

I turned around walking toward her door bending my right arm back to flip her the bird. "Fuck you very much Julia. See you tomorrow morning you nosy, hostage taking, non-empathetic, greedy bitch. Have a nice motherfucking day mooch." I slammed the door behind me.

I got into the Taurus still grumbling about the forced morning coffee visits with Julia Stubbs. There were very few things I hated about my job more than having to sit at Julia's kitchen table every morning listening to her babble on about how badly treated she had been by DCFS. To hear the woman talk she was the only one who suffered a hellish fate in all the universe. I had once felt sorry for her. That was no longer the case. She had lobbied Sheryl into granting my

126

sorry ass to her every morning from nine to eleven am as a sympathetic ear.

I was overloaded with more than forty-five cases on a weekly basis. I was working as a hybrid DCFS investigator and State police officer. I was only called if the report allegedly was going to be a criminal case. I handled the worst of the worst child abuse cases. I had a deadline of immediate response on every call in, no matter how far away. I handled a five-county area that was well over two hundred and fifty miles wide from north to south and over one hundred west to east.

You could be assured when my pager went off, some kid had been beaten to shit, raped, committed suicide or murder, or was killed. If the case was a valid one someone was going to a foster home, prison or the grave every time. I testified in court up to three days a week, worked all hours and didn't have the weekends or nights off. I was not even permitted holidays for a break.

I had to quit my job at the funeral home before I ended up being fired for never showing up. My job with DCFS had effectively ended my career as a mortician, for now.

My personal life was also suffering significantly. I almost never got to see my own fucking kids as I was always off dealing with another's kids. My Master was constantly pissed off due to my never being home to serve his needs and being almost unreachable most of the time. Sheryl had been very successful at causing Master Boyd many a headache and nights with blue balls.

In her great haste to break my Master and I apart by overworking me, she had forgotten that kind of stress without rest would have serious repercussions for her star Investigator. It was really no surprise she had no empathy for the damaged her little manipulations were causing in my dark world. I never saw her anymore.

Since moving over one hundred and fifty miles away she had become nothing more than another voice shouting commands into my overwhelmed ears. She was not there to make sure I ate, bathed, rested nor keep an eye on my tendency to self-injure. I had again started wearing electrical tape but was careful not to insert wires yet. As October rolled off becoming November, I was again considering the possibility of robot repair work that was more than just surface deep (uh oh).

Even my beloved Temple of the Green Rings had been forced to function without its High Priestess for most Esbats and Sabbats. I either had to rush off during rituals or was off hundreds of miles away arresting offenders, trying to sooth screaming crying children while the doctors patched them up, or filling out court reports to make deadlines so I could stay out of jail.

In only five weeks since my return to full duty my significant acute stage psychosis had degraded to a dangerous level yet again. No one was able to catch me long enough to realize it, not even my vigilant Master Boyd.

He was constantly demanding that I quit the job. My continued refusals always pissed him off to no end. My

Master did his best to keep from disrupting his service to me by enforcing daily phone calls and even chase me from county to county to make sure I was eating. On weekends, he would insist on coming to every priority case I was called in on. He would drive demanding I sleep to prove to him I was resting at least a little during the weekends.

Master Boyd already worked over forty hours a week as a police officer himself. This added weekend work was starting to wear him out almost as much as it did me. He too was showing significant signs of wear and tear to a near psychotic level. His own mental illness was starting to kick up a notch, and soon enough everyone would see just how perfectly matched he and I were when it came to being bat-shit crazy.

Despite his close watch, he had failed to discover my most severe symptoms. There were many signs of the seriousness of my break from reality. However, I cleverly hid my attempts to correct the errors. His biggest mistake was he would warn me of his approach by cell phone. I would remove the tape before he got to me. I always kept extra rolls in my purse to replace the discarded repair casings the second he left.

My strange speech patterns, and aggressiveness toward everyone was causing him much concern. No one was safe from my chronic flipping the bird, foul language, insults and even threats of physical attack from Julia to my Masters, the clients and even Simon. I would pull over on my way to calls to dance in a field, drag offenders and kick them into the back of police cars, and commonly threaten to do worse.

Everyone on the DCFS side turned a blind eye to my strange rants and odd appearance. I had begun to wear my signature white makeup and heavy black gothic gear twenty-four, seven again even to court.

I was doing an amazing job cleaning up the filth, corruption and my caseloads followed federal guidelines. So, no one cared how fucked up I looked or talked. As long as my bottom line was perfect no one gave a fig that I was obviously psychotic as hell.

Master Boyd was still calling every mental health system and psychiatrist in the state, but no one would listen to his pleas for assistance. He was frustrated beyond imagination. No matter how much he railed, he may as well have been butting his head into the wall.

No one wanted my case, and since I was testifying in court, and working full time, no one would admit my adaptive functioning abilities were tanking. So, what if I wasn't eating, bathing or sleeping? I could work. Therefore, I was fine. No reason to be worried. Everything was going awesome.

You know what? I had decided I didn't even have schizophrenia anymore. That had been a total misunderstanding. If I ever had it, I had managed to outgrow it. This Psycho was super lucky. Whew! For a while there we thought maybe we would be cursed to a lifetime of madness, abuse and exploitation.

Thank the Gods it was all over now. I, for one, was grateful to be cured. I didn't even need the stupid collar nor the Key. I was powerful. No one could stop me now. Simon was right. All I ever had to do was get that college degree. That paper said I was valuable in society.

There was no way I could be some filthy, unloved, stupid, street living, mentally ill creature only good for a fuck, then passed on to the next horny asshole. I mean, look at my incredible work as an investigator. I was a hero, not a psychotic zero.

Well, good thing we finally got that all cleared up and none too soon either. I was really sick of being told what to do.

We were fine. We felt great. There was nothing wrong with us. We did not have problems. The world was insane, not us.

I was on my way to the FINS (Family In Need of Services) case to check on the psychopathic teenager known as Samuel when the cell phone began to ring. I looked at the number realizing it was Master Boyd again. I groaned but picked it up to answer before he blew a gasket.

"Yeah, I am on my way to a very important case Master. What can I do for you," I said trying not to sound as irritated as I truly was by his constant need to be told he was still loved.

"Psycho baby, I just got off shift and wanted to check to see how you are feeling. You didn't come home last night again," he said sounding concerned.

I snorted. "I was there for a while. I got called out. I decided to do some paperwork after, you know, there was no reason to drive all the way back when I was already in Cumberland anyway."

He cleared his throat. "Uhm, the bed is still made up. You didn't sleep, I take it. This must stop Psycho. You are going to get really sick. You have to sleep, eat, and I noticed the tub is dry too. Did you even bother to shower?"

I chuckled. "Don't worry Master, I will still suck Your dick when you ask me to. Let it go man. I am perfectly fine. Who the fuck takes a shower everyday anyway? That is just overkill. Look I must go. I have reached my destination. Love you Master, have a great sleep." I hung up on my Master while he was attempting to argue his concerns at my ignoring commands for the thousandth time.

I pulled into the drive of the Turnbols home. They were a therapeutic foster home known at that time as a CASA house. These often very loving homes were approved for a single foster child placement at a time. The reason for this restriction was because any child placed there was deemed a troublemaker or handful by their history, medical/psychological problems, or behavior in other regular foster homes. Children who were placed in these kinds of homes of last resort were facing group or residential home settings if the CASA home placement failed.

The most dangerously ill or criminally behaving children often ended up with the Turnbols at some point before going on to jail, hospitals, or group homes. Mister and

Missus Turnbol were amazingly patient, loving, respected, and well-rounded parents to many children who no other could love. They had been working the circuit for over twenty-five years without a single serious complaint and had even managed to turn a few kids everyone had given up onto a path towards a better life.

The child in their care currently was one Samuel Moses. This young man of fifteen had seen his fair share of group homes, foster care, and even jail. Samuel like many kids who ended up in therapeutic homes was there because of his own bad behavior and not that of his biological parents.

He had been born to loving folks who celebrated his arrival in their lives. As the years wore on Missus Moses noticed her son was not like other children. Samuel was more aggressive, and hard to potty train. He would often bite, scratch or kick his parents and others when he didn't get his way. By the age of five it was clear Samuel was likely full of demons.

By the age of eight he had killed three of the family's pets after torturing them first and attacked a young lady at school trying to rape her in the hallway. The Moses sent Samuel for testing and inpatient treatment trying to curb his violent, cruel behaviors only to be told their beautiful son was a full-blown Antisocial Personality Disorder with Psychopathic tendencies.

The years wore on with his parents seeking out treatment after useless treatment. Samuel kept getting more aggressive and his behaviors more criminal and more dangerous. Then at the age of fourteen he broke into the local grocery store and robbed the safe after casing the place for months. He just sneered at the cameras that recorded his every move. The next day when he was picked up for the robbery, he bragged to the cops, he would rob the bank next time. Samuel was now a felon.

The Moses looked to DCFS to aid them. Samuel was far too rough to handle in their home any longer. With tears and heartbreak, they handed him over to the State praying that somehow, someone there could show Samuel the way back to redemption. His poor parents had no clue that Samuel's very serious personality disorder would assure he was cursed to live a life of non-empathetic criminal behaviors followed by long prison sentences, and maybe even eventual murder of himself or another. Sadly, there is no more a cure for Antisocial Personality Disorder than there is for schizophrenia.

The writing was on the wall. Samuel was a bona fide monster from birth. A true blue, demon seed. You had only to look into his vacant eyes to see the long string of victims of his thirst for perpetual thrill in them.

I for one hated visiting the creature. I more than anyone understood one day I would be digging up his latest victim from under his house. After all Debbie, my own mother, has the very same diagnosis as Samuel did. I knew personally what he was capable of and what he would eventually do if not stopped by incarceration for life.

I knocked on the door and Missus Turnbol answered. The lady looked worn and tired. Her long salt and pepper hair was disheveled in a loose bun. She had lost weight making her already thin, willowy frame appear so much frailer. Lucy was still a handsome woman at sixty, but I could see this latest placement was taking its toll. She had aged years in only months.

She smiled at me with relief filling her cloudy grey eyes. "Ah, my God. You are a vision. Come in, come in. Samuel is in his room, grounded again." She stepped back so I could enter the house.

I snorted while I walked inside. "Well he must have done something hideous indeed for you to say I am a vision, Missus Turnbol. What is it this time?"

She shook her head appearing very sad. "Well, I caught him on the computer trying to look up a way to make pipe bombs. He called in a threat to the school last week. He is suspended for the remainder of this semester. Tom and I are at our wits end with Samuel. He is just, well I never want to give up on any child but the more we try to help him the worse he gets."

I nodded. "Lucy, are you and Tom ready to give it up? Samuel is not going to get better, hon. It is time you face the facts and send him to residential care. I am worried his aggression towards you two may result in your injury. He is drawing pictures of the two of you impaled on spikes and cut to pieces. I would ask you once again to consider giving up this case. No one can say you didn't try. It is not a failure

Lucy, it is nature. Samuel is what he is. There is no fixing it," I said pleading with the good-hearted foster mother to finally realize the placement was doing no good.

Lucy's eyes teared up slightly. "Not yet. Tom and I want to give it a few more weeks. Samuel has so much potential. He is smart, handsome, witty and oh so creative. If we send him away to one of those child pits he is finished. We just can't bare it until we have tried everything."

I chuckled. "Okay, you know I can't make you give him up. However, you have been warned Lucy. Samuel doesn't love you the way you and Tom love him. It is not his fault. He was born without the part of his brain that understands love. He would just as easily kill you both as he would pull the wings off a fly, laughing while he did it. You can pity him all you want, but if I were you, I would do it from afar. Can I go back and see him please?"

She nodded. "Yeah, he has been waiting for you. I already told him twice to get back to his room. I am glad he seems to like you so much. He always kicks out the FINS caseworker. Samuel doesn't usually like authority figures as you well know. You seem to have some magic with him. Maybe you could talk with him about leaving the bomb idea alone?" Her eyes were pleading with me.

I laughed hard. "Oh Lucy, I have a way with the psychopaths. I know their language. I learned to speak it fluently when I was just a little one myself. You could say I was raised in their country, darling. I can talk to him for you but I promise you it will be useless. You think about what I said." I walked down the hallway towards the room that the Turnbol's had kindly granted to Samuel.

I knocked on the door chuckling at his 'Keep out' and 'Fuck off' handwritten signs plastered all over it. He had added yellow caution tape to his décor since my last visit the week before. Teen angst mixed with hormones and criminality. Samuel was just a nightmare waiting to happen.

"Fuck off Lucy, you stupid cow. I am busy flogging my dong. Unless you want to come suck my dick so I don't have to work my wrist so hard," Samuel yelled out angrily.

I stifled my giggling at his foul statement. "You can't afford my service, darling. Now open this fucking door," I yelled back.

Samuel was a looker even at the young age of fifteen. He was blond, blue eyed, light skinned and already almost six foot tall. His jaw was strong and square with deep set cheekbones. He wore his mane in a spiky fashion and was very careful to groom in the finest of clothing he could afford.

Vanity was another vice this budding crook engaged in. He already had a long list of broken-hearted young ladies. He also had more than a few allegations that he tended to be touchy feely without permission with his numerous girlfriends. So far, he had only been accused of unwanted groping. I assumed the word rapist was not far from being a word used to describe him.

Samuel immediately opened the door with a big sheepish smile on his handsome face. "Ah Psycho, I was just thinking about you."

I winced. "Yeah, I believe you made that clear to me and the entire house. Get out of the way Sammy. I am coming in. You better have your shit covered up. I am not interested in seeing your Vienna sausage thank you." I pushed past the teenaged psychopath.

Samuel grinned maliciously. "Ah now baby, don't be like that. You should check me out. I am hung like a bull. Just think you could help me out with my future career. I could show you my talents for entry into DCFS Investigators." He chuckled looking me up and down while licking his lips.

I rolled my eyes at him. "Cut the shit lover boy. Not interested. What is this crap I hear about pipe bombs? Really? Shouldn't you be working your way up? You know, start with sparklers or something? What is your hurry to hit the big time, I mean the big house like that?" I sat down in his desk chair glaring at him without emotion.

He smiled looking at the floor feigning embarrassment. "Ah, I was just fooling around having a little fun with the scaredy cats at school is all. I'm not making a bomb. That would be silly. I am a lover not a killer, baby."

I snorted. "And I am the Queen of England. Seriously Samuel, if you don't cut your shit I will personally make sure to place you in the Boy's Home. I have a special connection to the worst one in this state. I can contact an old resident that can testify to their heavy-handed practices. I am sure he can pull a few strings to make it happen. I know you have a need to get into trouble, but I suggest you stick to the petty stuff and stop threatening the Turnbols and school. You don't want to test me. I can be a real bitch when I want to be." I growled irritated that I was having this conversation at all.

Samuel frowned. "Really? you would put me into the Boy's Home, Psycho? I thought you and me were friends," He said faking his feelings had been hurt.

I laughed heartily at that. "Bullshit, you can save that acting job for the stage, cupcake. I am not one of your little doe eyed girlfriends. I mean it Samuel, keep fucking with me, and I will make sure you are out of my hair for good. I have better shit to do than babysit your ass. Are we understanding each other here fella?" I stared at him hard.

He nodded. "Yeah, I hear you. You likely to tell that ballbreaker Sheryl about my fun?"

I nodded. "Damn right I am."

He glowered at me. "You know when I am done killing the Turnbols, I am going to murder that red-headed cunt too. Then I am going to hunt you down and fuck you till my dick falls off. I will make you love it too." He grabbed his crotch smiling diabolically at me.

I smiled evilly back. "Oh yeah? Then what big man? You better call a friend because otherwise I will be left unsatisfied. You don't scare me Samuel so save it. I eat little bad boys like you for breakfast and I don't even wash them down with water. Now give me the bomb parts or so help me I will haul your ass off right fucking now. All of them!"

Samuel looked up appearing surprised. "What? Bomb parts? Me?"

I stood up. "Okay asshole, pack up. We are headed out. I have other cases and you are pissing me off."

He snorted while shaking his leg trying to wait me out. I made a move for the door and he rushed to block it.

"Okay, shit, okay. I am getting them. Fuck. You always call my fucking bluff. That is why I love you. God damn would I like to love you, demoness, all night long." He walked to his closet and retrieved a black bag full of items he had read that were required to make his pipe bomb.

I took the bag. "I doubt this is everything. No problem. I will get the bomb squad over here to confiscate the rest and your ass right to the clink while they are at it."

Samuel laughed. "Shit. You are clever. Okay, fuck me, please?" He ran to his bed and reached under the mattress grabbing more items he had been collecting then handed them to me.

I rolled my eyes. "Samuel, you are an honest to God asshole. I feel sorry for the world just knowing you are in it."

He smiled proudly. "See, I knew you loved me. Damn are you sexy when you are pissed. Now, before you leave how about a blow job?"

I took off for the door but turned around and blew at him. "There you go sport. Enjoy your wet dreams because that is all you will ever get. Leave the Turnbols alone. I mean it." I left with him standing there grabbing his chest smiling at his pretending to be broken hearted.

I slammed his door shut and walked down the hall looking for Tom. I found the worn-out foster father sitting at the kitchen table his head resting on his crooked arm snoozing over his newspaper.

"Tom, sorry to wake you but we need to talk." I sat down dropping the confiscated bomb parts on the table in front of him.

He snorted and woke up appearing mildly groggy. "Uhm, oh hey Missus Voss. Did you talk to Samuel? Lucy said you were. What is this stuff," he said suddenly noticing the numerous pieces of metal pipes, cotton and other things I will never repeat (you need not know how to make one). Just have faith Samuel sure as shit did know and had all the parts too, twice over.

I growled. "Samuel is making bombs, Tom. It is time to send him out. I am calling the local cops to search this house. If I were you and Lucy, I would rent a hotel until the boys in blue clear this place. I will call Sheryl and start the paperwork immediately. I know you and Lucy want to try longer but this is not okay. Samuel is trying to kill you. So, I am letting you know as a professional curtesy only, get out of the house now."

Tom was handling some of the parts appearing stunned. "Are you sure Missus Voss? I mean how can he have a bomb planted in the house when you have all his parts here?"

I shook my head. "I can assure you he has a third set already in place. You all keep making excuses for this kid. He doesn't care; he can't ever care. The trouble everyone has with these types is they want to project empathy and a soul. Samuel has neither. Take it from someone who knows this shit personally. I must go make the phone calls. Get Lucy, and that beast and rent a hotel room until the authorities come to pick him up. Tell him you decided to go on a fishing trip or something to get him out of town to cool off. Oh, and keep him away from sharp objects." I stood up to leave.

Tom grabbed my coat arm. "What if they don't find a bomb in the house? What if you are wrong?"

I grimaced. "I am not wrong, Tom. Do what I told you to do and let it go. You can't save them all. You won't save anyone if you ignore my warning. Good luck and for what it's worth, thank you for caring. Too bad this time it has been wasted." I left and got on the cell phone before even leaving the driveway calling the police and Sheryl.

I arranged to have Samuel moved to a residential care facility designed to handle budding criminal youth in Dallas, Texas. The local police in Cumberland assured me they would get right on the job of searching the Turnbol's house for the hidden pipe bomb.

I was half-way to Wheatly when the call came in. The pipe bomb had been located. In the Turnbol's mailbox in fact. Samuel had set it to go off that very afternoon when Tom went to check for the postal carrier's deposit. The bomb was discovered when it went off blowing the mailbox right to hell and the person opening the lid lost both their hands to the elbows.

Turned out Tom had disobeyed my instructions. After I left the man went to Samuel demanding to know where the bomb was hidden. Samuel of course told Tom I was lying and full of shit. Tom was angry. He told Samuel that thanks to his little trick the cops were coming to turn the house over while looking for a bomb that didn't exist. Tom, taking the little liar's word for it, went to find Lucy. The foster parents were calling in a complaint on me to Sheryl when the explosion went off in their front yard.

They rushed outside to find Samuel lying unconscious, bleeding and mangled next to a large hole where the metal box once stood. Upon hearing the cops were coming and he had been caught the idiot had run to try to undo his handiwork. It went off while Samuel was trying to remove the evidence. He had been rushed to the local emergency room where they would have to spend many hours patching him up to save his pathetic life. In the end he lived, but his hands and half his arms went buh bye, gone in the blast meant to kill the kindhearted Tom.

Oh well, looks like Samuel had annihilated himself from a life of debauchery and hardcore criminality. Kind of hard to rape and murder without any fucking hands.

Sheryl ordered that I visit the now mutilated psychopathic Samuel as soon as he was stable and able to speak. She wanted me to break the news to him that the Turnbols had decided to keep his unworthy ass on in their home despite the State being more than ready to send his butt right to Texas.

I groaned when Sheryl told me that. I realized at that point there was such a thing as being goodhearted to a fault. I doubted Lucy or Tom realized that while Samuel had done this to himself he was going to blame them. There was no doubt in my mind that eventually, he would find a way to retaliate. Samuel was just too fucking smart to allow a little thing like no hands stop him from destroying his loving foster family.

Sheryl snorted. "Well, so Julia called me a bit ago. She said you were rude to her and told her I am a liar."

I chuckled. "Did she? Huh? Wonder what crawled up her keister."

"Did you tell her you don't have schizophrenia," growled out Sheryl.

I chuckled even harder. "Did you say I did? I do believe that was a breach of confidentiality and a bullshit lie to boot if you did."

There was a pause on the phone. "Are you saying you don't have it? Seriously?"

I sighed. "Yes, that is what I am saying Sheryl. Schizophrenics wouldn't be able to do the job you are asking

144

me to do and I am doing well I may add. So, either I am loony toons or I am not. You can't have it both ways, darling. If I am out here working this job then I must not be sick. Duh, it was a simple misdiagnosis apparently. No harm done. I am not angry, just tired of everyone trying to convince me I had something I simply do not have."

Sheryl chuckled nervously. "I never thought of that. I suppose you could have just had a little nervous breakdown a while back. Hell, anyone could have one with enough stress and all. That Boyd would sure drive anyone nuts. I will have to make sure to remove that wrong diagnosis from your records. Whew, actually that is the best news I have heard all day. My darling Psycho isn't. That is just wonderful. Now if you just could kick Boyd to the curb, I bet you would never have any other problems at all. Think of all the work you could get done then."

I rolled my eyes and made a fake stroking motion from my crotch with the cell phone in my hand. I put the thing back to my ear. "Yep, that sounds about right. Are we done here boss? I have lots of cotton to pick before the overseer calls quitting time you know."

Sheryl growled. "Yeah, get to Wheatly and watch out for those Gypsies. They are nasty customers. I wish they would stop wintering in my catchment area. Fucking circus people. Freaks the whole lot of them."

I laughed out loud. "Wow. Damn ma kettle, did you just call the pot black cause I seem to recall you putting a collar around my neck. You also hired someone you thought was madder than a hatter and gets turned on by bruises. I think maybe you'd better be keeping those stones in your pocket baby. Anyway, got to go. I see my turn off, ciao." I hung up on Sheryl.

I started up the long dirt driveway to the top of the steep hill. It plateaued at the top with acres of real estate that was uninhabited miles in every direction. Well most of the time uninhabited. Once a year in the winter for eight to twelve weeks a troupe of people referred to as Gypsies would come to town and claim this area for their winter headquarters.

The rest of the year this group of displaced families of Romanian decent would travel the United States. This homeless mass all worked together and shared every penny they could earn with each other. They moved from small town to tiny hamlet camping out in tents as squatters until the locals ran them out of the city limits.

Every member young to old worked at making money by doing circus performances such as fire eating, impossible looking tumbles and seductive dances. The elderly members would offer fortune telling and magic spells. The children of the group would pick your pocket while you watched the adults entertain the audience. Even the dogs that traveled with them were trained to sneak into local grocery stores and run off with choice hunks of meat for the commune to share among its many hungry mouths.

The Wheatly folks had viewed this troupe as a plague they could not seem to exterminate for the last decade. Every November, like the winter rains, the brightly painted camper trailers would arrive in the darkness and park on the outskirts of town. The sounds of their lively fiddles, and sights of their bright fires would stick in the craws of the deeply Baptist or Pentecostal townsfolk. They could not stand the thought that in their very midst there were heathens who enjoyed dancing, music, laugher, drink, family and fun. Perish the thought.

When the Boswell Gypsies lit into Wheatly, calls from the locals into the police station and DCFS would be as common a sight as cows in the fields in that sleepy town. The Boswells had only struck camp seven days earlier. Master Boyd told me he and Dennis had already been out there three times that week on reports of petty thievery.

That morning I received my first hail out too. It was only a matter of time. In fact, I was counting on that call. I admit I had always wanted to meet the Boswells. This was actually a teenage dream come true.

I had never even seen one of the infamous Gypsies thanks to my chronic homelessness, isolation by my many Masters and of course inpatient treatments that tended to happen that time of year when the Boswells were in town. I had heard all the stories of their acts, their criminal activity and colorful exaggerations of their association with the Devil.

I knew that last part was untrue. I knew the Devil personally. Debbie told me once she had never met a Gypsy. So, I was a bit more than thrilled to answer the silly report that the Boswells were beating their children day and night.

I pulled up and parked just outside the circle of handmade tents, and painted camper trailers.

I sat in the car enamored by the sights before my eager eyes. Bright blues, reds, orange and greens mixed with yellows and pinks were everywhere. Even the makeshift tents seemed to be made of colorful skirts I had seen in picture books about the Gypsy peoples. My heart was thumping fast and hard. I had never felt so charged. I opened the door walking almost in a trance toward the encampment.

An incredibly tall man with long black hair pulled into a pig tail and deep-set black eyes immediately came out blocking my path to the center of the tent grouping. He was holding a sawed off shotgun like the one Micky Voss had lost his head to. That got my attention. I stopped dead in my tracks.

"Who be you? State your business. You don't belong here," said the man in a thick Romanian accent.

I raised an eyebrow keeping my eye on the shotgun. "Uhm, I am here from the DCFS. They called me, told me to come check to make sure your children are healthy and well-treated. I don't want any trouble just doing my job Mister Boswell."

He spit onto the ground. "How you know my name? I never seen you before."

I chuckled. "I was told in the report Mr. Boswell. May I please see the children so I can get out of here and leave you to your business?"

The man said something in Romanian to a humped over old woman with many colorful scarves and a large skirt who had shown up behind him. She looked at me saying something back. I noticed she didn't have any teeth and her long white hair was brushing the ground. Both were glaring at me suspiciously.

The man growled. "Momma says to prove to us you be the law or you get out of here now. I would leave if I were you. We don't like snoopers."

I nodded now feeling very nervous that I would be in a shallow grave by dusk. "I am going to pull out my badge slowly. Don't shoot please? I am only here to look, then be on my way. I know the call is a lie but I must look or they will fire me. Just look not touch, okay?" I held out my badge while the pair strained to see it from their distance.

The old woman said something else in their native tongue and the man nodded looking me up and down. "Momma says that you have proof, but you look like a Moolo. We don't need your kind here. You be gone Moolo." He shooed me with his gun.

A teenaged girl dressed modern appeared and grabbed the man's arm. She said something in their language then looked at me appearing embarrassed. "My father is old school Romani, ma'am. Forgive him. Of course, you can see the children. We don't want any trouble. Momma will call them and bring them here for you to see. I am Lavinia, this is my father Shady, and my great, great grandma Kenzia. You are?" She came forward offering her hand to shake.

I smiled brightly. "They call me Psycho. It is truly a pleasure to meet you Lavinia. I have waited my whole life to enjoy such a gift of meeting the Boswell's troupe."

She looked surprised. "Are you for real? I don't know what is more disturbing to me, a Gadjo called Psycho who looks like a Moolo but is a cop or your wanting to meet our family. You must be Dinler."

I chuckled. "I am a lot of things Lavinia, but I am no Dinler. Now I assume that means crazy or fool. But what the hell is a Moolo."

Lavinia laughed loudly. "It is a dead person possessed by a ghost. It is Romani legend. You are very funny. Here are the children Psycho or should I call you Dinler?"

I winced. "Call me whatever you like darling, just don't shoot. I didn't come to cause trouble. Even I am not that Dinler." I winked, which made even the dower Shady laugh as he told Kenzia what I said. She laughed too.

I saw a large group of very handsome dark skinned, dark haired and dark eyed children start to appear just in front of Shady Boswell. They were all dressed in stark, very clean white shirts with flowery skirts on the girls and brown pants with cowboy boots on all the boys. The children were well behaved, well-groomed, well-shaped, well fed and not one had a scratch on them.

As promised, I only looked them over while writing down the report was unfounded. I allowed Lavinia to release the kids. She said something in Romanian and they all ran off laughing and scattering like fireflies on a hot summer night. I smiled as I watched the amazing sight truly enjoying the most unusual, and unfounded, call for a change.

"Well that was it. You folks have a nice day. Thank you so much for your time. I would apologize to you for the ignorance of these hateful Gadjos but what good would that be? They will never change and you shouldn't have to." I smiled while waving at Shady, Lavinia and Kenzia turning to leave when…

Shady called out to me, "You said Gadjos. Do you know what that be?"

I didn't turn around. "Dumb white people I assume Mister Boswell or perhaps assholes. That is what I call them."

The whole camp broke out in laughter at my most foul statement. "Come back here Dinler. We like you. Come sit by our fire and tell us how you become a Moolo," yelled out Kenzia.

I turned around stunned. "Huh? you want me to hang out with you?" I stared at the old woman who was smiling as was Shady.

"Yes. Yes. Come tell us a tale Dinler. We always love a good Dariav. Come, I make you a gypsy Kaymak coffee. You like a coffee, yes?" The woman moved fast for her age already at my side grabbing my hand pulling me back to their camp.

I smiled almost overjoyed at my good fortune. "Coffee is mother's milk to me Kenzia."

She laughed. "Long as you no drink blood Moolo." More waves of laugher erupted through the camp as I followed the ancient woman to sit on a rock next to the campfire.

I watched the Boswell clan moving about, interacting with each other and listened to their conversations for about two hours. Their love for each other and tight bond was obvious. To outsiders these people were a nuisance, a plague of thieves and freaks. Within the center of this commune was many units that had a single heart that beat as one.

No one was left out, made to feel less or mistreated. I listened to them talk of lands far away, legends of their world, and tease each other lovingly while laughing till my sides split. The Boswells were everything I had dreamed they would be and so much more. I could spend chapters talking about what they said, did and the stories they told, but maybe another day in another life. For now, I will keep those rare gifts for myself. The Boswells were private people. I doubt they would have told me what they did if they knew I would repeat it.

I was served an amazing coffee that was made in a most odd fashion manner. I saw Kenzia boil sugar, coffee grounds and water in a pot. She then spooned off the top into several cups and kept boiling it for a while. Once satisfied it was boiled enough, she sat it to one side allowing it to cool slightly, then poured the liquid into the cups and handed one to each adult at the fire including me. It was amazing and called Kaymak coffee apparently.

I almost greedily accepted a second cup before realizing that others had been waiting to have their first. I saw the look of approval on many faces when I passed my cup to a Boswell girl on my left who smiled and took it with many thanks. My training in submission served me well. I knew how to be polite, patient and quiet when it mattered. It took me no time at all to become accepted as a 'trusted' Gadjo with the Boswells.

My pager went off indicating it was time for me to move on. I begrudgingly bid a fond farewell, until next time. I did tell Lavinia other reports would come in no doubt. The roars of displeasure that I could not stay longer settled with my most ominous prediction.

Lavinia looked at the ground while walking with me and two curious children to my car. "Why won't they just leave us alone?"

I smiled at the little Boswell children who laughed and ran from me. "Because they are superstitious and ignorant around here, darling. Anyone who is different must be bad. Tell you what, with Kenzia's and Shady's permission I will stop by once a week to check off the box saying that your children are under state observation. That will end the false calls to DCFS. I can do nothing about the local cops but do know they know you are good people. They are just doing their job."

Lavinia smiled brightly. "You would do this for us? Of course, do it. We would love to see you once a week until we leave. Thank you Psycho."

I got into the car laughing. "You know Lavinia, you are the one Dinler this time. No one has ever been happy to have a case opened on them."

She smiled. "Ah, then they don't know how to live. See you next week, Gadjo."

I waved smiling at her insult while backing up. My heart was light, still filled with the laughter and mirth of some of the kindest people I had ever met. I briefly wished I had been born a Boswell. Things would have been very different. Sure, the world would still hate me as an outsider, but at least I wouldn't be alone in my exile anymore.

My call was over one hundred miles away and not a priority. Someone had mistakenly called me into a case of child neglect not one of abuse or rape. I sighed as I argued with the secretary on the hotline. No matter the mix up, they expected me to see the allegedly neglectful mother by the next afternoon, and report back to the DCFS head of that county and foster mother Cheryl Rutgers.

The fact that Sheryl was my boss didn't matter to the idiot who had misassigned the case. I finally hung up realizing it would take me longer to fight the job order than to just drive to fucking Wells and assess the situation. I looked at my gas tank with a moan. I needed to gas up to make that long trip. I had burned the hell out of the petrol all week. This was my third stop to fill up in only two days.

I pulled into Night's station in Carter. The quick stop Mistress Ginger and I had once worked at down the road was closed permanently three months before. I drove by it trying not to feel the heartbreak that always seemed to rise each time I looked at that now locked up place. I still ached for my D/ss sham of a family even though Matthew had now been dead for over two years, and I was sadly celebrating my second year of Mistress Ginger's own cruel abandonment.

I had made peace with Master Boyd and had even come to understand I had some true feelings for him. That didn't mean I felt for him the way I did my one true love. I would have sold my soul to have even one more day with my lost brother collar. I finally understood the tears Mother Delleh shed the day of the Great Rite when she spoke of her own grief when Kevin was lost to her. No matter how much time had passed, I never stopped missing or wishing to be with Matthew.

I was dreaming of his arms and kisses while pumping my gas. I was jolted from my fantasies of Matthew when arms went around my waist hugging me tightly.

I let out a yelp as Master Boyd put his mouth to my ear and whispered, "Psycho, I wanted to see if maybe you might want to, I mean if you are not busy, I would pay and all if you are not in a rush somewhere. I would want to, I mean, maybe you could go to the movies this weekend with me? Like Saturday night? I have the whole weekend off." He was faking a nervous stammer.

I opened my eyes wide. "Uhm sure, but just dinner or the movies. Nothing else okay?" I recognize this line from long ago when Master Boyd had caught me at this very same pump and started his chase to gain my collar.

Master Boyd laughed. "I wish you had said that the first time I asked."

I grimaced as he groped my breasts still hugging me from behind. "Me too Master. What is done is done. What are you doing here? Shouldn't you be in bed?"

He groaned appearing in pain. "Yes, but Dennis made me get up and file some paperwork for the Windbush case. The man never lets up. I was driving by and saw your car. I am up. You are in town, come to lunch with me. You need to eat something, and I have missed you something awful. I never get to see you. Come on baby, no matter where you are headed you can spare thirty minutes for me can't you?"

I put the nozzle back into the pump pushing my Master off my unit. "Alright, lunch only. I don't have time for special services Master. I have a lot to do."

He grabbed my arm pulling me into a passionate kiss. "Don't tell me no, Psycho. I'm warning you baby, you know I hate that. Let's keep this pleasant, shall we? I do believe I am still your Master and you can't deny me my services if I request them when I request them," he said sternly in caution after releasing me from his lips.

I nodded realizing he was correct. "Yes Master. I apologize for overstepping my bounds. I would beg mercy.

However, to make this quick, I have a lot to do yet. So a trip home unless we hurry would be a bit much to ask me to do."

Master Boyd smiled mischievously. "Oh, we could grab a bite at Wanda's to go then hit the logging trail and take care of both at the same time. That work for you?"

I winced. "As you wish Master. Let me pay Dale and move my car. You can drive, I assume you would need to. It would be kind of hard for me to steer with my face in your lap."

Master Boyd began to laugh at my most true statement while I went inside Night's station to pay. When I came out my Master was staring looking irritated at the side street next to the building. I walked up next to him and followed his sightline.

Sitting in a car parked just off to the left shoulder was Trenton, Will and Mark. They were getting out and coming our direction. I felt panic surge within realizing this was bad news.

"Come on Master, let's go get lunch and take that ride to the logging trail." I tried to move his unit toward his car, but he pushed me off hand motioning me to be still.

I looked at the ground hoping the off-duty city cops would leave me and my Master alone. Of course, they actually had only stopped by Night's station to bully Master Boyd in the first place, much to my disappointment. They began the insults before even getting close enough to see the color of their eyes.

"Well, will you look at this. I just found my new girlfriend. Baby girl where have you been hiding? Oh, that is right. The nuthouse again. Maybe this time they managed to get you to come back to your senses. Come over here Psycho, you have tried out the creep, now let me show you what a real man can do. You don't need old Boyd here to make you scream and cry. I will be happy to fill that slot since you must like it that way. Only when you are with me, you'll be doing it in joy instead of fear. Come on girl, it will be nice change, I can promise you that." Trenton sneered out while walking toward Master Boyd.

I looked at Will and Mark who were flanking Trenton. The three of them reminded me of hyena's trying to surround a lion and his lioness. There was no doubt, fur was just about to fly. I saw my Master's hands ball into fists. Sweat was breaking out on his brow and his breathing had become shallow.

His anger demons were rising and these idiots couldn't have picked a more inopportune time to set it off. My Master had not had his cork pulled, sex or violent outburst, in more than a week. The trio had also made the mistake of interrupting his sexual liaison with me. So instead of me doing the job, he was going to end up blowing instead in the worst way. Okay, clever play on words there if do say so myself. Nurse, meds over here. Where is that bitch.

"Trenton I have told you before not to disrespect my fiancé like that. I hope you are ready to have your ass kicked. We are not at work this time. Psycho, get in the car and wait for me. I am going to take the boys around back and teach them a lesson in manners around a lady." Master Boyd said in an eerily calm fashion.

I looked at the off-duty city cops. "Uhm I guess telling you these pigs don't matter is not going to talk you out of it," I said under my breath.

He growled, "In the car now."

I didn't mess around but turned and ran for his black car getting into the passenger's seat. I rolled down the window terrified that at any moment the cops would come to arrest my Master. I couldn't stand the thought of seeing him taken away in cuffs. I looked around the car for any weapon I could find. I had determined that if the police did come I was going with him.

I would follow his directive to stay out of my Master's fray with these bullies. Trenton, Will and Mark had tormented him for years making his life pure hell. Master Boyd had never done a damned thing to deserve any of it. However, I would be hauled off myself before I would let any God damned cop stop my Master from getting his well-deserved vengeance.

While I was not happy to see it happen in broad daylight, I did believe Master Boyd had the right to defend himself and his collar. The clash was noticed by more than just the four potential combatants and one silly schizophrenic. Dale, and several nosy customers, had all rushed out taking their places to watch the show.

I noticed right away no one was calling the police to intervene. Instead they all seemed very eager to see blood. They all chattered and pointed grinning and watching with intense fascination the unfolding battle of testosterone. I even thought I heard a few making bets on who would win if this altercation came to blows.

It was then that I understood that the city cops and the county cops were already on the scene. Why would anyone call for more? Besides, getting to see police on police brutality, now that is entertainment folks. The three stood there eyeing my Master while he stood his ground staring back. I could only see his back but even from my vantage I noticed his shoulders were out wide and he stood up tall. It was a definite sign of aggression. I briefly closed my eyes. I silently asked the Mother Goddess to give Master Boyd strength to knock down the big mouths once and for all.

"Well? Are you just going to stand there asshole? I am waiting. If you think I am just going to let this go, you have another thing coming Trenton. Apologize to my fiancé or I will knock your fucking teeth out," called out Master Boyd as he spit on the ground.

Will laughed nervously. "Ah come on Trenton, I am hungry. Leave the pussy and his loony girlfriend alone. Who cares?"

Trenton looked at Will with irritation. "I care, Will. I am not afraid of this baby rapist. Besides, I want to see what that girl has under her hood. He is in my way."

Mark shook his head. "You would have sloppy seconds after Boyd? Jesus man, ain't no piece of ass worth that."

That was it. Master Boyd flew at Mark punching him right in the mouth sending the five-foot nine overweight cop to his knees holding his mouth in agony. Then like a viper he turned and grabbed Trenton bending the fat ass over his knee Master Boyd plowed him right into the back of his skull sending him face first into the pavement next to the gas pumps.

Will jumped onto Master Boyd's back. Will was six-foot-tall himself and in better shape than the other two portly officers. The two big men struggled landing blows into each other's faces and chest bouncing off the wall several times. Mark got up still holding his bleeding mouth he ran to try to interfere with the battling cops by sucker punching Master Boyd in the kidneys.

However, Master Boyd was tossed backward by Will. Boyd smacked into Mark sending him back on his ass. My Master felt the collision and without a bit of emotion on his face turned and kicked Mark in the head sending the idiot right to unconscious town. Will had grabbed Master Boyd from behind again struggling to subdue him. I saw him staring down at Trenton while rocking back and forth trying to get free of Will's tight grip.

I too looked at Trenton who was trying to get up. He was moaning and up on all fours. Master Boyd reared back his right foot and planted a kick into his fatty sternum from below. The bully yelped out losing all his wind, then rolled on his back kicking the air like a pissed off baby waiting on a diaper change. I admit that made me laugh like hell.

Will let Master Boyd go while kicking him in the back of his knee. My Master nearly fell from the force but recovered turned and head butted the shocked officer while punching him in the breadbasket. Will fell to his knees gasping for air. I sat there in unable to believe my eyes. Three cops were on the ground. One was unconscious, one was kicking on his back and one was on his knees unable to breath. My Master stood above them all panting, sweating and bleeding but was clearly the winner of the law officer's brawl at Night's station.

He looked over his fellow officers appearing satisfied that he had given them a taste of what they could always expect the next time they insulted him or me. Then without saying a word he stormed to the car, got inside and took off headed for the logging trail.

I have to say this about my role as his submissive the day Master Boyd finally got his revenge on those assholes. I was more than happy to grant him his special service in return for his protection and defense of his collar. I even ignored my pager that was going off wildly while he vigorously took me on the hood of his car that afternoon.

Despite his ragged appearance, bloody mouth and nose, and bruised up unit his lovemaking that day was stellar. I didn't argue with attending his every request until he was well satisfied and completely spent, twice believe it or not. You know what they say, to the victor goes the spoils.

After he was given his, uhm, prize, I had him sit down in the passenger's seat so I could effectively assess the damage to his unit. I was lovingly wiping the blood and gore from my personal gladiator while he continued to try to playfully grope, the man never stopped, I swear it. He was not being an easy patient. He continued to block my attempts to clean him up telling me to stop worrying so much that he was fine. The only touching he wanted me to do to him had nothing to do with his numerous cuts and bruises.

I was engaged in this game of clean up combat with Master Boyd when my pager went off yet again. Irritated that I couldn't even get thirty minutes of peace and quiet I checked the machine. I immediately recognized the number and almost fainted. It was Dennis. I looked at my Master sitting there smiling, glassy eyed, and feeling very relaxed.

"Master, Dennis is trying to hail me. He must have heard about the fight." My eyes were wide with fear.

Master Boyd closed his eyes wincing. "Shit. Well baby, it was totally worth it."

I let out a sigh. "I will remember you said that when I come visit you through the glass."

He smiled and pulled me onto his lap. "Cigarettes for my boyfriend, Psycho. Remember that is a directive. I mean it. Hey, are you wearing, you are wearing electrical tape again. Oh, sonofabitch," he yelled out appearing suddenly very horrified and afraid.

I tried to hide my arms. "No wires, Master, not this time I swear it. Just tape, please don't be angry," I whined out also terrified.

"Baby, I am not angry at you. I am scared, God damn it. We must get you some help. You must quit this job. I can't lose you damn it," he said softly while reaching out to stroke my cheek trying to re-assure me, he was concerned not angry.

My pager went off without pausing. It began flashing one number after another. First Sheryl, then Dennis, and now Cathy. I looked at the monster machine then back to my grieving Master. Uh oh, this could only mean trouble, big trouble.

Chapter 70: Touched Too Much
The Tragic Fall of Psycho
Master Boyd and the Absent Interim Master Sheryl

You have all have travelled with me such a long time. You are all experts in the game of madness. Bravo, congratulations, wait, are you very sure you learned everything there is to know about schizophrenia? It is a tricky disease you know. Often hard to spot. The funny thing about the Queen Mother of Madness is that every single expression of it is different. No two schizophrenics are the same.

Some of us can function independently, some need help, others are downright broken. For many years I was able to hide my monster disease from the world. I did that by keeping most out of my inner circle, not that anyone was in a hurry to get inside it. I had no friends, no identifiable true associations. I had to find a normal to follow whether they were good, bad or ugly. It was necessary so I could navigate the reality I was forever shut out of, even when not psychotic.

I was viewed as quiet, odd, strange, weird, explosive, and someone to avoid. I never could watch TV or be around religious stuff. Both would set my delusions off. I am a generous and nice person, but I have a dark psychotic side.

I am high functioning. Despite my illness, I had careers in places you would never expect to see a loony like me. I was even allowed to work as a State Police DCFS Investigator. Talk about weird jobs for a nutball to hold.

Violence, explosive temper, and given to misunderstandings. I even broke the law sometimes to get revenge or what I thought I was owed. Believe me when I tell you, I tried to control my anger demons, but you see there is no cure. No matter what I did, I was stuck, unable to get away, unable to move. I had to be careful about my aggression. It could get me locked up forever. I needed one single normal to follow behind. Someone to protect me from myself. Like a father or mother figure. Someone to help me hide my troubles.

Thank goodness I found the perfect match in Master Boyd. Ah, we were so much alike him and I. Same hatred for TV. Neither of us drank or did drugs. We both were kind and had a deep-seated need to be loved. We both thought sometimes God hated us. He and I even had the same sex drive. You know he totally got me. Did you know when he was fifteen, they put him in the Snake Pit too?

Master Boyd was taking medication to control that nasty tempter of his. He was doing all he could to fix his issues. I wonder why that wasn't working yet. Shit, he even took his punishment without complaint. He figured out equal service for equal service. His heart was good; he just has those demons inside. We totally get that. Wow, talk about empathy for each other.

My mirror for him was so strong, correct and without blemish. It was exact. I have no idea what Dennis's problem is. Why is he still bitching about this stellar match? Isn't it obvious that Master Boyd and I are like two sides to the same coin.

My Master understands my pain. He too has been shunned, misjudged, wrongly convicted, and viewed as odd. He has suffered years of loneliness and isolation. Not even a single distraction to keep him company. Over the years he learned how to keep his head down, so they all forget what they said about him. He knows how to keep a secret; he is the Master of them in fact. Fun fact, he even taught me how to hide my illness. He was a great teacher.

Sure, he and I started out on the wrong foot. You see, he had this weird ass delusion that he had to find his One and Only. Once he found her, he could have everything that had been taken from him. He tried to get me to understand I had been identified as his correct mate. That this unholy union was ordained by God. I wouldn't listen. He did what he had to do to get me to hear him. Now I get it. There simply was no choice. You see God promised this to him. Wait a minute. God talks to Master Boyd? Uh? Did we miss something here?

"Only this one-time Psycho and only because I can't say no for some reason. I don't know if it is your beauty or the moon, but I feel powerless. I must be under a gypsy spell."
--Master Boyd to Psycho at the Boswell encampment, December 1998.

Master Boyd was driving like a bat out of hell. We had to get back to Night's and use the phone. I had stupidly left my cell phone in the Taurus. The pager was still buzzing like an angry bee freaking both of us out to no end.

He glanced at me his blue eyes bright with terror. "Jesus, I am so dead. Let's just run, Psycho. Fuck it. We can start somewhere else where no one ever heard of either of us. I don't want to go back to, I can't go back Psycho, please baby."

I patted his shoulder. "Take a breath Master. It is going to be okay. Surely that little fight isn't stirring as far as old Sheryl. It has to be something else."

Sweat was breaking out on his brow. "Bullshit Psycho, they are going to send me away and you are just trying to help them do it. You of all people should understand," he yelled out now panicking as the terror inside him started to rise.

I glared at him speaking in a calm, soft voice. "Master, that is not true, and you know it. I won't let them take you away. You must learn to trust me. If they try I will fight them tooth and nail. This must be something else. You are being paranoid and you know it."

Master Boyd growled, "Take that back. I am not paranoid."

I glowered feeling my anger demon rise. "Fuck if you aren't."

He looked at me and the car almost went off the road. "Fucking take it back or so help me I will…"

I snorted. "What? What will you do Master? Masturbate for a lifetime? You aren't going to kill me so don't even threaten it. You want to be stuck in a collar too? I think not. You are being paranoid. If you don't cool it, they will lock your ass up and me with you."

He shot me a hateful look. "You'll see, they are going to send me away. You will have to break me out. That's a directive," he yelled.

I started laughing. "God damn you and the fucking directives, loon."

He looked at me initially angry, but suddenly a smile broke across his face. "Yeah, I guess I do make a lot of those." He started to laugh maniacally right along with me.

QUICK NOTE: *Now had you been a fly trapped in the window of that speeding black car that day, you would have wanted out for reasons other than just being free. I am sure that whole scene has been replayed a thousand times in mental institutions all over the country. Yelling followed by insane howling laughter. Looking back on it, it is kind of creepy. Okay, it is downright bone chilling.*

We pulled into Night's station still laughing like the fucking loons we were. Dennis was there on the pay phone apparently calling my pager. I looked over at my Master who spotted him too. The laughter stopped dead. Fear filled the void left behind.

"It will be okay Master. Stay calm or they will get you. Stay calm." I reached out and touched his shoulder causing him to jump slightly with nerves.

He nodded but I could tell his mouth had gone dry. I watched him trying to swallow as the sweat poured down his bruised-up face. His arms were trembling with terror. I felt a pang of sympathy for him. I had been there. Worried the authorities are there to take you kicking and screaming to do only God knows what. Just because you finally defended yourself. So unfair.

We pulled up next to the Taurus. Dennis saw us and hung up the phone and spit on the ground glaring our direction.

Master Boyd looked at me wide eyed. "Let's see who is paranoid." He nodded at my door indicating we were getting out to face the music no matter what the tune.

Dennis came slowly toward us. "Boyd, Psycho, where the Sam Hill have you been? Everyone is looking for you two. There is trouble."

Master Boyd and I both looked at the ground. "Yes sir," we said in unison shooting a quick nervous look at each other.

Dennis snorted. "Well never mind, you are both here now. Look we got a fellow named Dirk who run off with a woman's little girl. He is holed up in a house outside of Carter. Now Psycho, you are to take custody of the child if we can get her out alive."

I looked up startled. "What do you mean if?"

Dennis shook his head, "Dirk is drugged up on some acid or some shit. His girlfriend Jenny is fucked up too. We got her down at the station. The kid's name is Kerrie. Dirk took off with the baby demanding we release Jenny or else."

I gulped. "Jenny from the grocery store?"

He nodded. "Yeah that is her. You know her?"

I thought back to the day she was nasty to me when Jonathan was trying to get my phone number. "Not really. Okay, so Boyd and I will follow you?"

He nodded. "Sounds good. Now you stay back and let Randall handle it. They are standing him off now. Sheryl wanted you there, but you stay back. Boyd, you keep her safe. You hear me?" He looked at my Master not appearing to notice his busted-up face.

Master Boyd nodded. "Yes sir."

I went to the Taurus grabbing the cell phone then jumped into Master Boyd car again. We tore off speeding after Dennis headed to the standoff.

I looked at Master Boyd who was panting in sheer relief even though the real problem was really just as bad. "So, you are paranoid, Master," I said flatly.

He winced. "Apparently so. I will just take more medication."

I snort laughed. "It isn't working and you know it, Master."

Master Boyd gritted his teeth. "It will. This time it will."

I shook my head in disbelief. "Now your delusional too? Wow! Are you trying to get taken away to the psyche ward, Master? The medication doesn't work, damn it."

He groaned. "It will work Psycho. It must work. I will just take more of it."

I shook my head. "Okay sure, go ahead. Taking too much medication shuts down the liver. Happened to me back in 1993. Liver flushes are nasty things, Master. Won't stop the problems but you will get a nice clean gut."

Master Boyd looked at me concerned. "Really? Too much medication can do that? Bet that hurt like hell."

I laughed. "Fucking right it does, Master. When was the last time it got out of control?"

He grimaced. "Uhm, when I started chasing you. Then it got really bad around last May." He trailed off looking embarrassed.

I rolled my eyes. "Are you fucking kidding, Master. Really, you mean the whole white cell bullshit. Oh, forget that noise. Look I don't want to hear another word. Besides, none of that matters. You have me now. We will help each other." I smiled brightly without a damned bit of understanding of the seriousness of the very dangerous situation developing.

Master Boyd smiled and reached out taking my left hand then kissed his engagement ring. "Yeah, you are right. I have you now. Everything will be perfect. No more troubles. God promised me that. I have my One and Only by my side. Nothing can stop me or you." He held my hand to his face rubbing lightly, appearing in a trance.

I heard the Looper growling. "He is never letting you go, run, run, run." I waved my free hand around my ears.

Master Boyd glanced at me. "What are they saying?"

I snorted. "Stay out of my head, Master."

He let my hand go. "Dirk will kill that little girl you know. He is a fiend."

I shook my head feeling sad. "God I hope not, Master. I can't deal with burying another little girl."

Master Boyd sighed. "Me either baby."

We arrived at the scene to find more than a handful of squad cars, two ambulances and a fire truck. Luckily, Dirk had given up without much of a fight. Master Boyd and I pulled in behind Dennis ready for disaster only to be told by a dayshift cop the fray ended peacefully. I sighed with relief as I was handed a healthy but very frightened Kerrie. I smiled at the infamous Randall, Dennis's original partner, who was holding the baby girl making funny faces trying to calm her down.

Kerrie was a little girl of five who looked just like a living porcelain doll. Her hair was brown; her eyes were hazel and her chubby cheeks rosy. She was dressed in a red polka dotted dress with empire waist and puffy sleeves. Her Mary Jane style shoes and white tights made one think she must have been the model for every doll ever created and that sat on a store shelf.

I looked her over finding not even a scratch on her little unit. I silently thank the mother Goddess that I would not be attending a funeral this time. Kerrie smiled at me with her perfect pink lips and called out for her drugged-up mother Jenny. I stared at the child wondering what drug could be so powerful to make a mother risk such a rare gift for it. I decided Jenny didn't deserve this precious girl. What an asshole.

I called the Fairbanks foster home and had Kerrie placed and secured within only two hours. It was a case that appeared deadly but ended well. Jenny and Dirk were going to jail for a long while or so I hoped anyway. I was beyond grateful that no one got hurt and the bad guys were being held accountable. Not many of my cases ended up so cut and dry. I reveled in this being one.

Dennis called all his employees back to the station for a follow up discussion including my Master. I was stuck tagging along with him until he was released by his commanding officer. We followed Dennis back to the station while Sheryl called back and chewed me out for not answering my pager faster. I just listened and rolled my eyes at her bullshit. Master Boyd chuckled at my less than interested facial gestures.

"When I fucking page you I expect you to answer God damn it. You ever do that again…" I interrupted Sheryl's ranting.

"You'll what, Sheryl? Fire me? I don't think so. Maybe you'll cane me? Ah, you coming one hundred and fifty miles to do that? I don't think so. Look, I didn't have access to a phone. I will answer a page when I can. If you don't like it then I suggest you get someone else to do this shit job. As it is, the baby is safe. All is well that ends well. Are we done here," I yelled back at her.

"Uhm, yeah okay, so good job, bye." She hung up before I could on her being her typical prick self.

I just snorted, "Stupid bitch."

Master Boyd laughed. "Psycho quit the job and stay home with me. You are stressing too much. Oh, and about that electrical tape, no more electrical tape, that is a directive. I want all of it, the stuff on your arms and the tape hidden in your purse too. I know you." He smiled knowingly at me.

I pulled up my sleeves removing the tape. "Shit, I was hoping you forgot Master. I wasn't doing anything, just wearing it is all. PC said it would help the short circuit. Don't you want me well?" I said while putting the spent tape into his consol.

He snorted. "You know the tape doesn't work, Psycho. The medication doesn't work. Only time works. Now until this shit passes, I want you to quit, please? I need you at home." He glanced over to make sure my arms were not injured under the tape. They weren't, yet.

I shook my head. "You promised I could finish Sheryl's term. A deal is a deal Master. Please show mercy and stop bothering me with demanding I quit."

Master Boyd paused looking deep in thought,. "Okay, a deal is a deal. I want to see your arms every time we see each other. Every day in fact. That is a directive."

I grimaced. "Yeah, I kind of figured that Master. Anything else?"

He smiled diabolically. "Yes. For me, I want to watch you dance."

I groaned. "Yes Master. You are about to miss our turn lover," I pointed as my Master just nearly drove right past the station.

Master Boyd laughed as we squealed tires whipping into the parking lot of the jailhouse. "I guess I was headed to our secret spot at the edge of town."

I snorted. "You wish, Master."

He laughed while getting out. "Damned right I do. Get out of the car and come with me. I want to keep an eye on you while I still can."

I groaned and bitched but got out as he ordered. I followed behind him while he went to the conference area with the other officers to get their orders from Dennis and Randall. Master Boyd sat me in a chair next to his desk smiling the whole time as Linda and a few of the other officers watched us while looking jealous. Everyone was chattering and mumbling, but you could have heard a pin drop when Will, Mark and Trenton came through the door. The three looked worse than Master Boyd.

Mark's mouth and side of his head was swollen so bad he couldn't open his left eye. Will was cut across his nose and had a black eye. Trenton had numerous scrapes on his forehead and chin. The cops all looked around at each other than over at Master Boyd who also had bruised cheeks and a cut across his forehead and busted up knuckles that kept seeping blood. The others assumed Master Boyd who was at the standoff had gotten into it with Dirk. Will, Mark and Trenton had not been there, so now the group was realizing this was somehow linked, but how?

Hushed murmurs and whispers broke out as the three bullies took their seats just behind me and Master Boyd. My Master looked at his desk not saying a word. I just listened to the numerous voices in the room all wondering if the four of them had finally come to blows. They were of course right, but the story of the Night's Station Police Brawl had not circulated yet. For now, there was evidence but no reported crime.

Dennis and Randall came in closing the door behind them. The room went silent. I sat listening while the two old bulls talked about ways to improve performance and praised the officers who ended the standoff without incident. Dennis then handed out job duties to his night officers. As he walked around passing out his assignment sheets, he was yapping about things to be watching for. He looked over toward my Master and the bullies. He suddenly trailed off in his discussion appearing stunned to see his boys all looking like busted up prize fighters.

He raised an eyebrow and looked directly at me. I looked at the floor realizing he was trying to read my mind. Dennis let it go and went back to yammering. However, as he released everyone, he called me to the front with him and Randall. Master Boyd started to follow but Dennis hand gestured him to stay seated. Will, Mark and Trenton walked out with everyone never even hazarding a look toward me or my Master.

I walked up to the front desk as the two old bulls surrounded my unit like predators.

"Okay out with it Psycho, why do my cops look like raw meat," whispered Dennis while Randall leaned in eager to hear my answer.

I stared at the floor shrugging. "Beats me Dennis. Why are you always bothering me? What makes you think I know anything about anything?"

Dennis snorted. "You know everything that happens in these towns and we all know it. Fess up girl or so help me. Did Boyd and the fellows get into it? That is what happened, isn't it?"

I glared at Dennis. "Really? You think I would tell on my fiancé even if he did?"

Dennis smiled at Randall who was also grinning like a madman. "Did Boyd whoop the shit out of those blow hards? He did, didn't he?"

I shrugged. "Well, seems to me that maybe they started it and someone finished it. That is what happens to big mouths. They get shut the fucked up, don't they."

Randall chuckled then covered his mouth. "Dennis, your boy finally kicked their asses. Shit I wish I had seen that. Oh, what I wouldn't have given to see it. Damn Psycho, did you see it?"

I smiled looking at the floor. "Ah, you know me Randall, I see a lot of shit. Some real, some not. I maybe hallucinated some fat ass cops getting what they had coming at Night's earlier today, but that couldn't have been as I was off having lunch with Boyd. Must have been in my head."

Dennis appeared excited. "Ah, so did you hallucinate the officers got whooped or did the whooping?"

I laughed. "Oh, one beat three from what I saw. See totally insane. Couldn't have happened. Just so you know Boyd was with me. So, it was all just my wishful thinking."

Dennis looked at Randall. "Hey partner, I need to get downtown and check on that uhm, case, talk to you later." Dennis rubbed his moustache then took off for the door.

Randall yelled after him, "Hey Dennis, pal, call me later with the details on that case."

Dennis waved and nodded never missing a step as he hauled ass out of the station to his car. I just stood there smiling. "Are we done here, Randall? I have shit to do you know."

Randall chuckled. "Yeah Psycho. Thanks for the help today. Give my regards to Boyd." He took off to the parking lot after Dennis.

Master Boyd rushed up to me. "What did they want?"

I laughed. "To hear about your fight."

He looked frightened. "Shit. Is that why they took off? To call in IA or something?" He looked toward the door as if a monster would jump out.

I laughed harder. "Paranoid much? No, Master. Those nosy old bulls just rushed off to ask old Dale what he saw. Dennis and Randall were proud of you silly."

Master Boyd started to wring his hands. "Nah, that can't be right. Dennis told me to never hit one of them or else." He started to pace.

I glared at him. "Stop that. Damn. I need you to take me back to my car Master. I have a case in Wells. What if someone comes by and sees you acting a fool?"

Master Boyd realized himself and nodded. "Alright, come on baby. I think I will come with you."

I followed him as we headed for the car. "Uhm, don't you need to sleep?"

He shook his head. "Nope, not tired. It will be fun. We never spend time together anymore."

I didn't argue with him realizing he was scared to death that Dennis was about to put the hammer down on him. I was my Master's security blanket. I really didn't want him tagging along but if it kept him calm, I supposed it didn't hurt. Besides, Wells was a simple priority two neglect case. Not a big deal and not my job.

My Master drove while I sat listening to him blather about running away again. He was really freaking out over that fight. Nothing I said would calm his crazy ass down. We sped past Night's station. He saw Dennis and Randall out front with Dale drinking bottled cokes and laughing. That really set his imagination into overdrive.

"Shit, Dale is telling them," Master Boyd yelled as we passed by.

I nodded. "Duh. That fight story will be a fucking epic battle in a week instead of a little scuffle, Master. It is a small town. The old Bulls told me they wished they had seen you beating the assholes up."

He looked at me. 'Bullshit, stop lying to make me feel better, Psycho. Dennis is going to send me off and you know it. You don't even care."

I looked at him startled. "Okay, that is it. This paranoid shit is getting on my nerves. No one is sending you anywhere. You keep this up and they will. Stop acting stupid, Master."

Master Boyd got quiet, but his breathing was shallow and ragged. He was still stressing. I was beginning to be sorry I had bothered to stop for gas. Shit.

THE STORY OF THE BUTT BABY

We arrived at the reported address. I groaned realizing the beat up single wide trailer with broken windows and its front door hanging by one hinge was my girl. I looked at Master Boyd who rolled his eyes blowing out his breath.

I nodded knowingly. "Yeah, do me a favor and call the Fairbanks, Master. There are two children in this home. Looks like the Fairbanks just got their dance card filled all in one day. Tell them we will be there in about two hours."

Master Boyd nodded. "Will do. Be careful. Who knows what you will find in there?"

I snorted while getting out. "Hopefully that the family moved away earlier today..." I laughed then headed to the door.

A skinny woman of only twenty-five with stringy brown hair and only a few teeth came to the busted door. She had mildly crossed brown eyes and spoke with a very significant speech impediment. I realized very quickly Missy was intellectually disabled.

"Can I come in and see your children Missy," I asked politely.

She smiled. "Oh sure. Marcus and Marcus are in the back playing." She stepped aside.

I began to step inside but paused in horror. The entire floor was covered with refuse, half full trash bags and dirty diapers. The furniture was also covered in garbage. In fact, the entire trailer was just a big dump. The smell wafted nearly knocking me to the ground. I took a deep breath and stepped inside. I immediately nearly busted my ass slipping on a discarded diaper covered in shit.

I stayed my stomach and nerves as Missy asked me to sit down. "Uhm, I think I will stand. I have been ridding for hours. My backside could use the break," I lied, sort of.

She sat down pushing a mound of foul items out of the way as if it was not reeking and fly covered. "You wanted to see Marcus and Marcus," she slurred out.

I nodded almost stunned to stupid. "Uhm, uh huh, Marcus and, uhm, Marcus?"

Missy nodded. "Yep. Marcus. Marcus come here, now," she screamed out almost sending me running for the hills.

Two dark headed children came running. They were very close in age, one appearing four the other close to six. One appeared female the other male. They were filthy and wearing only diapers. Both looked well fed and healthy otherwise. They were far too old to be in diapers, and I could see that despite getting the largest available the tape was rubbing the kid's upper legs raw.

They giggled and pushed each other making grunting noises. Neither appeared able to speak other than single words and those were poorly pronounced. The female had crossed eyes and the male a cleft palette.

I blinked my eyes in shock. "Uhm Missy, is one of, I mean, is Marcus a girl?"

She giggled, "Yes silly. Marcus is a girl and Marcus is a boy."

I nodded trying not to drop my jaw. Mainly because to do so would drag it in the garbage below, yikes! "So uhm, why Marcus? Why not Sally and Marcus?"

Missy snickered. "Cause they are brother and sister, duh."

I nodded again. "Oh, hahaha, yeah, silly me. Uhm, so where is the father?"

I was hoping he could help me out to answer my questions about the condition of the home, the children's obvious environmental and education neglect, and tell me why the fuck he had two kids named Marcus.

Missy snorted then blew a snot rocket across the room. "Uhm, he should be here soon. He is off collecting cans and stuff to sell. But I ain't supposed to say he is their daddy. Cause we is kinfolk. He is my mother's brother you know? He says that isn't right, us having babies."

I stood there sure I was fucking hallucinating. "The father is your uncle? Oh my, okay. Missy honey, I am going to have to take Marcus and uhm Marcus with me for a little while. Just until you can get this house cleaned up and talk to some people for me?"

Missy looked at me in shock. "Oh shit. You is one of them child buster people. Damn it. Bobby told me not to open that door for no one. Shit, you gonna take my other one too?"

I gulped. "Other one?"

She nodded appearing upset. "Yeah the one inside my belly. I got another one in there too." She pointed at what I had missed, a pot belly of pregnancy.

I almost fainted. "Uhm, how long till Marcus comes?"

She snorted. "This one ain't no Marcus. I have to wait and see what he is. Cause he ain't no brother or sister to Marcus."

I looked at her surprised. "Oh? This child has a different father is what you are saying?"

Missy looked at me as if I were stupid, she did. "No, the father is the same. But this one was made in my butt. He will be coming out of my butt, so he won't be a Marcus. I am not even sure he will even look like me at all. I done told old Bobby not to making babies in my butt, but he did. Now we might have a monster."

I started looking around at the roof of her trailer searching hard. Missy looked up too. "What are you looking for?"

I groaned. "The camera. This must be a joke, right? You think that you got pregnant by having sex in your butt and now the baby is not related to Marcus and Marcus or your uncle the father. Is Sheryl fucking with me? I don't think this is funny. Are you working for Sheryl? Is this retaliation for my telling her to fuck off?" The confused look on Missy's face told me this was no joke.

I moaned. "Sorry Missy. I just need a rest is all. I want you to stay calm. We are going to get you some help with the kids, okay? You would like some help I bet?"

She nodded. "Yeah that would be nice. They are bad kids."

I told her to hold tight while I went and got that help. I immediately went to the car and called the Manager of the County, Cheryl Rutgers.

"Cheryl, this is Psycho Voss Sheryl's investigator. I seem to have gotten your case by accident. Well I am out here with Missy Links and we have a problem."

Cheryl yawned. "Marcus and Marcus again? Yeah, she has been a problem for years."

I gasped. "You fucking knew. Okay, send help out now. This is not acceptable. The uncle is taking advantage of his retarded niece and the kids are severely in need of aid as is Missy. This house is a fucking case of typhoid waiting to happen. Send a caseworker right fucking now or so help me I will have Sheryl on you next," I yelled beyond angry at this lazy manager.

She paused. "Alright, okay. I will send Paula. She will relieve you."

I growled. "No, Paula will do her fucking job while I take these kids out."

Cheryl groaned "We don't have room for these kids. Where are we supposed to put them."

I almost lost it. "You fucking drive to Cumberland and take them to the Fairbank's home. There are no homes open her in Wells, but there is a big old state out there, Cheryl. Try getting off your ass and visiting it once in a while."

She sighed. "Paula ain't going to like driving to Cumberland, you know."

I sneered. "Then I hope she don't mind driving to the fucking unemployment office, Cheryl. Good day to you." I hung up beyond furious.

I called Sheryl and reported Cheryl and Paula for insubordination toward an investigator, Paula took two hours to drive fifteen minutes from her office, and neglect of duty. Paula was fired and Cheryl busted down to caseworker the second the Marcus children were examined. Not only were they severely intellectually disabled, in the forty IQ range, they had worms along with a cleft palate and one had a partial bowel obstruction. The child was slowly dying. The problem was caught in the nick of time. Thank the Goddess.

NOTE: *The Marcus children were adopted by the Fairbanks eventually. The male was to keep his name Marcus; the girl was renamed Marcella. The third child*

was also taken into custody, a boy named Billy. He was of course the full sibling, so the Fairbanks adopted him too in time. The kids were all significantly disabled, but last I heard were happy, doing as well as could be hoped and Marcus got his palate fixed. All three children can now speak, are potty broke and are pleasant people I am told.

What happened to poor Missy? This sad figure was a long-term victim of her sexually abusing uncle. He was jailed for rape of a severely disabled person. Missy was taken to live in a residential home where she could receive the much-needed protection and aid someone with her significant difficulties required. Last I heard she was doing well and adjusting to residential life with much joy. She was friendly, affable, and eager to have friends.

In that State there were several very solid reputable residential centers specially designed for the intellectually disabled. Round the clock, well screened and trained staff aid these folks with socialization, recreation and life skills. If you were mentally ill, you were fucked. If you were intellectually disabled, the state had tons of money, help and treatment just for you. Do you know why? One of the important politicians of the time had a sister with a low IQ. He lobbied and won tons of state funds to change the way the intellectually disabled client is treated. Bravo fellow, now how about the schizos and nut balls? Could we get a taste of all that cash?

Once we had Missy and the two named Marcus settled, we rushed back to Carter. Master Boyd needed to get ready to head to his own shift. He was still acting paranoid and nervous though he had a good laugh at the story I told of my encounter with the Links.

I followed him back to the house and made him supper while he paced and wrung his hands in the living room. I was wondering if I should call Dennis to settle his ass down. Maybe if Dennis told him all was well, he would get this bullshit idea out of his head that they were going to haul his ass off. I had not even seen a police car. His chronic checking of the door and windows was making me nervous too. It was, well, insane.

I couldn't take it anymore. I called Dennis and informed him I thought he should come by and talk with my Master. Dennis seemed concerned but I wasn't at liberty to say what the problem was with Master Boyd, only that I thought it would be wise to make a house call.

When only twenty minutes later Dennis pulled up, I almost had to chase Master Boyd down. He was making a break for the back door because he was just sure that the old bull was there to do only God knows what. I managed to talk my Master into sitting the fuck down and waiting to hear what Dennis was there to say.

I opened the door making eyes at Dennis indicating there was some nutball shit going on. Dennis nodded and came inside taking a seat in the armchair. I got him a coke while making small talk about the weather with him chuckling and trying to act naturally. Master Boyd didn't say a word. He said there staring at the floor looking as if he may go catatonic himself.

Finally, I sat down next to my Master smiling at Dennis. "So, I guess you heard about Boyd's little show down."

Dennis looked at me smiling. "Yeah, everyone in town knows about it."

Master Boyd let out a gasp. "Am I in trouble Dennis? Just say so and stop fooling around. I can't take all this bullshit stress."

Dennis laughed. "Yeah you are in trouble for not letting me watch you beat the stuffing out of that blow hard Trenton. Damn boy, three of them. Now that is something else. I am not condoning what you did. We have discussed keeping your hands to yourself and your anger in check Boyd. This was different. Dale said the boys came looking for trouble and you gave it to them. You did it on your own time and away from the station. They aren't calling in any reports and you aren't. I think that should be the end of it. You got your licks in. They bug you anymore, you call me. I doubt that they will. I heard tale today that you are one hell of a fighter. Those boys won't be fooling with either of you again is my guess."

Master Boyd looked at me appearing stunned and relieved. "This is real? I really am not in trouble?"

I hugged him tightly. "Yeah it is real, lover. You didn't do anything wrong. Told you that you would not be in trouble."

I felt him release his tension and relax in my arms. He hugged me tightly back taking long deep breaths. He had been beyond frightened no doubt.

Dennis watched us frowning. "Psycho, Boyd, I think it is time we all sat down for that chat I wanted to have. I was hoping to put it off a while, but I think that is not possible. Sunday, come by the house around five. We can all have a nice dinner and discuss things. That is an order you two. Now I must get going. Carla has a pot roast on and if I am late, she will kick my ass. Boyd see you tonight." Dennis got up while I let him out.

Master Boyd was back to his old self grabbing and chasing me around the house. I was for a change glad to see it. His stress was not good for either of us. He had the right to defend himself no matter what had happened in his past. It was great to see Dennis back his play and give my Master a chance to be the hero for a change. It had been such a long time coming.

We had dinner together and then despite his arguments I demanded he get some rest. He had not slept all day or the night before. I had realized he was sleeping less lately with all the worry about my mental health. It often is very stressful and worrisome for my Keyholders when my psychotic shit comes on. It was no different for Master Boyd, except he loved me for real. That was making watching me get ill so much harder for him than any Master before.

We laid in the bed while I allowed him to cuddle me. No matter what we did the sandman was not coming for either of us.

After an hour I rolled around to face my Master smiling. "You know what they say works to help one sleep?"

He laughed. "No what?"

I sat up on my arm. "A glass of warm milk is supposed to make a person sleep I have been told."

Master Boyd stuck out his tongue appearing grossed out. "Sounds awful, but if it works then maybe we should try it? Go get us a glass of warm milk baby, that is a directive."

I giggled at his silly need to always give directives as I dropped down onto his lap beginning oral sex on him.

He grabbed my head appearing confused. "Wait, I said go get a glass of warm milk. What are you doing?"

I laughed. "Look if you want that milk from the fridge warmed up, do you really think that shit will work, I will go get it for you. I, however, realize I need not go that far to get something that is damned close, warm and much more fun to pour. So, you lay back and I will try out this old home remedy of warm milk." I pushed him back down and he didn't argue any further. In fact I had to stop him from assisting me in my getting my warm milk.

Well, the old wives' tale is true. After I got the warm milk, we both quickly fell asleep. We sleep so deep we almost didn't wake up to the fucking alarm.

We groggily fell over each other while I got him showered and dressed for his shift. I kissed him goodbye while I put on my own jacket headed out to yet another page call that came in during our measly three-hour nap.

That night alone I had to sit through two rape kits on two little girls under ten and one young boy that had to have stitches put into his head thanks to a beating from his drunken father. By morning I was beyond tired. I drove back to the house seeing shit rushing across the road as my brother the sun rose to a height indicating it was time to visit Julia.

It was Friday and I had worked non-stop for seven straight days. I was worn out. I stopped by the house to find Master Boyd wasn't home yet. I snuck into his closet stealing back some of the electrical tape hoping he had not counted the rolls. Without hesitation I took off headed for Cumberland to make my daily visit to the annoying Julia and do my paperwork with PC and Fax.

I was only a few miles out of Wheatly when I saw Simon thumbing it, laughing at his already long worn out joke. I stopped and picked him up happy to have a passenger to help keep me awake.

"So? Are you giving up sleeping for good or what," snorted Simon while he rolled a smoke.

I snorted. "Really? I barely see you these days and you want to start a fucking fight? Too early man." I whined.

"You know Master Boyd finds out about you stealing that electrical tape, you're fucked right?" Simon looked at my wrist now wrapped up once more.

I pulled down my sleeve. "He won't find out, Simon. Why did you pick Master Boyd? You know how stupid that was right?" I glanced at him with a look of seriousness.

Simon shrugged. "Hey, I thought he was going to kill us, so did you I seem to remember. Sheryl sure turned out to be a winner. No choice babe."

I narrowed my eyes. "What you did was cruel, and you know it, Rachel. We will break his heart. Why did you do that?"

Simon's eyes went wide. "What did you call me?"

The Chosen One growled, "Rachel, you knew he can never be. Now he is going to get hurt. You picked him knowing his problems. Why? It was cruel. You are like her. The Devil is what you are."

He shook his head. "No, I didn't know. I swear it. I am not like her."

I glared at him. "You suspected it. For how long? I know you, Rachel. I can read your ind. You suspected it in the hospital back in 1989. You did. Admit it, liar. That is why you never picked him for sure."

Simon sighed. "Yeah, you are right I suspected him, but I didn't know. I swear it. Timmy came and I chose him, no ties, better choice."

I started laughing at that. "You mean better genes. Timmy was way better than Boyd? Why Rachel? Well no matter. Lie all you want. We know better. You will hurt him. Hope you are happy, devil."

Simon and I pulled into Julia's driveway still arguing about his choice of Boyd as our Master. She came out to find me yelling obscenities at him wildly.

"Mother fucking liar. God damn, why do I even talk to you, nut ball. Get out of the car. We are here. Shit, just shit," I yelled back at him while getting out.

Julia snorted. "Yeah, you are totally not a schizophrenic. Who the fuck are you yelling at?" She smiled smugly at me.

I glared. "Simon, don't you see the bitch sitting right there. God damn, you are blind and an asshole." I stormed past her headed for the kitchen table for my coffee.

Julia came in after me appearing unaffected by my yelling. "So, rough day at work I take it?"

I snorted. "Just pour the fucking coffee and start your blathering, bitching and poor me song and dance. I am not willing to start anymore shit today. I have a headache and the fucking turkey is going bad in the refrigerator."

She looked at me bug eyed. "Huh? Okay, sure, whatever you say, Psycho."

I snapped my head at her snarling. "What did you say bitch? If I were you, I would stick to dead babies and feeling sorry for yourself. I ever hear you call me that again, well I will show you fucking psychotic, got that?"

She smiled. "Oh yeah, I sure did loud and clear. So, have you ever been to Maryland? It is such beautiful country. The Northerners are just better people you know. My mom lives out there in a small town. I miss her a lot. Especially now with the girls gone."

I rolled my eyes. "Geez, then why don't you go the fuck back? I wouldn't mind. Hell, let me help you. How much do you need for a bus ticket?" I started reaching into my purse.

Julia started laughing. "Damn you are funny as hell. Well, I need more than a bus ticket Psycho. There is no work in that town. Just strip clubs, beer joints and hookers you know. I can never go home, not until I can afford to retire."

I looked up from my purse. "Well that ain't gonna happen with you sitting on your ass now is it? I suggest you get a job."

Julia sighed. "Yeah, never was much for a nine to five. Nah, I would have to sell all my shit, hope to get a good price, and well pinch my pennies. The hubs, he hates Maryland. If I divorced him, I could go home, but then I would have to share half the money we don't have with him. It is a real quandary you know?"

I took a drink of the coffee she put in front of me. "Sounds like a personal problem to me. Not interested in hearing about it either. I really don't care about you Julia, and you don't care about me. o why the fuck do you keep dragging me here?"

She looked startled,. "What? I thought we were friends. Wow, you are one cold bitch, Psycho."

I shook my head. "Friends don't drag friends over to hear sob stories when one friend is overworked and had more important shit to do. You got Sheryl to make me come here every morning. That is not friendship, that is taking someone hostage Julia."

Julia took a drink of her coffee and cut her eyes at me. "Oh? So, you have to come see me because Sheryl says so huh? You can't just tell her to fuck off. Now why would that be?"

I growled. "Because she is my fucking boss moron. I am her investigator. Did you fall and hit your head or something?"

Julia chuckled. "Why not just quit the job if you hate doing what Sheryl says so much? Hey, do you really have a husband and fiancé? What happened to your parents?"

I shook my head. "Unfucking believable. Not your fucking business, nosy bitch. Would you like to know my bra size too? Fuck me, stay out of my life, loser." I looked up to see Simon motioning me to come away looking worried.

I glared at Julia who was leaned forward appearing interested to hear the answers to her probing questions. I didn't say another word as I got up abruptly. Julia sat back appearing startled and frightened while I stormed out the door getting into the Taurus. I backed up wildly looking at a very nervous looking Simon while I hastily left with Julia standing looking very confused in her doorway.

"Okay out with it. what was that about," I said glancing at the still nervous Simon.

"Something, Psycho. Don't go back to her house. Something is wrong there. I can sense it." He shuddered.

I looked at him startled myself. "Really? The questions? Her staring? She is fishing for something isn't she?"

Simon nodded. "Yeah, collars. Stay away from her. She is talking about needing money. Psycho she is poaching out collar. Sheryl has blabbed perhaps or maybe she has just figured it out. No matter don't go back, ever. That woman is looking to sell us."

I snorted. "She has to get the collar first silly."

Simon glared. "Sheryl could maybe sell it to her. Or maybe she will just hurt us to get it?"

I nodded. "You are right on this. It feels bad. Poacher no doubt. She reminds me of Joyce, right?"

He nodded with big eyes. "Yeah. That is who she reminds us of, Joyce. Maybe that is how Sheryl knows her? From the clubs?"

I laughed out loud. "Ah, clever Simon. Clever Sheryl, the clubs, poacher of the collar. Yeah, Julia Stubbs is no more. Now, I have paperwork to do with PC and Fax. If you want to come inside be quiet this time. Jane is getting freaked out with all your yapping."

Simon snorted. "Uh dingbat, she can't see or hear me. You are the one freaking her out."

"Christ all mighty, can you just fuck off and stop disagreeing with me," I yelled out as I came storming into Jane's office in another fight with Simon.

Jane looked up appearing worried. "Oh shit, Psycho. Hey, you aren't going to kick over my new plastic plants today, are you? Seriously, when will they give you your own office to fuck up?"

I looked at her blankly. "We are happy to serve you. Have a nice day." I sat down flipping on PC.

He whirled to life appearing nervous. "Hey Psycho Tron, I overheard the office tech the other day. He said they are going to replace all the outdated electronics in the offices in a few weeks."

I stared at him in a trance. "You are not obsolete PC. There is no reason to malfunction. We will update your software and hard drive. We are happy to be of service. Take a number please. All lines are currently busy. Have a nice day." I moved very slowly reaching for my forms.

PC looked at me appearing even more worried. "Uh oh, Psycho Tron. The script is running long. You need a reboot soon or the system will crash."

I blinked still trancing. "Negative PC, systems are functioning at maximum capacity. Please delete all non-essential programs. There are still open windows do you still want to shut down? Please hold, all our service representatives are currently assisting other customers. Thank you for holding. Have a nice day."

Jane walked over to stare at me. "Okay wow. You are messed up, Psycho. I am not Sheryl, but I do manage this office. You are wigging out bad babe. Go home. Take the day off, or I will write you up myself. I will handle Sheryl. This is not okay. Out." She pointed at the door.

I looked at her without emotion. "You must enter the correct password to deselect this programming. Please take a number, hold please, we are ready to serve you now. How may we be of service?"

PC gasped. "Psycho Tron, leave now. Jane is not kidding. She is about to call Charlie. Sheryl is gone. Run that through your fucking memory hard drive, fool."

I nodded. "Affirmative PC. This computes. Thank you have a nice day." I flipped off the PC and packed up my things just as Jane reached her desk ready to call the cops if I didn't leave her office immediately.

"Have a good weekend Psycho and for Christ sakes get some sleep. You look like hell," said Jane as I opened the office door to exit.

"Thank you have a nice day," I called back in monotone.

I got into the Taurus feeling very odd. The light was just too bright. I decided I need to go home. Something was just wrong. I sped off headed back for Master Boyd's house. I ignored Sheryl's attempts to call and Master Boyd's too. I needed a moment without all the noise. Just so much of it everywhere.

I kept trying to change the radio station on the Taurus radio but was surprised each time to find it was not even on. I could hear the music. I could hear the weather report, the announcers. It didn't make sense. I suddenly realized I was hearing radio wave in the air. Shit. I pulled over and plugged up my ears with tissues and taped them inside. I didn't recall I should remove the electrical tape from my arms much less add more by putting it over my ears.

I went flying into Master Boyd's driveway almost hitting his car that was parked sideways itself. I found that odd but didn't think much of it. We were both very tired. I went inside the house to find him not in bed as I expected him to be. He also was not in the shower or kitchen. I went out back and found him pacing appearing to be in duress. He didn't see me, so I stayed hidden watching him walking back and forth going nowhere and wringing his hands.

"She isn't answering the phone," he said sounding upset.

"Maybe she is dead? No, that can't be. Not again." He looked up into the sky and rubbed his forehead which was very wet with sweat.

He stomped. "Not fair, not again. Do you hear me? I know you are listening, you bastard," he yelled at no one.

He began to babble, ramble and talk incoherently while moving like a trapped lion in a cage. He wrung his hands and kept hitting his forehead while appearing angry at something he mumbled.

I stood there wondering why he was so angry. I finally decided to see if he would tell me.

"Master?" I step out where he could see me.

He looked over appearing not to recognize me at first. Then he smiled and came running. He picked me up hugging me tightly seeming beyond grateful.

"Oh you are okay. I thought, I thought they got you too, like Maddy." He was tearing up appearing very upset but relieved too.

I nodded. "Yeah, they sent me home. I am sorry Master. I messed up talking to Simon at work. Jane got mad."

He laughed. "Well fuck Jane. We have the day together. Come inside and eat something. I want to tell you about Will, Mark and Trenton."

I smiled. "Ah, see you were paranoid. You won and everyone is proud of you."

Master Boyd looked at the ground. "Please Psycho, don't call me paranoid. I don't like it. That is a directive."

I nodded then yelled out, "Don't call me Psycho. I don't like it either."

He looked up stunned. "Oh. Yeah, no that would not be, oh." He appeared confused as he pulled me by my hand inside.

We went into his kitchen. He sat at the table still mumbling and sweating while I made breakfast. He was talking to someone about the name Psycho. My Master thought that was not very nice to call someone by such a derogatory moniker. He didn't like to be called a rapist. I listened to his babbling, agreeing with most of it. Then he was talking to God and I really listened in. God and I didn't speak much anymore so I had been wondering how the old fellow was doing as of late.

Some of the shit God was telling him though, I wasn't buying. I never thought God had much to say of worth. I always ended up with either a cracked noggin or houses getting burned down when he used to talk to me. I put my Master's plate down in front of him chuckling.

He looked at me surprised. "What is so funny?"

I rolled my eyes. "Master, don't you believe what God says. He will get you into trouble. I know plenty of us schizophrenics that get locked up for that shit."

Master Boyd nodded at that. "Yeah they do. Don't tell Dennis then?"

I got up and kissed him. "Do I ever betray the collar, Master? I don't. Hey, did you take your medication yet?"

He shook his head. "Nah. Did you?"

I shook my head back. "I see no reason to. It never works. If I take it I get sick. If I don't, I still get sick."

Master Boyd sighed. "Mine isn't working either."

I laughed maniacally. "No shit."

He smiled while blushing. "Want to hit the shower?"

I laughed even harder. "I would rather hit Julia. But the shower sounds fun. Race you, Master."

He knocked his chair to the floor trying to grab me and get ahead, but I tripped him. He fell to the floor laughing while I won the race to our bath fun.

We spent all day Friday copulating and talking about pretty much nothing. We ignored the phone, the pager and made a pact not to check the mail. We both tried to sleep but neither of us could. Then that night Master Boyd sat on the porch watching Simon and I dance for Mother moon. Again, sleep didn't come for either of us.

By Saturday, our lovemaking had become violent. We broke several things in his room and one kitchen chair. Okay, I broke it trying to hit him with it in our struggling to maintain dominance during our trysts. Our tempers were flaring pretty hot. He and I were kicking, biting, bruising and scratching each other to shit. Plus I cold cocked him with a kitchen chair. When not arguing and fighting, we were again having sex all over the house like wild animals. It was, well insanity, pure and simple.

When Sunday rolled in, we could barely move. Still no sleep, but now we were docile and fatigued. I spent the day sewing up the rips in our clothing from the day before. He attended the yard work.

Both of us were rambling and mumbling to no one. He paced back and forth mowing the grass. I paced back and forth mopping the floor. Both of us had cotton in our ears, taped in.

QUICK NOTE: *Have you figured out what you missed yet? Go ahead and take a guess. It is okay, I have chapter after chapter for you to put this puzzle together. I can wait longer, but no worries. I am about to spell this out for you. It was always there but you never saw it. Just like no one ever sees me.*

At five we arrived at Dennis and Carla's for Sunday's supper. We sat down at his table keeping our mouths shut so no demons popped out. Dennis noticed our subdued stance and lack of hunger. He looked at Master Boyd.

"You are getting too skinny again, boy. Are you eating? Psycho, is he eating?" Dennis looked at my Master's untouched plate then at my own full one.

He threw down his fork and leaned back. Carla reached out and touched his shoulder appearing to be pleading with him not to get angry. He put up his hand to stay her attempts to calm him.

"Now enough, Carla. Someone has to say it. Boyd, Psycho this match is not going to work. Two of you together is like Nitro and Glycerin. Look, you both need help. What are you going to do? Take turns being inpatient? Your cycles are running together. Your both are damned psychotic at the same fucking time. I knew this was gonna happen. Boyd, I told you a schizophrenic and a schizophrenic cannot have a damned sound relationship, God damn it."

I looked up gasping. "Uhm Dennis, please, we don't like that word."

My Master kept looking at the table as if in a trance but nodded.

Dennis laughed appearing incensed "Oh? Is that so? Well face it, Psycho, you and Boyd are touched sister. You both got the damn thing. I have told Boyd for years to leave you alone. He wouldn't listen and now here you two are engaged. Boyd is smacking around officers; you are yelling at everyone. Both of you are off the medication I am willing to bet."

Master Boyd looked up at Dennis. "You can't tell me who to love or not. I don't care what you promised mom. I am an adult. I don't need a guardian, Dennis. I have been on my own all this time. No more trouble has happened. Trenton started that fight. He was saying nasty shit about Psycho. Why do we have to keep taking abuse from everyone? Why? Because we are sick? That is not fair. Why is it okay for everyone to call her Psycho? How about we call Trenton fat ass or Linda gay. It isn't fucking right." He was panting appearing very angry.

I grabbed his arm and he flinched. "No more Psycho. It is time for a fucking change. We do our job. We care more than you normals do, but we are the fucking monsters? Why? I have never hurt anyone, well except Psycho, and she forgives me but no one else does. I am tired of it." He sat back in his chair about ready to cry from the stress of it all.

Dennis looked at Boyd appearing to truly pity him. "Look Boyd, you are right. We all know you didn't do that nasty business with Maddy. We all know it was because they all heard about your disease that you got blamed. There is nothing that can be done about it. Psycho here, well she has had a rough road to hoe too. That shit family of hers, I'm not even going to start on that. You can change it all but not if you fall apart on me, son. The two of you together is just wrong. You can barely look out for yourself, and Psycho can't do it at all. She is too much for you to handle is what I am telling you. Now if you would just want to date a girl who could help you take your meds, bear you a couple of youngsters. Let Psycho do what she always has, things would settle down."

My Master glared at Dennis. "Dennis, there is no girl who is going to have kids with me. First, everyone thinks I am a damned rapist. Second, I am a schizophrenic. Third, well I am Boyd, now aren't I? Creepy, weird, obsessive, odd, quiet, Boyd. When I cycle then what? Do you think some nice girl is going to put up with that? Ask Psycho. She can tell you all about it. She is the One and Only for me. We understand each other. We see the tapestry and hear the transmissions. We are the same. She is the one made for me. I have told you this for years. I should have been with her all these years. I should have never listened to you. I am finally happy. I am never giving her up. Forget it." He began to rub his forehead getting agitated.

Dennis realized he was stressing Master Boyd too much. "Okay, I will stay out of it. You treat her right though boy. I am not going to stand by if you start getting too rough. Same goes for you girl. I know you too. Both of you have tempers. I expect some day to be at your place in a damned standoff while both of you knock the shit out of each other. Tie two cats by the tail and hang them over a wire, well the fur is gonna fly. I already heard about your fights and make ups at work."

I started giggling. "Oh Dennis. That was just play. We get along great. We were just having fun is all, I swear it."

He looked at me stunned. "Uhm, he isn't beating the piss out of you? Nor you him?"

I looked bashful. "Now Dennis, our sex life is none of your business. You know I like it rough. Maybe Boyd does too. But that is private. We don't go snooping into your bedroom, now do we?"

Dennis snorted. "God help me, you are both fools. Okay, I am not going to warn you again. The two of you are a mistake. You'll be sorry mark my words. Boyd you look like shit. You sleeping?"

I looked at Master Boyd. "Uhm, well he has had some troubles, but I have been using an old home remedy on him. You know, warm milk."

He smiled back realizing my private joke. He reached under the table to take my hand.

Carla had been sitting there quietly suddenly pipped up. "Wow, so that really works?"

My Master grinned evilly never taking his icy blue eyes off me. "Well not if your wife is lactose intolerant it doesn't." We both began giggling wildly while Dennis and Carla sat there looking at each other confused.

We sat there while Dennis continued to warn us that our high functioning schizophrenic love affair was doomed to fail. We sighed but endured it. I had suspected my Master was a very high functioning Schizo as far back as 1989, but it wasn't until I move in with him that I discovered his records while cleaning the house.

I was blown away. I was collared by one of my very own, likely while he was in a long prodromal and acute psychotic break from reality. I had assumed everything from OLD, to IED to PTSD. The last two of which he has due to his unfair incarceration. I knew the symptoms he expressed when residual sure looked a lot like my own, but no way he could be one of us, right?

Ah, but if you think you can see he is indeed. Everything I ever told you about him smacks of the Queen Mother of Madness. He is just a genetic, male and natural schizo. I have brain damage too so mine is actually more severe.

He is in the upper twenty percent of all people affected by the genetic expression of our disease. He is much higher functioning than me, capable of understanding basic adaptive functioning. My Master could function independently with some observation to watch for his cycles. He is a Schizophrenic, Paranoid Type, high functioning, age of onset at fifteen years old. He was hiding right in plain sight. No one could see him. A police officer in a small town with the old Bull watching out for his troubled adopted son.

As Master Boyd and I left Dennis and Carla's that afternoon he looked at me thanking me for not freaking out that I had discovered his secret. I just chuckled reminding him I couldn't cast a single stone at one of my own. We laughed while walking hand and hand to his car.

He opened my door for a change then whispered in my ear. "I love you, Niemand."

I looked at him puzzled. "Who the hell is that Master?"

Master Boyd smiled brightly. "The name God picked for you. I asked and he told me. No more Psycho. My One and Only is called Niemand."

I laughed as I got into the car and he closed the door. Niemand is such a pretty name. I think I could learn to live with it.

We are cooking with gas, pipe bombs and Gypsie campfires. Master Boyd is also a high functioning schizophrenic. Now that you know his real diagnosis, does that change what you think about him in general? He is a genetic, natural schizophrenic and I did know it the whole time.

Chapter 71: "That's Paranoid Boyd" Part 1
The Fall of Psycho & the Rise of Niemand
Master Boyd

What is real and what is fantasy? Ah, such a hard thing to figure out when your channels are all mixed up. Faulty perceptions are certainly not the sole property of the schizophrenic, but we are experts in the field. It is just too easy for us believe a lie until it become a truth. Our fears often take on a life all their own in a symptom called delusions.

In December 1998, Master Boyd and his submissive Niemand were losing their battle to maintain their grip on reality. Not like either of them had a solid hold on those slippery slopes anyway. Before Christmas both would be helplessly caught in a raging dance to the tune of madness.

It would be one cruel hard winter for the psychotic D/s pair. Sadly, normals can't fix the insane couple's white nightmare. It really is too bad that never stopped the well-meaning idiots from doing their damned best to make it so much worse. Oh well, it sucks to be the Master and his collar.

"Boyd is schizophrenic. Holy shit, he is sick just like Psycho. How could I not have realized that? I mean, well shit. The symptoms were right there in my face the whole fucking time. I just thought he was creepy or weirdo religious or something. Oh, my Goddess this explains everything. Boy do I feel like an idiot."

"I don't give a fuck if Jane did tell you to go home Psycho. You have not returned a single call or page in three motherfucking days. Your caseload is building up and I had to call in a relief worker. You know what, I am coming to Cumberland to kick your ass," yelled Sheryl through the phone.

I looked at Master Boyd who was staring back appearing to be looking at something behind me. "Oh fuck you Sheryl. Come to Cumberland. I will be waiting on you. You'd better bring an army if you think I am just going to stand there and take your shit. Your refrigeration sucks. I don't even have an office and you don't even know the fucking password," I yelled back stealing looks behind me worried my Master could see something I couldn't creeping up on me.

"What the fuck are you talking about you loony asshole. Refrigeration? Office? Passwords? Jane told me you are talking shit. Looks like she was right. Go to the fucking ER and have them increase your medication right now. Then get your ass back to work you God damn lazy nutball," she growled.

I took the phone receiver and beat it into the wall several times, hard enough to crack the casing. Master Boyd took off running in terror knocking over his kitchen chair startled by my sudden movement and loud noise. I started giggling at his hyper vigilant behavior then put the near busted phone back to my ear.

"Fuck you right up your hairy ass, Sheryl. I also will tell you I have figured out your little game with Julia. You know what? I am cutting off your collar. You are out of here baby. I don't need you. I don't need anyone. I am smarter than you and God. You should bow before me and hope I don't crush your fucking square head. Hahaha, you don't even know the grid. Did you hear me? I am off to work now. Oh, and don't have a nice day you stupid cunt." I started to hang up the phone.

"Psycho, wait, cut off my collar. Psycho, what was that loud noise? Put Boyd on the phone. Psycho, I want to talk to Boyd," Sheryl screamed out in desperation.

I rolled my eyes "Hey, Sheryl wants to talk to you," I yelled out at my Master who was now pacing in the living room while mumbling and wringing his hands in an extremely agitated state.

He looked at me. "Tell her to fuck off. I don't have to talk to anyone. Shut up, shut the fuck up. Do you hear me? Shut up." He went back to pacing while sweat broke out on his forehead mumbling that it was too loud in the house.

I chuckled at that agreeing it was far too loud. "He says fuck off. Go bother someone else asshole. Who is this again? Why are you bothering me?" I had already forgotten what the phone call was about.

Sheryl gasped, "Psycho, you are fucking with me right? This is a joke? Look honey you are seriously sick. Go get help. I will come to Cumberland tomorrow and visit you at Jane's office and straighten this whole mess up. Take the night off. Go to the ER. See you tomorrow."

I raised my eyebrow. "Uhm, okay? See you tomorrow I guess. Wait, why?" I hung up the phone unsure what was going on as the static began to eat the room edges. I wandered past the agitated Master Boyd out into the yard to dance with Simon in a deep trance.

I was twirling and stomping when Simon finally joined me. "Psycho, you must stop this. Master Boyd is inside the house tearing up the kitchen. He needs our help. There will be time for this later. Dennis will expect him at work in only a few hours and he is going off the deep end. Go inside and calm your Master down. It is your fucking job," he said while spinning me around him.

I groaned. "Not now Simon. We can feel the electrical grid calling us. Another time. It can wait."

Simon glared. "No, it can't wait. Go now, do your job."

I stopped dancing and looked back at the house. I strained my ears and could hear thumping and pounding. Simon was right. Master Boyd was tearing something up inside. He had been very upset since the dinner at Dennis and Carla's a couple of hours before. Dennis calling him out on his disease had set him into a tizzy. Master Boyd didn't like anyone reminding him that he has schizophrenia. His onset of the prodromal stage of the cycle made him irritable and easy to upset.

Dennis should have known better. Questioning Master Boyd's choice to maintain a relationship with another of his kind was not real smart. No right that minute anyway. A residual Master Boyd may have taken this disapproval of his union without freaking. A prodromal and paranoid Master Boyd was irrational, unreasonable, and completely pissed off.

I groaned again and looked at Simon. "Fuck me. He is ripping the house apart. He is God damned crazy Simon. I don't want to go inside. Insane people are dangerous you know. I don't want to be around that kind of bullshit. He needs to be in a hospital. I don't know anything about schizophrenia. What am I supposed to do with him?"

Simon's eyes went wide. "Seriously? Did you just say that? Oh fuck. We are gone too. Shit. Oh, this is bad. Call Dennis. Get help. We are all in trouble. You, me, and Master Boyd. Get help Psycho. Hurry, call Dennis. He will know what to do."

I nodded. "Yeah, Dennis. He can help get Master Boyd to calm down. Okay, I will go call him." I rushed inside to call for our father figure to help two drowning psychotics but already forgot what Simon told me before I even went through the door.

Master Boyd was in the kitchen throwing everything out of the drawers and cabinets. I stood there watching as he tossed the silverware, plates, and glasses onto the floor sweating and babbling.

I finally couldn't take not understanding the strange scene any longer. "Master? Why are you doing that," I asked calmly.

He turned and looked at me appearing frightened. "They put the bug in here somewhere. They are trying to haul us away, Niemand. You take that side and I will check over here." He pointed to the cabinets on the right side.

I nodded. "Okay, but Master, what would a bug look like? What color is it? Does it have legs?"

He grabbed the sides of his head. "I don't know damn it. Just start looking. We will know it when we find it. Just fucking look for the bug. That is a directive.." He then ripped open another cabinet door throwing the stuff out while cursing.

I went to the cabinets on the right and joined him in the hunt for the bug. We tore that room apart for the next thirty minutes. I think only thirty, but it may have been shorter or longer. I finally found a small round silver pebble no bigger than a pencil eraser after knocking a hole in one of the upper walls.

I gasped as I pulled it from the hole. "Master. I found it. It is a bug. Just like you said."

He stopped throwing everything out his refrigerator and came running to see what I was holding.

I handed over the small pellet to a horrified looking Master Boyd. "Shit Niemand. The Bastard was right. They are watching us. Fuck, just FUCK. Look let's just run away. If we don't, they are going to come and split us up. I heard Sheryl. She is coming to take you away too. Dennis is going to send us both away, he said so. It could be anybody." He looked at the bug closely.

I shook my head. "Have faith Master. I won't let them take me or you away. We need to flush that down the toilet and then cut off Sheryl's fucking collar. It is the only way. Simon says Sheryl is trying to sell us to Julia. I believe him."

Master Boyd looked up startled. "What? She is? No, no, no. Fuck her. I will kill her first. You are mine. God gave you to me, not her." He stormed off to his bathroom to flush the bug.

I stood there looking around at the piles of discarded and broken dishes in the floor. I groaned realizing I would have to clean all that up. Damn psychosis is a lot of work.

He returned still mumbling angrily. "Come with me Niemand. Let's cut off that stupid ass collar. I have your real one anyway. You don't need this dumb thing." He reached out and grabbed me by the collar roughly dragging me out the back door to his banged up shed.

I bitched that he was hurting me, but Master Boyd couldn't hear me over all the damned voices. He let my collar go and went inside the shed. I waited for his return rubbing my throat now cursing under my breath as heavily as he was.

He came back out holding a big pair of bolt cutters. "Here this should do the trick." He walked over and adjusted the tool around the front of the silver circle to make a clean cut.

I held very still while he applied the pressure to the metal band. With a sudden clank the cutters busted the ring and cut the hell out of my neck in the process. Blood began to pour down my chest from the superficial but painful cut. I yelped but smiled as I reached up and felt the large separation that officially ended Sheryl's authority.

He smiled at me. "There, Sheryl is not a Master anymore. Now I am the only Master." He reached out and ripped the broken collar from my unit and flung it behind him not even looking to see where it fell.

I reached up to feel my naked neck. A smile spread across my loony face. I felt the wetness from the cut. Then I laughed while looking at my crimson coated fingers. Master Boyd threw down the bolt cutters and started laughing too. He reached out took my hand and pulled me after him back into the house.

We tripped and rushed through the destroyed kitchen right to his bedroom. He told me to sit on the bed while he got his collar. I sat down as told holding my bleeding neck.

"Master, I am bloody. Can I have some electrical tape please? I need to stop the seepage before my pistons fail," I said while wiping the crimson tide from my hands onto my pants.

He nodded while digging in his closet. "Sure baby, just a second." He closed his closet door returning with both his collar and a roll of electrical tape.

I took the tape from him and with his help we wrapped my neck to end the flow from the open wound. Neither of us had any sense to the dangers of infection, nor to clean up the mess at the very least. Yikes, we were gone.

My Master smiled brightly. "There, it is all better now. I want to put my collar on you. Kneel and let me put it back on." He opened the metal ring.

I knelt while he locked his collar which effectively ended Sheryl's reign by collar but not by right. I didn't cry as I heard it snap closed. I already belonged to Master Boyd. This was not a collaring. Just a collar change. The emotionality of being submitted didn't affect me like it usually does when a Master is taking possession. He laughed maniacally pulling me back to my feet by his collar. He then forced a deep, passionate kiss.

"Now you belong only to me Niemand, just like God promised me. Everything is the way it was. I have it all back now. Nothing can stop us. Not even Dennis or they." He kissed my neck and his collar.

I closed my eyes feeling my sexual drives kicking in. "Shouldn't we consummate this collaring Master," I panted out.

Master Boyd had begun to breath heavily as well. "Oh hell yeah. I intend to consummate often. I told you the first time, day and night, Niemand. I want you to make love to me and that is a directive." He began to tear at my clothing as I tore at his.

We were right in the middle of a violent and loud tryst when someone began to bang on the door with vigor. Master Boyd had been pinning my arms to his headboard by holding my wrists tightly. He let me go and stopped his harsh thrusting. My Master stared into my face with a sudden look of suspicion. I looked back at him realizing he had heard it too. Fear began to rise in both of us at the same time.

"Did you hear that," he whispered.

I nodded. "Yes Master. Who do you think it is? Dennis?"

He shook his head. "Couldn't be. It is they. The figured out we found the bug," he said under his breath.

I felt terror race down my spine. "Already? Oh shit. What are we going to do," I said almost in a blind panic.

The knocking came again, louder this time. We looked at each other about ready to die of heart attacks.

He put his finger to his lips motioning me to be quiet. My Master dismounted my unit and stealthily got off the bed gathering our discarded clothes. He then motioned me to follow him. I got up and both of us went to the bedroom door. He took my hand, nodded at me, then we took off through his house running for the back-door sky clad and terrified.

We almost fell in the kitchen but made it out without stopping hand in hand. My Master kept pulling me behind him heading right into the woods behind the house. Neither of us looked back. We ran like idiots until both of us were nearly dead from exhaustion. We had not slept in three days.

Finally, sure we had outrun the they, Master Boyd fell to his knees and I collapsed right next to him. We panted, fighting for air unable to go any further deep in the darkening woods at the foot of the Giant's belly.

We stared at each other gasping but straining our ears listening for any noise. Both of us hoping we had indeed eluded our predators. My Master threw my clothes toward me while he put on his own. He had not grabbed our boots, but we at least could shield our units from the thick brush. I helped him button his shirt while he aided me to pull down my own.

Once we were dressed and had caught our breath, my Master stood back up. He looked around appearing unable to determine our location.

He looked back at me upset. "I think we are lost, Niemand." He rubbed his sweaty forehead.

I stood up brushing off the leaves from my clothing. "You can say that again Master. What just happened there?"

Master Boyd shook his head. "Not sure. I think we were being chased."

I chuckled bitterly. "Uhm, that is paranoid."

He looked at me suddenly irritated. "Take that back. It is not paranoia. Someone was at the door. You heard it too."

I walked over to him staring at him hard. "You are getting sick Master. That was probably Simon or Bastard at the door. We just ran from a trick. That is paranoia."

Master Boyd growled, "I am not paranoid, Psycho."

I narrowed my eyes. "I am not Psycho."

He laughed. "You are too."

I pushed him. "Take it back."

My Master pushed me back. "No, you are a psycho. You are a fucking schizophrenic."

I jumped onto his unit scratching and biting, knocking us both to the ground. "Fucking loon. So are you. Plus, you are paranoid, Boyd."

We rolled around on the forest floor kicking, scratching and slapping each other. All the while hurling insults about the insanity of the other. Truth was we were both fucking nuts. There was no longer any doubt about that.

Our struggling was violent enough to send us both to the ground several times. I would get up and he would pull me back to the ground. He would try to stand and I would trip him. I knocked him down a third time. Without hesitation I crawled onto his lap. I was straddling a very angry Master Boyd about to backhand him again when a bright light blinded my eyes. I covered my face yelling out in pain as my brain lit up from its intensity.

"What the Sam Hill are the two of you doing? Get the fuck up now," yelled out Dennis from behind the demonic light.

Master Boyd threw my unit off his lap with force and stood up. "Dennis is that you," he called out also shielding his eyes from the offensive glare.

"Yeah, it is Boyd. Psycho, get up. Now tell me what the fuck is going on. What happened in the kitchen? Jesus Christ, start talking or so help me," Dennis yelled out sounding very angry.

Master Boyd reached down and took my hand helping me to my feet. "Uhm, just fun and games Dennis. Not really your business. Kinky stuff, you know," he said while shooting me a look of caution.

I looked at the ground. "Yeah, just being rowdy. We kind of got a little too excited. You know, shit happens." I forced a chuckle, but it sounded nervous.

Dennis lowed his flashlight. "Bullshit. Boyd, you are supposed to be getting ready for work. Did you forget? Do you even know what time it is? I came by to pick you up early and I must have banged on that door for the last half hour. Then I see the two of you running off into the woods naked as jaybirds. I find you out here bloody, fighting and barefoot in the middle of the God damned mountain. This is not kinky. This is fucking insane behavior. Are you taking your medication? Either of you? I told you this relationship was going to set you off Boyd," he yelled beyond furious.

Master Boyd reached out and took my hand keeping his gaze at the ground. "We are taking our medications Dennis. I admit we got a bit carried away with our affections. I lost track of the time is all. How we like to fuck or where we do it on my property is not your business. I am sorry that we got caught up in it so close to time for work. Now, we can go back to the house and I can get ready or we can just stand here arguing till we are late," he said sternly.

Dennis spit on the ground. "I have just about had enough of this. I know you are full of shit, both of you. You are both thin as bean poles. Psycho babbles all the damned time and Boyd you are irritable and trancing. I know God damned well the two of you are going off your decks. I think it is time to send Psycho to the hospital and let you get a break from the stress before you end up joining her in the nut hut," he growled out.

I gasped feeling terror fill my unit like static electricity. "No, I didn't do anything Dennis. Don't let him take me to the hospital Boyd. Please, I didn't do anything." I started to hyperventilate from panic.

Master Boyd grabbed me hugging me to his unit tightly. "No, Niemand isn't going anywhere Dennis. She is fine. She is even doing better. Leave her alone."

Dennis snorted. "Niemand? Who the fuck is that?"

My Master looked at Dennis. "This is Niemand, Dennis. All of you are going to stop calling her Psycho. She has a real name, you know. Niemand isn't going to the hospital. She is going back to the house with me where she belongs.

You may as well get over it. She is never going to leave. Niemand is my God given wife. Deal with it."

Dennis looked shocked. "What? Boyd, I will stop calling Psycho. Errr, Niemand is that her name? You are right. It is rude and cruel to call her by that nickname. You know I have always thought that. I will call her by her name from now on happily. That said, you had better rethink the rest of what you said. She is sick and you are getting sick because of it. You are talking about God again Boyd. You keep that up and well, enough said. I want to see your medication, both of you. Get going to the house. This has gone far enough. I am not going to argue with you in the middle of the fucking woods in the middle of the night."

We all walked back to the house with Dennis fuming the whole way about our most irregular behaviors. He warned us that if we continued to act nuts he was going to have both of us committed to the Snake Pit for our own safety.

Master Boyd never let go of my hand the whole walk back. He would squeeze it harder whenever the State mental institution crossed Dennis's lips and shoot me a worried look. I too was frightened by his threats. I decided it maybe was best to try not to hit Master Boyd or help him tear up the kitchen in the future. A trip to that hell hole was not something I was in hurry to visit again. Apparently, my Master felt the same way.

I had been incarcerated there over half a dozen times by 1998. Master Boyd had graced their cells three times himself prior to his twenty-first birthday. He had been super lucky since the early days of his onset. He not been hospitalized in a decade thanks to Dennis's vigilant care and a calmer expression of the disease than normal for most of us. Dennis had become an expert at watching for the signs of psychosis over those years.

Master Boyd's cycles had been benign and not deep enough so Dennis had managed to hide his son's disease from the public by grounding him at home on sick leave. When my Master would cycle in, Dennis would just keep a baleful eye on the pacing, mumbling, paranoid Master Boyd until the acute cycle passed.

So, what happened May 28th and December 2nd in 1997? How did Boyd end up raping, then collaring me to become the 28th Master without Dennis knowing?

In late 1996, Carla had developed breast cancer. The loving Dennis was spread thin trying to care for his ailing wife and keep track of the cycles of his schizophrenic adopted son. To Master Boyd's horror, and my detriment it turned out, his usually light cycle began to run deep for the first time in a decade that year.

By the winter he was already stalking me full of violent delusions and unable to refuse the command hallucinations from God to take me as his wife. By May of 1997, trapped in a rapid and heavy cycle, without someone to keep a close eye on his symptoms, he had become acute and dangerous. I became a victim to his madness late that same month in the white cell.

I myself had been acutely ill with my own disease symptoms. He was as helpless to stop himself from attacking me as I was in stopping him. Believe it or not we were both hostages that night, I just didn't know he too was kidnapped by the very same illness at that time. After the incident, his acute stage finally wore off and he became residual as did I. He broke off his stalking and attacks finally coming to his senses barely recalling what he had done.

Master Boyd thought he had possibly been hallucinating the entire mess. He was too terrified to ask me to see if what little he did recall had really happened. Hell, I would have avoided him too had the situation been reversed. Especially if I had already served six years of my life for a rape I had never committed. When I never said a word, he figured it was just delusion. That it never happened.

However, his residual was as short as my own. By December that same year we both were cycling into psychosis yet again. This time by sheer accident Dennis was off with Carla aiding her in her treatment when the once again stark raving mad Boyd caught me with my Key and Collar at Darling Cemetery. The rest of that story of this psychotic nightmare had led to our walking through the darkness barefoot in front of a very upset Dennis that night.

The Queen Mother of Madness herself had brought me and Master Boyd together in an unholy union. He admitted that his collaring me was never meant to happen but did literally by sheer insanity. Master Boyd had never intended to go chasing my collar but once it had happened, he did his very best to make it work and try to make up for his many cruelties during his psychotic cycles. His love for me was very real, even if his belief that God had specifically made me for him was total delusion.

It was not secret that Master Boyd had been completely enamored with me since we first met that fateful day in the barbed wire. It should be understood, however, that it was his delusional command symptoms that caused him to act on his interests in being my lover and spouse. My Master had not willfully come after me with a full understanding of his actions.

In other words, he had no fucking idea what he was doing at the time of the white cell rape, or when stalking me and the other mean shit he did in the beginning when I told him no. He could not stop himself that night any more than I could have stopped myself from kicking in the door at the Freewill Baptist Church to preach. When in residual, he was more than happy to grant choice and equality.

When sick he could be a real monster sometimes. Then again, the same goes for me. After all, I had raped him back while he was residual and I was acute, now didn't I? Master Boyd and I really were perfect mirror images, believe it or not. A truly unholy union made right in schizophrenic hell.

Now that Carla had survived her sickness, her cancer was thankfully in remission, Dennis was just discovering the usually mild psychosis that Master Boyd demonstrated had become much more serious. Dennis erroneously assumed it was his dating another schizophrenic that was causing this sudden increase in strength of Master Boyd's cycles. It really had nothing to do with me. It is just the nature of the disease. Every one of us can go for years with light to no cycles at all then suddenly see rapid, deep and violent changes without knowing the cause.

Since Dennis didn't know Master Boyd had already been through almost two years of strong psychosis this appeared to be new to Dennis. But my Master and I knew the truth. We just couldn't tell the old bull. If Dennis knew what Master Boyd had already done it would have been a disaster no doubt. To keep our father figure from finding out about the rapes, mine and his, and my collaring we had made a pact to never speak to anyone about the incidences of those two years. A promise I kept till I wrote that all down to all of you.

Master Boyd and I had no choice but to keep our heads down while the old bull made the wrong assumption that we were in fact bad for each other. No matter what anyone said we knew we were a perfect match. One God had ordained himself. I loved my Master and he loved me. We had figured out the normals were trying to keep us apart because they hate our kind. They don't want to see us have a happy life because we are monsters to them. That much Master Boyd and I could truly understand. We knew it was us against them in a war to stay paired despite all the odds predicting our total failure as a successful couple.

Dennis walked in behind us though the back door. He looked around at the mess in the floor. He let out his breath while staring in disbelief at the open cabinets and drawers strewn everywhere. Master Boyd took off to the bathroom to get our medication bottles.

Dennis glared at me. "So what is the story with this shit? Don't give me kinky sex caused this mess Psycho, co, ah, Niemand."

I looked at the floor trancing slightly while shrugging. "We were looking for something. I was going to clean it up afterwards, you know."

He let out a sign. "Okay fine. I didn't really expect you to tell me. You never have been one to just volunteer any information. I want you to consider going inpatient Niemand. You know you are setting Boyd off. If you love him, you will do this. He needs a break from the stress your sickness is causing."

I growled. "Yeah, sure Dennis, because my going to the hospital will cure his loony ass. Forget that noise. I have work tomorrow. I am fine, so is Boyd. You worry too much."

Master Boyd came into the demolished kitchen and handed our medication bottles to the old bull. We both took Thorazine and Lorazepam at ungodly levels. The medications did help but only when we were residual. When the prodromal and acute cycles came, there was nothing that would stop them expect time or increases in the medication at hospital levels which only worked sometimes.

My Master picked up an overturned chair and sat down. He motioned in my direction to join him. I took his extended hand while he pulled me onto his lap. I snuggled my head into his chest immediately closing my eyes. I was starting to break out in a sweat while fighting back the fear that was rising within me.

I truly believed that Dennis was going to make Master Boyd put me into the back of the squad car. I doubted my Master would listen to my pleas of innocence while hauling me to the Snake Pit. Dennis always had complete authority over him. My Master would never dare to stand up to his demands. To my relief it turned out I didn't know my Master as well as I thought I did.

Dennis's eyes went wide as he realized we had been taking our medications properly, and we were. "Boyd, what is going on? Are you throwing out the meds instead of taking them?"

Master Boyd grumbled. "Uhm no, Dennis. We are both taking that poison just like it says to. It is not working. I don't know why."

I winced. "There is no cure Dennis. The medication doesn't work," I whined out.

Dennis snorted. "Boyd what is with this mess? Why is this kitchen torn up?"

My Master sighed appearing very tired. "I was looking for that stupid gravy boat of mom's. Niemand and I got a bit carried away in our rush. I was going to give it to Carla. he has done so much for me. I was trying to be nice," he lied smoothly.

I hid my smile in his chest and stifled my giggling at how clever my Master truly was. "We still haven't found the damned thing," I added quickly.

Master Boyd wrapped his arms around me and laid his head on mine. "I need to get ready for work, Dennis. We are going to be a bit late even if I rush it. Are you done bitching or what?"

Dennis hitched up his pants then put the medication bottles on the table. "No Boyd, I am not done. I think it is time for you to take your sick leave. I am going to call in Linda and ride with her for the next week. You stay home and rest. I will come check on you in the morning after the shift ends. Niemand says she will be at work so someone will need to monitor you till this cycle passes." He rubbed his moustache looking at us as if deep in thought.

Master Boyd sighed. "Sure Dennis. Whatever. I am fine but if you want to make a big deal out of this you are the boss. See you in the morning then. Be careful and tell Linda, Niemand and I said hi." He kissed the top of my head.

Dennis stood there for a few more moments staring at us. "Alright then. I will see you in the morning. Take your medication and get some rest boy. You look like hell. Niemand, fix both of you something to eat for Christ's sake. I mean it. Eat something, both of you." He stormed out of the house slamming the door behind him.

The noise of his exit made us both jump. A monster psychotic episode was making both of us her bitch that night.

Master Boyd and I didn't move from our spot in the chair even after we heard Dennis's car leave.

A stone like trance had overcome our units at the same time, likely due to extreme exhaustion and stress. We were not asleep but in a place between wake and mental shut down reserved exclusively for the insane. An hour or perhaps two passed before finally Master Boyd stirred, able to move once more. His struggling to come back from catatonic stupor rousted me from my own.

"Baby? Niemand? Oh shit. I am late for work," he said slurring slightly still groggy from the brain fog.

I moaned. "I am too Master. Did you put the turkey back into the refrigerator? It is going to go bad so don't eat it. It has been poisoned. Everything has been poisoned." I was grateful that I was able to move my stiff limbs feeling relief to be able to break free of that statue-like hell.

Master Boyd gasped. "That makes sense. I noticed the food tasted funny lately. Okay, they are probably trying to kill us. They want us apart and they don't care how they do it. Don't eat the food. In fact, throw it all out. That is a directive." He helped me to stand.

I nodded while stretching, feeling my head rock slightly. "Yes Master. I will do it now. I am taking it to the ditch. The fumes could get us too."

He stood also flexing his stiff muscles, then stomped his feet several times while rubbing his forehead. "Yes, take it outside. Hurry, I will help you." He walked to the laundry room to get a basket to help us haul out the tainted materials.

I picked up the discarded food stuffs off the floor while he loaded the basket from the fridge. Together we cleaned out every morsel of eatable material from the house and tossed it all into the ditch across the road. He worried we could die from even breathing the stuff while packing it up. So, we covered our faces with handkerchiefs Master Boyd brought from his dresser.

After finishing our disposal of the poisoned groceries, the darkness called to me. In only moments it had sent me into a wild dancing fit. Master Boyd sat on the porch to watch Simon and I twirl, stomp and prance under the black sky. He had already forgotten he was supposed to be at work. It had slipped my mind that I needed to rest for work the next day myself.

I suppose my Looper was off having coffee with his Bastard and God. None of his or my many shards, command hallucinations or inner selves were helping either of us get our shit straight. It should be clear that one or both of us needed to be inpatient, but without a normal around watching it would get way out of hand soon enough, as if it hadn't already.

QUICK NOTE: *Master Boyd is like most high functioning schizophrenics in that he also has a Simon. His Simon has a name, but I am not at liberty to tell you what it really is since it is not mine to share. Master Boyd is still alive and his inner self's identity is his private* *business. I will always refer to his Simon in these stories as 'Bastard' because Master Boyd often cursed that word when arguing with him. Just understand that is not really his name.*

Master Boyd also spoke to and was spoken to by God. To keep down any misunderstandings, please note that this voice is his 'Looper' or shattered memory he is hearing. While Master Boyd did recognize Bastard as his shattered inner self. He didn't realize God was his memory that he could hear, like I hear my own named Looper, outside his head. This confusion is what made his delusions dangerous at times.

Think about this.: If you thought God was talking to you and telling you to do shit, you might be afraid not to do what you were told. Master Boyd also has a Dude voice called by a personal name (when that happens, I will tell you) and several other shards too just like me. As these things come up in the chapters, I will do my best to point them out and show the parallels to my own expression of the disease. Now you can see just how very schizophrenic he really is.

Around two in the morning my urge to dance had abated. Master Boyd decided the house was now clear of any poisonous gases that could have escaped the befouled foodstuffs. He told me we could go back inside the house safely. I went to his kitchen to start cleaning up the mess while he paced, wrung his hands and yelled at Bastard about the bugs in the house yet undiscovered.

I bitched at Simon about the pile of broken dishes and glasses while I worked. If you had been a fly on the wall in that house that night, you would have packed up and gotten the fuck out. The only difference between Master Boyd's home with us in it and a mental asylum, hmm, well his house had more windows. It was beyond fruit loops with the babbling, yelling and incoherent speech we hurled out at no one as the night wore into morning.

Still, neither of us slept. Only the two-hour catatonic stupor and a three-hour nap three days before guaranteed big trouble. I had gotten his kitchen cleaned back up to near normal looking when I heard him go out the front door around five in the morning. I didn't bother to follow him as I grabbed the mop to finish the job of putting our house back into order.

I saw him rush back inside. He came running for the entry to the kitchen appearing very startled. "Niemand, come here now. You have to see this." He grabbed my upper arm dragging me to the porch panting in panic.

I looked across the yard seeing the transmissions rising from the ground in greens and yellows like wildfires everywhere. I let out my air stunned into silence.

Master Boyd looked at me concerned. "You see it too? It is real?"

I nodded. "Yes Master, what are we going to do?"

He started shaking. "Run? I don't know? How do we make it stop? I don't know what is going on." He started hitting his forehead with the palm of his hand like I do sometimes when I get confused.

I looked at him wide eyed. "We decipher the codes Master. That is what we do. I remember, solve for X and it will stop." I grabbed his wrist and pulled him back inside to find paper and a pencil.

My Master stood at the window peeking out from time to time while watching me collect what I required to solve the issue. I finally sat down on the couch and looked at the walls. The codes began to erupt everywhere when I focused hard. I began writing down what I saw.

Master Boyd became interested to see what I was writing. He sat down next to me watching the symbols.

"Ah. I see it. Okay, okay, now where is the deciphering item? Do you have it in your purse?" He grabbed my purse and poured it into the floor sifting through it for the Rosetta Stone.

I shook my head. "No Master. We can decipher them by solving for X. See here is the equation." I wrote it down for him.

He picked it up while appearing confused. "Shit, that looks pretty hard. Let me find my calculator." He got up and went into his room to find the machine while I continued to write down the coding.

Master Boyd returned with his calculator and tape. He grabbed more paper and began to try to solve for X. When he got any part of his equation completed, he would tape the pages with the answers on it to the wall where I could see it. I then began to attempt to decode the symbols using his work. The two of us spent the next two hours arguing, mumbling, rambling and decoding our madness while taping the results to his living room walls.

At eight, the phone rang. I didn't want to answer it. Master Boyd decided he was going to tell the caller to fuck off. He stormed toward the kitchen bitching that our important work was not to be interrupted by some damned crank caller. I just kept on writing symbols and decoding but strained my ears to hear his conversation.

"Yeah, what the fuck do you want," yelled out Master Boyd.

There was a pause then he said, "Fuck, whatever, okay. Yeah I will tell her. Stop calling her Psycho, you dumb bitch." He slammed down the phone receiver and walked back in heading right back to his equation work without saying a word.

I looked at him. "Well Master? Who the fuck was that?"

Master Boyd looked up from his wild writings. "Oh, that dumbass Sheryl. She said you are due at the office in an hour or some shit." He looked back down mumbling numbers.

My eyes went wide. "Shit, I have to get to work Master. It must be Monday already."

My Master jumped at my sudden yell. "Huh? It is? Okay, let's get rolling then. We don't want to be late." He stood up still looking at his paperwork.

I shook my head. "Do I have a mouse in my pocket Master? What is this we shit?"

He looked at me angrily. "Do you think I am going to let you go without me, Niemand? No fucking way. They are just waiting to catch us apart. We are staying together until they fuck off. We haven't even solved the God damned codes. Grab Simon and let's get going. I am driving, that is a directive."

I looked at Simon sitting there with his head in his hands. "Fucking loon wants to come with us Simon. Oh well, get your drunk ass up. Looks like we are going to town asshole." I started laughing wildly.

Master Boyd frowned. "I am not a loon. You are. Stop calling me names."

I pretended to wipe my eyes of tears. "Ah, so sorry Master. I forgot you are sensitive. Call me what you want but you are the one with schizophrenia, not me." I got up and put on my coat.

My Master glared. "Fuck you. You have it too. I saw your records. And mine is not that bad anyway. You are a God damned train wreck. I am barely sick at all. I think I may even be over it by now."

I looked at him alarmed. "Seriously Master? You have got to be kidding me. Look at you. Searching for bugs in the walls. Watching out the windows. You are fucking cracked. My records lie. I was clearly misdiagnosed. It was a brain tumor. They took it out. Now I am well. I was never

239

schizophrenic at all." I started putting all the shit he had dumped back into my purse.

Master Boyd appeared stunned. "Can they do that? Misdiagnose someone with schizophrenia I mean?"

I nodded. "Well yeah. They sure did it to me Master. Fucked up my world till I got it all fixed in college."

He looked at the floor. "They misdiagnosed me too then. Shit, those assholes. I knew I wasn't sick. I am so stupid. I fell for it too."

I laughed. "Yeah they are good. Fucking doctors know it is just a brain tumor. They like to torture people is all. Well, now that I think on it, they probably misdiagnosed you too. No way you have it. How could you be a cop? No loony toon could do that job. See I figured it out when they hired me to be one. Sorry I called you a schizo, Master. Likely, they just said that about you to be mean over Maddy and all." I smiled at him.

He looked back at me smiling., "Yeah that makes a lot of sense. Oh well, I have you now. God said everything will be fixed as soon as I found you. I shut up those assholes Trenton, Will and Mark and now I find out I never had schizophrenia at all. See it is already happening. God was right. Everything is getting straightened out. Let's go before you are late." He rushed for the door with me right on his heels.

We decided to take his car since he felt more comfortable driving it. He took off out of his driveway spinning tire and throwing dust for miles. My Master drove at high speeds ignoring all the red lights, stop signs and passing every car between us and Cumberland. We laughed maniacally telling lewd jokes to entertain each other. Damn, did he know a lot of them.

From time to time he drifted too far to the left and ran off the road. He would wildly pull back onto it while we both howled in laughter. It is amazing that no cop stopped us and that we were not killed. Nor did we run over anyone. His recklessness was beyond crazy. Oddly, I never felt a second of fear from the mad driving of my psychotic Master. We made it to Cumberland and the DCFS office in record time and in one piece.

Master Boyd nearly missed the drive and had to slam on the brakes. We flew into the parking lot nearly sideways squealing tires and giggling like loons at his near miss of the large drainage ditch. He pulled into a space and killed the motor still smiling widely.

"This may be the best day of my life. It is like a huge weight is off my chest. I still can't believe I fell for the lies. I am a fool but not crazy. That should upset me, but somehow it doesn't." He chuckled then grabbed my left hand kissing his engagement ring.

I smiled at that. "Time to go deal with Sheryl. You want to stay in the car while I get my assignments Master?"

He looked at me with mischief in his sky-blue eyes. "Hell no, I want to see that bitch squirm. I wouldn't miss this for the world." He got out while I did the same giggling at his childish need to see me read the riot act to the failed Master.

We walked in the door holding hands while everyone stared at us looking nervous. We ignored them and went right through the wooden door headed for Jane's office. I was excited to introduce PC and Fax to my Master. They had heard a lot about him, but never officially met. I hoped I would have time, after telling Sheryl to take a hike, to say hi to them both, then head out to my many cases.

We entered the office to find Sheryl and Jane talking while looking at PC. The women looked up both appearing startled to see me and Master Boyd standing there grinning at them.

"Holy hell, look what the cat just drug in Sheryl. I am going to take a break. This is your nightmare sister. I haven't had enough coffee for this insanity," breathed out Jane wide eyed still staring at me and my Master.

Sheryl nodded/ "Uhm yeah, no wait Jane. You better stick around. I may need Charlie here or the Marines. This is not looking good."

Jane groaned but went and sat down behind her desk while Sheryl walked toward us. "Okay Psycho, uhm Boyd, what is going on here. Why is he here and why are you covered in blood and wearing electrical tape around your neck sweetie? Boyd, did you do that?" She pointed at my neck but looked at my Master appearing upset.

Master Boyd nodded. "Yeah I sure did. Cut it right off, Sheryl. See, it is gone." He snickered into his hand while I elbowed him motioning toward Jane.

Sheryl looked harder at my neck. "Ah, it is, so I see you put yours on. Very clever Boyd. I always thought it was you who had fucked her up that night she showed up. You are a real asshole. I see you have brainwashed the little schizo on top of all the rest of the nasty shit you have done to her. I hope you're proud of yourself. Now you may leave so she can get back to work, assuming you are done gloating that is." She crossed her arms looking at Master Boyd hatefully.

I growled. "I am not brain washed and I am not schizo Sheryl. And stop calling me Psycho. I am not Psycho. I am Niemand. Now I am going to work, but you are not going to tell me what to do anymore. You don't even have the proper coding or functions. I can't work under an idiot who can't even tell me where the dead child foster home placement forms are. I will work for Jane now. She at least puts the turkey in the fridge before it goes bad. She should be Area Manager, not your dumb ass." Master Boyd snickered still covering his mouth while looking at the floor as I yelled at Sheryl.

Sheryl gasped. "Oh boy. Okay, you know what? Boyd you are her Guardian. It is time to take Psycho here to the hospital and let her get some rest. Just this once try to be a fucking decent human being will you? She has blown a gasket. I am taking her off for the rest of the year. Get her out of here and get some help. It is the least you can do, idiot. She is nuts like this because of all that bullshit you pulled. I

243

believe we are done here. Jane call in an order for a relief worker. Psycho is effectively on leave until January 1st. We can't have this crazy shit going on in court or running around the counties handling children," she said looking back at a very frightened Jane.

Master Boyd stopped laughing. "Stop call her Psycho. Her name is Niemand."

Sheryl growled. "I don't give a flying fuck what her name is at this point. Take the fucking loon to the hospital and get her fixed. Now out or I will call the fucking cops, Boyd. Both of you out." She pointed for the door.

I smiled. "Fine by me bitch. I am happy to have a couple of weeks off. You can go dig up the babies under the tire swings and have coffee with Julia. Hey, tell Samuel, I said I will give him a high five over his fine work as soon as I come back in a couple weeks. Have a very fucking Merry Christmas. Oh, let me give you ladies the gifts I got for you." I flipped her and Jane off while Master Boyd began to giggle again.

My Master and I turned to leave. "Get her some help, Boyd. I mean it," Sheryl yelled to our backs as we hoofed it out of the office.

He just snorted and flipped her off too without even turning around to look behind him. We rushed from the building and back to his black car. My Master pulled out, burning rubber, at a high rate of speed headed back to Wheatly.

We just giggled and snickered saying nothing to each other until we were over the county line. "Now where do we go, Master? I think Dennis took you off work for a week and now I am off for two. What does a person do when not working? I can't remember anymore, it was too long ago."

Master Boyd laughed. "Let's go to our special place and fuck."

I rolled my eyes. "Ah, what was I thinking? Of course that is what you would say, Master." I crossed my arms looking out the window to watch the transmissions flowing toward the sky.

He snorted. "So? What is wrong with that? We can't eat because they are poisoning us. We can't go home because the house is bugged. We can't go to work because everyone threw us out. You have a better idea?"

I thought about what he said. "No I don't. You are right. No one wants us around. Everyone wants to put me in the hospital for some fucking reason," I said while sighing.

Master Boyd nodded. "I know why everyone is trying to put you away. They all know you figured out they are lying to us. They are trying to shut you up, Niemand. Can't you see that is what is going on? That is what they did to me. I told them I didn't hurt Maddy. You know that I didn't rape her. They said I had schizophrenia and did it but didn't remember doing it. I didn't fucking do it. The more I told them I never touched her the more they said I was just crazy. Then they locked me up to shut me up once and for all. Now they are trying to do that to you too. Don't worry baby, I

245

won't let them get you." He grabbed my left hand holding it while stealing loving glances at me.

I winced. "Yeah, that makes a lot of sense. Shit. I shouldn't have told them I knew they are liars, Master. Oh hell, me and my big mouth. Can you forgive me for fucking this up so bad?" I looked at him worried he would be upset I had set 'they' off to try to kill us.

Master Boyd smiled. "I love you Niemand. You set me free. You don't need to apologize. I have never been happier. They won't get us. We will just hide until they realize we are not going to just walk into their stupid trap. Eventually, they will forget about us. You'll see." He kissed my hand.

I smiled back grateful he wasn't angry. "Okay, so we hide in your secret place till this blows over, right? That could work."

Master Boyd laughed. "Damned right it will. In a week we can go home, and I will go back to work, and you can hang out at the house until you go back to work. Then it will all be back to normal again. They will be gone, and you and I can get married too. No more fucking schizophrenia, and no more Psycho, and no more paranoid Boyd talk, that is a directive."

I laughed too. "And you will love me forever and I love you back, that is a directive."

He looked at me initially confused but then realized my joke. We both howled at my trying to make a directive, but he also agreed to follow it.

When we arrived in Wheatly, he slowed down careful to watch the speed limits. We didn't want to attract any unwanted attention. He slipped away down the old single laned dirt road then parked the black car off the road behind a large group of old tangled bushes. He opened the trunk and took out a tent, lanterns and other camping supplies such as blankets.

I raised an eyebrow in surprise while he sheepishly told me that he had kept this gear from the days when he was stalking me. My Master's disturbing confession should have bothered me, but it didn't, not at that time anyway.

I told him I was grateful he was prepared to hide out with me in the woods for seven days. It was a lucky thing he had the gear. Without it we would have frozen out there during the cold nights or suffered somewhat when it rained unless we lived in his car.

I aided him in hauling the gear along with two gallons of water to the clearing deep in the woods. Together we pitched the tent and carefully set up our camp. My brother the sun could barely reach out to blind us with his smile the area was so thickly wooded with pine trees. Master Boyd and I were completely exhausted. He teased the entire time we worked that he was going to ravish me the second we were done.

However, once finished we climbed inside the tent, crawled into each other's arms under the blankets and finally fell into a deep sleep. We had been running on terror for almost four full days. At last we felt safe enough to let our guards down so the Sandman could come hang with us for a while. We were so tired we woke up in the same position we had closed our eyes in. Neither had moved a muscle for a full day and most of that night. Only a dim lantern kept the darkness at bay.

In the wee hours of Tuesday morning Master Boyd woke up first to begin our psychotic spin anew. I was startled to consciousness by his kissing my face. At first, I didn't recognize him and began to struggle afraid I was being attacked. Thinking this was part of the rape game we often played – his weird fetish remember – he rolled over on top of me then pinned my arms above my head pushing his mouth onto mine forcing a passionate kiss.

I began to yell in a panic, now beyond terrified, while fighting to get away. My inability to identify my own damned Master set off his own inner demon for violent sexual interest. Master Boyd became very excited by my terror. He pawed and ripped at my clothing further setting off my alarms of distress.

He let my arms go as he tried to pull off my pants. I scratched at his eyes while hitting him with all my strength. Master Boyd ignored my screaming until I managed to hit him square in the nose nearly blinding him with the impact. In total psychotic response he backhanded my face hard sending me nearly knocked off my block right to my back. I was briefly stunned while he finished removing his barrier to his desired carnal interests.

Without a second hesitation he engaged roughly, then began thrusting violently which brought me back from my near brush with unconsciousness. I let out a yell and tried to hit him again. He grabbed my arms holding me still while he finished his coupling ignoring my pleas for him to stop. I could see the vacant look in his eyes while he reached his climax.

It was then that I recalled his identity. My fear quickly abated as my Master panted and moaned in pleasure spent of his lust. I calmed down feeling rather stupid that somehow I had mistakenly thought I was being raped. Master Boyd let go of my arms and rubbed his nose smiling at me while his unit relaxed, still intertwined with my own.

"Damn you are getting good at acting afraid, baby. I almost believed it this time." He giggled.

I gasped as the vaginal cramping began. "Oh Master, that was no act. You snuck up on me. I thought it was real." I tried to force a chuckle, but a moan of pain escaped instead.

Master Boyd looked at me suddenly appearing concerned. "Oh shit. Are you okay? I didn't mean to scare you. I thought you were playing. Oh fuck." He disengaged appearing distraught.

I reached up to feel the blood pouring from my busted lip. "Well, the backhand was a bit much, Master, but it is okay. I shouldn't have hit you in the nose. You just scared me is all. Please mercy. If you are going to want special services make sure I am fully awake next time." I sat up while he grabbed my chin to assess the damage.

"Yeah, I think I got carried away there. I will need to be more careful. Shit, I can't be busting up that beautiful face of yours. Damn it. I don't know why I do stupid things like this. I really don't even deserve you." He began to wring his hands getting more agitated by the second.

I winced at a new wave of cramps. "It is okay Master. I still love you. Forget about it. Our play gets rough sometimes. Accidents are bound to happen, just no choking okay?" I reached out and grabbed his hands looking at him lovingly.

My Master nodded. "Yeah okay, you are right. I lose my head when you struggle like that. I just can't control myself. So, until I can get that devil out of me, no more struggling, that's a directive," he mumbled.

I chuckled. "Okay Master, I will try harder and you try harder to believe me when I tell you I love you no matter what."

He stared at me with a look of gratitude. "You really were made just for me, Niemand. No one else in the world could ever love me. If something ever happened to you I would be alone again. I can't ever go back to not having you to hold and cuddle. You are all I ever dreamed you would be." He reached out and stroked my face.

I looked at the ground feeling afraid and despaired all at once. "I certainly hope so Master. I don't want to be without you either ever again. I admit I am scared they will break us apart like Bastard said they will."

Master Boyd smiled. "No baby. I won't let them do that. Bastard doesn't know shit. Simon is smarter. Simon says we are the right match. I believe him. Besides, no one can find us here. We are safe. In a week they will be gone. Dennis said so." He pulled me to his lap while wrapping his arms around me kissing my neck gently.

I nodded. "Dennis would know. He is one of the normals. Oh shit. Master, he said he was coming to check on you this morning. I just remembered that. What if he is still on the porch banging on the door?"

Master Boyd laughed. "Niemand, he will see my car is gone. He would have realized we left for a while. It is okay. We are adults you know. It is a free country. We can leave and go wherever we want when we have vacation time. We are just on vacation is all. Dennis can wait. Let's just enjoy our time together, okay? Forget about Dennis and Sheryl. They are not even going to miss us anyway. You know normal people run off to be alone all the time. It is not against the law."

I giggled. "Hey, you are right Master. I have never had a vacation before. The normals do it all the time. Jane went to Hawaii for two weeks this Fall, and Nora went to Aspen. We are camping out on ours. Dennis and Sheryl did say for us to rest and relax. That is what a vacation is."

Master Boyd smiled happily. "Well it is my first vacation too. We can do anything you want. Just name it and we will do it."

I thought for a minute then smiled. "I want to go to the Boswell courtship dance on Wednesday night Master. I was invited. Can we go? Please?"

Maser Boyd laughed. "A dance? With the Gypsies? Really? The whole world is ours and you want to go to dance at a campsite when we are already camping? Well, okay, only if I can watch you dance."

I hugged him tightly. "Maybe you would even dance with me? I would like that very much Master. God won't even see you do it because we are on vacation."

He giggled. "Oh we will have to see about all that, but for now let's get some water and clean up that pretty face of yours. I also think before we go to the Boswells we will need to go shopping for a few things. If we show up empty handed, it is bad manners you know."

I looked at him surprised. "How do you know that Master?"

Master Boyd smiled wickedly. "Because I have known them since I became a cop. I have hung out with them when they hit town for over a decade. They never treated me like there is something wrong with me. So, I went whenever I had days off, you know to listen to Shady's stories and for Kenzia's amazing coffee. Promise not to tell Dennis though, that is a directive."

I laughed out loud. "Master, you never cease to surprise me. You are just full of secrets, aren't you?"

He kissed me deeply. "I used to keep them because no one cared to know anything about me. I won't keep anything from you though, Niemand. All you have to do is ask. I love you. You are forever my One and Only."

He and I cleaned up as best as we could given the limitations of our supplies then drove to Wells, where no one would recognize us. We didn't want to be bothered by people who might know who we were. Master Boyd knew what store would sell items that would be viewed as proper gifts for the Boswell visit. I followed him through the store ignoring the stares of the locals who likely wondered about the bruised and cut up schizophrenic couple in dirty clothes. He and I didn't care what they thought. We were having the time of our lives. It was our very first vacation, at least inside our delusional heads.

In reality Dennis had come by that morning just as he had promised. When he found Master Boyd's car missing and still no return of his wayward son by afternoon, he had forced his way into the house. He called Carla and Randall immediately upon finding the disturbing large amount of scribbling and symbols taped all over the walls of his living room.

A quick and quiet search of all the known places Master Boyd would inhabit was done by the trio. When that too resulted in no sign of me or my Master, Dennis and Randall began to fear the worst.

Dennis put out an APB on both of us by Tuesday morning. The other officers were briefed on the situation.

The city and county cops were told that their police officer brethren may have been taken hostage by his schizophrenic fiancé during a delusional fit. No foul play was suspected, but everyone was asked to approach Master Boyd and I with caution if we were spotted. Dennis or Randall were to be notified immediately before anyone dared approach us.

It is most likely that the old bull now had realized Master Boyd was as deeply psychotic as I ever had been. I can imagine he was doing all he could in a last-ditch effort to keep my Master's dirty little secret under wraps from his fellow officers.

Up to that time, only Carla, Randall and Dennis knew Master Boyd was schizophrenic. There is no way Dennis could have believed it was possible to hide the secret any longer given the obvious proof that Master Boyd would need inpatient care when, and if, found. Dennis now had to deal with the fact that he had mistakenly thought I was the only one who needed emergency intervention.

Even as vigilant as the tough cop had been all those years, he had missed it when Master Boyd flipped rapidly from a nasty prodromal to an agitated acute phase of the cycle. It is likely that my Master's sudden break from reality was due to severe lack of sleep and significant environmental stresses that collided with his delusional belief system. The threat of taking me to the hospital, told to break up our relationship, and called schizophrenic to his face just to name a few. The reasons for Master Boyd's total meltdown could also be chalked up to the nature of the disease itself with no outside factors at all.

Each psychotic cycle is different in depth, progression speed and onset. It could have simply been his time to pay the heavy toll each of us who have the illness will before they lay us low. Even the luckiest of us can expect to see the white walls, strait jacket and restraining beds of at least a few mental hospitals or psychiatric wards.

Unfortunately for me and Master Boyd our bill was very close to coming due and schizophrenia does not tolerate late payments.

Chapter 72: "That's Paranoid Boyd" Part 2
The Fall of Psycho & Rise of Niemand
Master Boyd

Are we having fun yet? Why hell yeah. We are on vacation. It is about time. In all my miserable life I had never once taken a day off and just let all my stresses go. In many companies and even a few small business's they call having holidays imperative to ensure the good mental health of the employees. Well, now there in an interesting concept.

Master Boyd and I are doing the right thing based on this idea. Couldn't have come at a better time either. We really needed to get a break from our shattered minds. Oh, and did we ever take that break. In fact, you could when the vacation was over, both of us were busted right to hell.

ODE TO THE PARANOID MASTER BOYD:

Master Boyd, why are you watching the door?

Because 'they' are coming to take us away.

Master Boyd, why are you talking to the Lord?

Because God knows how I can make you stay.

Master Boyd, why look for bugs, there aren't any more?

Because I want to protect you Niemand May.

Master Boyd, why are you meaner than ever before?

Because you are not listening to what I say.

Master Boyd, why do you keep kissing your ring?

Because I know you are the only one for me.

Master Boyd why do always obsess on silly things?

Because I know you will leave don't you see.

Master Boyd why don't you accept you are my king?

Because It took threats to get you to agree.

Master Boyd, why did you betray me that awful Spring?

Because I have insanity in my family tree.

"Okay everyone. If Boyd takes off running, let him. Even I can't catch that boy. What you need to do is focus on Psycho. You grab that girl and Boyd will not run far. He is very protective of his sweetheart. He'll come back to try to save her. Now I don't know if he is armed. I pray to the Lord that he is not. The boy is a dead shot. I don't want to have to take him down like that so let's just hope he isn't packing. Understand, Boyd is strong, fast, and clever. He also has one nasty temper. Don't forget he is psychotic as hell right now. He likely will not listen to reason. So, you boys stay back unless we call you. Randall and I will handle this. You all focus on catching the girl and then we will take down Boyd."
--Dennis instructing his police officers before the standoff with Boyd and Psycho, late December 1998.

"That was a lot of fun. I don't think I have ever been shopping with anyone before," said Master Boyd while rubbing his forehead repeatedly.

I narrowed my eyes. "Master, is something wrong with our head? You keep rubbing it."

He winced. "I have the damnedest headache. It is getting so bad it is messing with my eyesight." He groaned.

I laughed. "Your eyesight? How Master? I mean what does that mean exactly," I said while digging into my purse looking for Ibuprofen for my Master's ailment.

He chuckled nervously. "Well, it is kind of weird. I keep seeing this fuzzy white stuff like in the corners of my vision, sometimes it looks like, nah, it is not important. Do you have something for a headache?"

I looked up startled. "You are seeing the static. Oh no, Master. We must go back to the house and get your medication right away. It will come and eat your world."

Master Boyd glanced at me appearing nervous. "What the fuck? Niemand honey, you are talking crazy stuff again. Just look for that Ibuprofen, that is a directive." I saw him watching the rearview mirror as he slowly sped up.

I looked behind us. A red care with a man and woman was right behind. I didn't think much of it. I found two of the headache pills and handed them to Master Boyd. He took them, swallowing them both without bothering to ask for water, which we didn't have anyway. I saw him narrow his eyes still watching behind us in his mirror.

258

"What is it Master," I said noting the sudden quiet and tensing of his unit.

He whispered, "That car has been following us for miles. I wonder if it is 'they?' I mean I don't even know what 'they' look like. It could be them, the car that is following us." H took a right turn onto the road that led back to Wheatly, the red car turned too.

Master Boyd's eyes went wide. "Did you see that? That car is following us."

I nodded. "Maybe. I think though maybe they are just headed our way. There are not a lot of roads going anywhere out here in the sticks, Master. Pull off on another road and see if they come too. Only way to know. The next town is Pace. Pull off onto one of the roads that go around a side street or two. See if they follow then."

He smiled. "Yeah, you are right. I will watch them until then. Fuck, my head is killing me." He rubbed his head again appearing to be very uncomfortable.

I began to yawn feeling very tight in my muscles. I stretched trying to keep my skin suit from shrinking as I too watched the red sporty car just behind us. The man and woman appeared to be talking, laughing and generally having an enjoyable time. In our own car the mood had suddenly turned paranoid and quiet. I had no doubt in my mind that Master Boyd was obsessing that this was 'they' coming for us at last.

I glanced at my psychotic Master. He had sweat beads beginning to form on his forehead. I looked at his narrow jaw which now had a few days growth of a heavy dark beard. Neither he nor I had engaged in basic hygiene in days. Despite his lack of shaving, somehow the more rugged looking Master Boyd was even more handsome than before. His sky-colored eyes pieced out from his well-formed skull full of life and madness. I looked at his chest noting his unit and face appeared haggard from many weeks of poor diet. We had not eaten in days.

My Master's dark brown hair was greasy and standing up on end. His sharp cheeks were bruised up from his fight with the city cop bullies. He had a dark healing cut on his forehead also from that brawl. I had helped him wrap up his busted knuckles in a ripped-up shirt. Due to continued fighting with me he kept re-opening the wounds. The blackish blood had seeped through it several times making his hands appear gory.

I looked in the mirror to see that as a perfect match to my Master, I was thin, dirty, hollow cheeked and my wig desperately needed a bath. I sighed realizing we both looked like a couple of street schizophrenics; dirty, unkempt, and beaten to shit. My own light blue irises reflected the insanity that was slowly taking me hostage from within.

We were approaching the town of Pace, a small town with a few red lights, and several businesses scattered about. My Master shot me a look as he turned on his blinker and took the first right turn available. We both gasped when the red car took the same turn. He looked at me appearing very afraid.

"Fuck, they found us." He turned the car abruptly making a sudden left.

The red car also took the left. My Master was now pouring sweat in terror and even I was starting to become afraid. I assumed my Master was just being paranoid, but I couldn't deny this red vehicle was trailing our every move.

"Calm down, Master. Go back to the main road. We can outrun them." I barely was able to breath out.

He was panting. "Yeah, okay we can outrun the, wait, we should maybe kill them. They may tell the others?" He looked at me his eyes glowing with terror.

I gulped. "Uhm, if that is what you think is best. Did you bring a shovel from the camp? If we kill one or two of them, 'they' will really send an army won't 'they?'" I looked back at the couple still giggling behind our car.

Master Boyd nodded. "I am sure they will. Shit, just shit. I don't have my gun. Are 'they' very strong do you think? What if they have guns," stammered out my Master now definitely terrified.

"I don't know. God damn it. Why are you asking me? Who the fuck is running this programing? Simon, help. We can't discover our location." I suddenly felt very scared, unable to figure out my location. What is happening?

He looked at me in a panic. "Calm down, Niemand. We will outrun them. No killing unless we must. Breath baby. It is going to be okay. I won't let them get you or me. Fuck them."

Master Boyd pulled back onto the main road and the red car went around us taking the inside lane on the four laned main drag through town. They pulled up next to us just in time to have to stop for a red light at the intersection.

Master Boyd rolled down his window. "Fuck off. Stop following us assholes. I am not scared of you. You are not going to take her from me. I will kill you first," he screamed at the couple.

The woman sitting in the passenger's side looked at my Master appearing afraid. She locked her door and looked at her male driver. She was avoiding eye contact with my Master who was still screaming obscenities at the car, threatening them if they dared to bother us any further.

When the light turned green the red car speed off at a high rate trying like hell to get as far from us as possible. My Master didn't give chase but just sat there fuming, mumbling and cursing under his breath about 'they.' Finally alone we traveled through Pace on the road back home once more.

I felt very strange. My speech was slow and slurred, and I continued to feel the need to rock my head and wring my hands. My Master finally noticed my agitation.

"What is wrong baby? Does your head hurt too?" He rubbed his forehead again and blinked his eyes hard as if trying to clear his sight.

I nodded still rocking. "Do you hear the radio waves? I like this song, but they play it all the time. Someday, maybe they will change the channel. Do you think they could change the channel?" I watched the transmissions begin to light up the fields all around us.

Master Boyd chuckled. "They never change the channel. I know what song you mean. I hate that one. Do you think maybe when we get home, we can find something to plug up our ears? I am tired of listening to God. He won't shut up. It is getting old."

"Yes, we can use the ripped up shirt and tape. I could use a break from Looper. I told him we are on vacation. He won't listen to me. Simon says Looper doesn't believe in vacations. Did we remember to put the turkey in the refrigerator?" I sighed feeling very fatigued as I continued to rock and wring.

Master Boyd looked surprised. "Well he and Bastard can just go play cards. We are on vacation. They can put that fucking turkey in the fridge for us. Tell them both to do so, that is a directive." He rubbed his head again then ran his hand through his hair appearing to become as agitated as I felt.

We managed to sneak back into our hiding spot without any further incident. Neither of us had any idea the entire police squad was out looking for us. Master Boyd and I had mistakenly assumed we were like any normal and could just take off on vacation whenever not working.

However, we were and are not normals. Despite our delusion that we did not have schizophrenia, and didn't need anyone's guidance, attendance nor observation. We were dead wrong. By late Tuesday night Dennis and Randall were fearing the worst. A search of Master Boyd's home done by the old bulls had indicated that my Master had been slowly slipping off the deep end for at least the last two months.

Besides the obvious symbols and codes taped to the walls, they found all his food in the ditch, letters he had written to Maddy, and lists of numbers written on the walls inside the shed. Master Boyd was notorious for getting obsessed with lists, letter writing and numbers. It was no longer doubted that this psychotic episode was the dreaded deep drop into insanity that Dennis had feared for many years.

Dennis was also very aware that neither of us had thought to bring our medication wherever we had fled to. Without that both of his schizophrenic wards would encounter probable and potentially life threatening seizures along with the 're-bound' effect of stopping the deadly shit suddenly. He had become frantic to find us, praying he could do it before Thursday morning when the Thorazine would have cleared our bloodstreams. If he couldn't, then both Master Boyd and I were going to be in for one hell of a psychotic surprise.

QUICK NOTE: *If you recall this re-bound effect has happened to me several times. One of the easiest to recall was the day I punched out Master Julie's teeth, and the day I saw the church windows bleed into the sky with Stephanie. Both incidences were caused by suddenly stopping my medication. Master Boyd and I have been on the meds now for many years. When we suddenly stopped taking the medicines our rebound effect would go like this: Whatever phase of the cycle we were in when the Thorazine left our blood stream in three days would be strengthened violently to the worst degree. We would become extremely dangerous while our brain chemistry struggled to re-boot without the aid of the powerful sedating antipsychotic.*

We left the Boswell gifts in the car and headed for the tent. Master Boyd and I were both feeling very irritated. The medication was starting to wear thin in our systems. The DT's had begun, and the misfiring of our neural pathways was starting to grow in strength. I found myself stretching and yawning unable to stop moving. I paced and wrung my hands. A powerful headache started to radiate from the back of my skull making it feel like it weighed a thousand pounds.

I looked over to see that my Master had also started to pace and wring his hands while rubbing his head. He was feeling the need to keep moving too. The rebound effect was already starting two days early. It is likely that is because both he and I had been taking our medication steady for more than five years. Any drop in the high levels would have been felt rapidly and viciously. Boy were we feeling it. *We were demonstrating a symptom called Akathisia. This is a movement disorder characterized by a feeling of inner restlessness and inability to stay still.*

We paced, yawned, stretched and even began to stomp wildly. I did my best to wear out the unit while my Master did the same. We shot frightened looks while we wandered past the other. It was a very helpless sensation knowing there was nothing we could do to help our partner.

The late afternoon passed into dusk then darkness and still he and I were trapped in our Akathisia hell. I could hear the panic in my Master's voice as he told Bastard he couldn't take much more of the nightmarish need to keep moving.

"God, make it stop. What is going on? Why won't it stop," he yelled out to Bastard.

I winced looking at my own Simon who was sitting watching in silence. He had been through so many of these episodes with me. I was very experienced at suffering. My Master had never encountered the true power of his disease before. The symptoms of it were starting to get to him. I saw Simon look up at me with worry in his eyes.

"Psycho, he is about to flip out. You had better do something," Simon yelled out.

I turned to looked at Master Boyd who to my horror was now run pacing. Uh oh, that is not good.

"Master, don't," I yelled to my now terribly upset Master.

Master Boyd flashed me a look. "Make it stop. I can't make it stop." He took off running headlong into a tree with his head knocking him backward onto his ass in a daze.

I rushed toward the now injured Master Boyd. He was sitting there stunned with blood pouring from his forehead. His staring vacant gaze indicating he was near unconsciousness from the blow. I bent down to cradle his head and lay him back just as the Grand Mal seizure onset. His eyes rolled back into his head as his unit began to tremble wildly. I grabbed a stick and shoved it into his mouth while the quake ripped through him sending him into the void of nothingness.

Several seconds passed before he was completely still. I removed the stick from his mouth and checked to make sure he could breathe okay. I waited for ten minutes but my Master didn't regain consciousness. Feeling worried I put my ear to him as I listened to his chest. I sighed grateful to hear his heart was beating slowly.

I laid his bleeding head onto my lap while I began crying silently. I still felt the terror within demanding that I get up and move, but I fought the urge. My Master was in trouble. I needed to attend him, but I couldn't focus enough to figure out what to do.

Simon walked over and sat next to us. "He is going to sleep for hours, Psycho. You need to stop that bleeding and clean the wound." He pointed to my Master's forehead.

I nodded. "Okay, yes you are right. He is sleeping. Master Boyd is tired is all." I sniffed back my tears while gently moving his mangled head of my lap so I could get the water and a rag for his injury.

Simon looked at my unconscious Master appearing sad. "Psycho, this is from the medication. He will get worse and so will you. You must call Dennis or Linda. We need help. All of us. He could die. We could too."

I shook my head as I brought back the water and a section of an old shirt then began my nursing of his gaping cut. "No, I will not betray my Master. He thinks they are his friends. They are not. We are not going to turn this poor schizophrenic over to the normals Simon. Remember what they did to us when they thought we had that disease? Well Master Boyd does have it. They will fry his brains out. This is all your fault anyway. We cannot love a mentally ill person. We are normal and he is not. He will hurt us on accident. We can never understand him; he is too crazy for that. Now he loves us, his heart will be broken. You fucked up." I cleaned off the blood and applied pressure fighting a fresh wave of urges to pace.

Simon's eyes went wide. "Oh my God. I thought we solved this problem ages ago. You are a pack of dumbasses. How can all of you sit there calling his kettle black, Psycho? We are also schizophrenic stupid. Why else would we take the fucking medications? What is that drool pouring out? Hmmm?" Simon pointed as the drool began to run down my chin from my throat shut down.

I shook my head. "Noooo. Shatop. I'm…I'm…I'm…shhhhhit," I slurred out.

268

I went wide eyed staring at Simon's smug smile. I stood up helpless as the sky opened and thunder rolled along the ground almost sending me face first onto it. I threw out my arms to keep from falling only to be trapped in the position. Simon paced around me snickering as the tremors began in my legs.

"Buh Bye Psycho. Your turn. See you both on the grid, schizophrenic idiots," he whispered into my ear.

I tried to turn my head to say something as the lightening cracked through my forehead sending me almost backward. My spin popped as it was forced into an unnatural inversion. My eyes rolled back from the agony. My bladder released as the partial seizure ripped through my shattered brains causing malfunctioning and loss of consciousness.

A full twenty to thirty minutes passed while I stood there unable to move trapped in a C position while complex seizures raged on inside my mind. When at last I was finally released I collapsed next to Master Boyd falling into a deep trance unable to move.

If you had been a forest animal or a curious woodland dweller, you would have seen one crazy sight in that clearing that early night. Two schizophrenic fools laying side by side. One on his back with a bleeding forehead from head banging himself into dipshit status. Next to him his mate on her side, staring unblinking in a catatonic trance. Both laying in their own blood and urine, unable to understand the extremely dangerous situation they had put themselves into by trying to be something they were not normal.

When Wednesday morning arrived Master Boyd stirred first. I could see him but not respond. He sat up moaning. He almost fell back when the dizzy spell from his obvious concussion hit him. My Master shook his head then reached up and felt his gashed forehead wincing from the pain. It was then he noticed my staring unit next to him.

He let out a yelp of terror. "No, she's dead." He grabbed me rolling me onto my back putting his ear to my chest.

I felt the numbness start to wear off as I gurgled out, "He..he..lp."

My Master jumped up and grabbed the water jug from where I had left it when trying to clean him up. He immediately began to pour the water on my head. The shock of the cold water felt like electricity flowing through my veins. I lot out a scream and immediately began to jerk and seizure all over. The terrible pain filled my every part as my Dopamine starved brain finally was bathed in the chemical. My Master moved quickly to pin my arms and legs with his weight to keep me from harming myself as my muscles returned to my control.

NOTE: *Dopamine deprived brains will cause catatonic stupor. If you don't have enough of it you cannot move but will be conscious. When you suddenly gets it after much time has passed it hurts like hell. The pain is the return of the hormone being forced into the nerves and muscles so you can move again. It feels like your dead, stone-like flesh is returning to life, because it is (shuddering).*

Sometimes a sudden shock of any kind will cause the hormone Dopamine to be released (like cold water or ice in the face), sometimes it takes a lot of medication like lorazepam, and sometimes it takes ECT to stimulate the release. All bad stuff no matter which way you go.

My arms and legs began to calm. I looked into my Master's worried face. His forehead was cut deeply and a stitch or two would have been helpful. His thickening beard and dirty hair was covered in leaves and dirt. He no longer looked like the clean-cut, handsome, shy police officer I had known for years. This Master Boyd couldn't even be recognized as being the same man. He now had evolved into the rough, unrefined, wild-eyed psychotic he truly is.

"I am okay now Master. Please mercy, let me up," I said feeling parched and weak.

He nodded. "Niemand, what happened? Did we get into a fight again? My head is killing me and I can hear God so loud. He is driving me nuts. I hear music and other people, but I don't see anyone. What is happening?" He let me go sitting back down appearing very confused as he realized he had pissed himself.

I got up slowly. "You had a seizure, Master. I had several. We should be okay for now. We need our medication. You are hearing voices because you are off your medications. It is going to get worse. I don't know how long that data will go into the turkey, uhm, what? Wait, uhm, huh?" I began to hit my head with the palm of my hand trying to get the right words to come out.

271

My Master raised an eyebrow. "Seizures? Oh shit. Really?" He started to giggle uncontrollably at that, appearing upset by his inability to stop laughing.

"Christ, make it stop. Shut up. Shut the fuck up. Make it shut up," he covered his ears still laughing like a hyena.

I narrowed my eyes then stood stomping three times as I bowed to him over and over unable to stop my repetitive movements. My head rocked and my eyes kept rolling back into my head as my own Looper began to chatter like the sounds of a thousand cicada. I too covered my ears yelling for everyone to shut the fuck up.

Master Boyd sat there grinding his hands into the sides of his head rocking and yelling for it to stop while I danced and twirled also covering my ears begging for it to end. Our rebound was now in full force. A monster episode engulfed us both that morning. For hours we suffered the assault of complete sensory melt-down without any mercy granted to either of us.

QUICK NOTE: *We shared similar behaviors at the same time due to the exact same dosage of medication and same day of discontinuing it. Lack of proper food and water had hastened our date with the horrors of full-bore acute cycle nightmares.*

Had anyone been around in those morning hours and offered us a white cell, strait jacket and a shot of nasty antipsychotics, we would have taken it. It was that bad. Both of us were made bitches to the most horrendous parts of our disease. I had been through a few of these holy motherfucking shit moments in my eleven years struggling to get control of my symptoms.

Master Boyd, however, had never dealt with the horrific hallucinations, cognitive malfunctions, and motor misfires at such a hellish level before. He was beyond freaking out, terrified beyond all reason. I had to stop him several times from banging his head to a bloody pulp into the trees around the campsite while he tried to make the voices stop taunting him.

"They are not real Master. Don't listen to them. They lie." I grabbed him around the waist trying to stop my raging Dominant before he smacked his head into the tree for the second time.

"Yes, they are. I can hear them. Make them stop. Christ, fucking make them shut up. Help. Someone fucking help. Can you hear them? They are everywhere." He looked around at the forest then the sky trying to see the faces of those who were making fun of him.

I looked around too. "Yes, I hear them Master. They are liars. Do you hear me, you motherfuckers. You lie," I yelled out while laughing and twirling.

He grabbed the sides of his head. "No, make it stop. Please help. I didn't do that. Why are you saying that? Stop fucking laughing. Shut up. Fucking shut up. Please rip out my ears, Niemand. Make them stop." He fell to his knees drooling and crying while trying again to cover his ears to stop the noise.

I looked at him swaying and wailing. Pity washed over me for his situation while the band the Police played their songs in a loop. All around us were the clamor of those who hated us and wanted us dead. I could hear them talking over each other. Insulting, hateful, cruel and truthful. I winced as they reminded me that I am a loser and so is Master Boyd.

I walked to his struggling unit and sat down outstretching my legs. I grabbed him around the waist pulling him into me as if I were a chair.

He flinched. "Don't touch me, it burns." He tried to get away, but I held his waist tightly.

"It will pass. Let me help you Master. Lay back, let me help." I felt him relax and lean back still holding his head, drooling and crying.

I covered his ears with my own hands. "Now open your mouth Master and keep it open. Don't close it. The voices will calm. Do what I say and find relief."

Master Boyd moaned out sobbing, "It won't stop." He tensed up again.

I put pressure on his head. "Open your mouth, it will stop," I said soothingly then opened my own wide.

My Master opened his mouth allowing the drool to pour freely. He continued to cry quietly but calmed down as his auditory hallucinations began to soften. He stopped yelling out at his imaginary bullies and eventually his ragged breathing became smooth and even. I sat behind him also finding some solace from my own torment. We didn't move for most of the morning trapped sitting there with our mouths open like that. It was truly some of the worst hours of either of our lives, and I have had quite a few of those. So, trust me when I say this was bad.

QUICK NOTE: *When a schizophrenic hears voices, they can make the voices cool down a bit by opening their mouth and covering their ears as you see me doing here. It doesn't always work, and sometimes it only helps a little. However, that day it helped both of us a lot. The trouble is you cannot close your mouth for even a second or it will start again. Watch the homeless mentally ill one day when you are out and about. You will notice some of them walk around with their mouths slightly or fully open. Now you know why.*

Finally, around noonish based upon the location of my brother the sun, I tried closing my mouth. The Looper had calmed to his usual dull roar. I sighed deciding I would have to keep my mouth slightly ajar for likely many days thanks to this episode.

"Master, I think the episode has passed. Try closing your mouth to just a slight open and see if you can tolerate them." I said while removing my hands.

He reached out appearing suddenly frightened trying to put my hands back on his ears. "No. I can't take that anymore. Please I want it to stop."

I pulled away from his grip. "Master, we can't sit here forever like this. We need water. We will die if we don't drink something." My throat was sore from yelling, drooling and lack of liquid.

Master Boyd nodded. "Okay, okay, you are right. It is better but I still hear God and the others though they are not as loud, buy they are still there." He sat up looking around worried with his mouth half open still drooling heavily.

I tried to smile but found my face was frozen in a grimace. "I will get the water Master. Can you stand up?"

He nodded. "Yes, my head hurts so bad."

I chuckled without affect. "Mine too, but that is what head banging gets us." I stood up dragging my heavy limbs to retrieve our precious water jug.

When I returned, we both drank from it almost draining the entire gallon. We both had to piss terribly, and both of us smelled like a urinal and blood. He and I aided each other in our calls to nature due to the stiffness of our long moments in stillness for the last twelve horrific hours. The worst of the episodes had passed for now. I warned him that more would come in time. That information appeared to scare him a great deal.

"Will the medication stop this?" He looked at the ground unable to make eye contact.

I nodded. "It would help Master. We need the medication. We have to go home to get that."

Master Boyd winced. "Okay then we will go home right after the dance tonight. We can finish our vacation at the house. Doesn't matter where we are long as we are together right?" He pulled me into a long kiss with him.

I felt my drives suddenly kick in. The medication had always kept a hamper on just how interested I could ever be in carnal congress. My monster sexual appetite has always managed to overshoot the nasty side effects of the sedating Thorazine. Now that the governor was off, my urges for Master Boyd were starting to look very inviting indeed.

My Master apparently also noticed his own lustful abilities were enhanced. He began to grope and paw at my befouled clothing pushing me backward trying to lay me on the ground.

I initially resisted his attempts, but he became frantic finally using his strength to subdue me to my back unable to contain his need for coupling. I didn't fight him as he feverously removed my clothing and his own forcing himself between my legs mounting with a sheer wildness in his eyes. He engaged me in deep kissing while he entered me and began his thrusting with fervor. The intensity of the sensation made me cry out while he moaned in absolute pleasure.

Neither of us had engaged in sex, well with a male for me, while free of the numbing medication before. I began to orgasm almost immediately. I yelled out in extasy while he groaned in pure thrill. His own climax came quickly as I began a second series of my own. He fell forward panting and groping my breasts. My Master stared into my eyes smiling while he enjoyed the feeling of my responding vaginal walls as they griped his spent manhood.

"That was what our life would be like without medication." He gasped out appearing pleasantly surprised.

I moaned out as the last of my pleasure spasms hit my unit. "Ah yeah Master, and voices, headbanging, is it worth it?" I closed my eyes momentarily while enjoying the only good moments of that horrid day as much as I could.

Master Boyd kissed me. "That is a tough question to answer. Being with you like this, knowing you like this, it would be worth any kind of hell. I didn't know it could even be like this." He looked sad as he stroked my face.

I grabbed his wrist watching him flinch from the shock of my touch. "It can't be like this ever again. We have to take the medication Master or they will make us go away. You know what they do in the hospitals."

My Master looked at me suddenly fearful. "The hospital? You think they would put us in there because we are off medication?"

I nodded. "Yes, they will make us take blood tests. It doesn't matter that I don't have the disease. If the test says I didn't take it they could send me back. You know it, you are my Guardian."

Master Boyd looked confused. "Yes, I did know that. Somehow I forgot it. Why would I forget that?"

I looked at him harshly. "Because you don't have to answer to one that is why. They make me. I got into trouble being stupid and young. Now I am ruined for life and they can tell lies about me having schizophrenia when I clearly am not sick."

Master Boyd winced. "Niemand, I do have to answer to one. Dennis and Carla are my court appointed Guardians. They can lock me up whenever they want."

I sat up as Master Boyd disengaged feeling suddenly very afraid. "What? Oh no, Master. If Dennis wants to break us up he can. What will we do if he says you have to stop being my Master?"

He looked at the ground taking up his foul clothing. "I will die before I let him break us up. He knows that. That is why he can't ever know I fucked up and took your collar. Then he would make me give you up. I must marry you, then he can't stop us. Don't you understand? I love you and want to spend my life with you always. You were made for me by God and I was made for you too. You are my One and Only. It is why I had to ask you to marry me in front of him and why you had to say yes. I didn't think you could ever love me back after I messed up, but I think now you do. Dennis is using your marriage to Timmy as an excuse to keep us apart, baby. I should have told you all this, but you were so angry with me. I just keep messing everything up." He began to sob again.

I got up and hugged him tightly. "It is okay Master. We will figure this out together. We are a D/s couple now, remember? You are going to have to have faith that if this was meant to be, it will be. Now, we must get ready for the dance tonight. Our clothes are ruined. What do we do about that?" I looked at the discarded pile of our befouled outfits.

He stopped crying for a moment still appearing deeply depressed. "We can't go with blood, dirt and piss on us like that. I don't think going naked is an option either."

I giggled at that without affect. "Well let's go home and get a change of clothes and our medication. We still have plenty of time."

Master Boyd shook his head. "The house is bugged and full of poisonous gases. They will be looking for us Niemand. We can't go home."

"We could take backroads, and one of us could cover our face run inside fast grab the stuff real quiet. Then we could sneak back here before they even see us" I said suddenly thinking this was the correct answer.

My Master paused as if in deep thought. "Yeah, we couldn't get a shower or anything but at least our clothes would be clean." He smiled suddenly at the thought.

We got dressed while laughing spontaneously. There was nothing funny, but our emotionality was as mixed up as our thoughts now that the Thorazine was almost spent in our systems. By morning our blood streams would be completely free of it, and so would the suppression of the symptoms of our disease.

Master Boyd took every single unknown backroad and logging trail possible to get back to our house. It took a full thirty minutes to go what usually took ten thanks to our bobbing and weaving through the wooded landscapes. Finally, his black car popped out of a little-known side road onto the road in front of the house. He pulled into the driveway. He took off his shirt and I wrapped it around my face ready to make my wild dash into the deadly space to grab our things.

We had argued over who would go inside to take the risk. My Master wanted to be the one to run through the fumes. I won the right to go inside by reminding him he was the getaway driver. If he was dizzy from poison, and by accident they saw us, we would be doomed. He begrudgingly gave in to my good advice on that decision.

He smiled as I gave him a thumbs up. He kept the car running while I ran into the house like the devil was chasing me. I went to his closet gathering fresh clothing for my Master. I picked my favorite outfit for him and grabbed fresh ones for myself as well. I cradled the entire wad and headed rapidly to the kitchen.

To my horror our medication was not where we had left it. I ran back to his bathroom, then did a quick search of the house. None of our medication was anywhere to be found. Panic filled me as I realized someone had stolen it.

I saw the static coming through the kitchen while I stood in the living room trying to decide what to do. The fear of the encroaching fumes filled me forcing me to run back to the car and my Master without our item of desperation.

Master Boyd took off back the way we came without even asking the second I got into the car. He didn't put back on his shirt either. We were safely hidden on an abandoned logging tail when he looked at me appearing to take his first breath in relief.

"Well, let's take the medication now, so we can feel better right away." He looked at me still holding our change in outfits on my lap.

I looked at the floorboard. "It was gone Master; they took our medications."

He gasped. "What? What do you mean they took them?" He appeared confused.

I shook my head about ready to cry "I mean they stole them. I looked everywhere. They mean for us to go to the hospital. You were right. They are trying to get us. They took away our medication. We must go to them or go mad. We are trapped. They even stole the fucking turkey. What are we going to do Master. They are going to get us for sure."

Master Boyd shook his head appearing upset. "I won't let them get us baby. We don't have schizophrenia. We never needed the medications. They fooled us and got us addicted to that nasty drug. What is happening is we are DTing. It is just the Detox is all, like all druggies you know? We needed to kick the habit. We can get through it together. In a couple of weeks, we will be okay. I have seen people kick drug habits before. We don't need it so we are going cold turkey. That is a directive."

I looked up shocked. "Master, they took the turkey. I told you that you are right. We are addicted to drugs. Just a couple of dirty drug addicts is what we are. We deserve whatever we get. We are stupid. That will teach us to use drugs. Simon needs to stop drinking and smoking too. Tell Bastard to stop taking him to bars all night. Ugh. I didn't even realize what a true pig I have been. I used to know better but I got stupid. It was the poison from the damned food. It fucked with my head you know," I babbled out.

Master Boyd nodded. "Yeah, druggies. I fell for that shit too baby. Anyone can fall for it. Look we will just quit now that we know. Let this be a lesson to all drug addicts. If I ever listen to them again then kill me. That is a directive. Hey, did you say you got a turkey?"

I looked at him confused. "No Master. You forgot to put it into the fridge. It went bad. Wait, did we forget something? Is there something we should know," I said now feeling very lost.

My Master smiled then giggled. "You said you would quit smoking and drinking if I feed the turkey and fix the refrigerator, didn't you?"

I giggled then hit my forehead. "Master, I think my brain tumor is growing back. It seems that the tapestry is very sticky today. Did you solve for X? I need that equation soon. There is a timeline on that fucking shit you know," I yelled now irritated he had not solved our problems yet.

His eyes went wide. "Yes, I did solve it. X is squared so that means it is equal to service for service. It is all in the electrical grid. Do you see that? Look at the sky. It is split down the middle. It is a storm, Niemand. We are going to get wet when that rain comes. Can you hear the thunder? It is the thumping, hear it?"

I investigated the sky and saw the world open. Master Boyd pulled off into a field while we got out to stare at the oncoming tempest. We stripped down and put on our fresh clothing. Throwing the dirty ones on the ground keeping a baleful eye on the world above us. We both could hear the thunder rumbling in the distance shaking the earth beneath our boots.

Master Boyd pulled me close while he and I winced at the shocking sensation of the others touch. "I am afraid, Niemand. What is happening to us? I can't seem to remember anything. It is like my mind is not right. Something is wrong, but I don't know what it is. Everything is mixed up. Why can I taste the ground and hear the colors? Was it always like this? Didn't something happen before this," he mumbled into my ear.

I shook my head "I don't know Master. I don't know what is wrong. Something about the program. Is it something electrical or is someone after us?"

He kissed me and I could feel him trembling in terror. "They won't separate us. I won't let them. Stay with me forever, that is a directive."

I nodded. "As you wish Master. We have a dance, don't we? You promised to dance with me."

Master Boyd nodded then took me by my hand back to the car. We got inside and took the back road that led right to the Boswell encampment. That poor troupe of Gypsy people had no idea they had invited two Moolo's to join them for dinner and dancing. I am sure that wherever they are today they still tell this story by their campfires on dark, scary night.

THE SCHZIOPHRENIC COURTSHIP DANCE OF THE GYPSIES

We pulled up and parked behind the Boswell's camp with the troupe members various vehicles. Master Boyd grabbed the bag of gifts for the family while we both got out and began walking toward the tents, and camper trailers. Shady was by the fire and saw us immediately. He walked out carrying his shot gun but lowered it when he recognized Master Boyd and the Dinler Psycho.

He smiled. "Ah, you did come. Momma will be so happy to see both of you. Come, come. Everyone is making ready now." He reached out to shake Master Boyd's hand, but my Master backed away looking nervous.

Shady looked at me confused and I looked at the ground afraid he was trying to read my mind. Gypsies have magic powers, did you know that? He looked closely at us realizing the cuts, bruises and disheveled appearance almost immediately.

"This is maybe not a good time for you? Maybe another time for dancing? You have changed Boyd. Something is different. Ah yes, the beard. It looks good on you. But this cut on your head is painful no?" He said appearing concerned while he looked our units up and down.

Master Boyd stole a glance at me. "No, it is okay Shady. Niemand and I are okay. We brought gifts for Kenzia and the women folk. A trade, a fair trade." He handed the bag to Shady.

Shady looked inside then smiled with delight. "This is very good Boyd. Kenzia she will want to kiss you with luck. Ah, come then sit by the fire. The night is getting cold. We dance after we eat. Come be with us tonight when the young are courting."

My Master shot me a nervous smile. I smiled back as we followed Shady and took a seat together on a small bench while warming our units from the onset of the cold darkness.

Master Boyd and I sat there both staring in a mild trance. We were helpless to do anything but listen to our voices while Shady excused himself to tell Kenzia of our arrival. He took the bag of fine chocolates, gold coins, brightly colored scarves, and numerous large ornate earrings and necklaces of silver we brought for her and the family. It was Kenzia's job as the phuri dai (leader of the woman and children) to hand out the appropriate portion of our gifts to each female according to their status within the troupe.

QUICK NOTE: *In the Romani tradition making a display of great wealth and prosperity is coveted. The* *women will often appear at celebrations and special gathering wearing gold and silver with expensive scarves and dresses made of fine material to denote her status. It is very proper manners to share your wealth with the entire family. Master Boyd and I had spared no expense to make sure to show great respect and honor by doing just that. Food, flowers and gold or silver colored jewelry is the kind of gifts one brings when visiting any camp or home of a Romani. We had spent a minor fortune to make sure every Boswell woman and girl would get her piece of our wealth to show off on her unit that night.*

Kenzia was thrilled by such an unexpected pleasure. She came out of her trailer to welcome us properly. Shady caught her pointing to us and said something in Romanian to her. She paused looked at him appearing unsure. Then she walked over toward us slowly. She stared at us while we looked lost in our insanity.

Kenzia gasped then spoke to Shady in her language. He nodded then sat down across from us tending the fire while she walked in front of us smiling kindly.

"Yes, you are dinilo. Boyd this is so? This we know already of this one, but you are dinilo too," Kenzia said softly.

He looked at her still trancing but nodded his head. I didn't need a translator to know that word meant crazy or mentally ill. I could see in Kenzia's eyes she recognized our state of deteriorating sanity. She was not a dinler (means fool by the way). She nodded back and sighed.

"The people believe that God touches some with special gifts, eh? You both have this second sight, no? This is okay. No one will be cruel to you here. I am surprised that the Moolo is your woman Boyd. You never say so before, but you maybe get dinilo because you love one so cursed eh?" She smiled with a bit of pity on her face.

Neither me nor my Master responded to her statement. I felt Master Boyd grip my hand tighter as she spoke. It was as if he feared her words would somehow tear us apart. He had nothing to fear there. I had no intentions of going anywhere. I wanted to dance with the Gypsies. It was my psychotic dream come true. I did wish I felt more clear headed, but I wouldn't have missed that chance had I been on my deathbed.

I did realize she had just told Master Boyd his sickness was because he loved me. Kenzia was right in a way. Had he never loved me so much and collared me, then he would have never tried to help me. The stress of losing me to my disease and threat of being forced to give me up may have been enough stress to cause such a deep break during his cycle. The truth is there is no way to ever know for sure. Unless you take the word of an old gypsy woman.

The catatonic trance was starting to clear as Kenzia sat down next to us and the rest of the family began to straggle out of their campers and tents. Master Boyd stole a glance at me and shot a nervous smile. I scooted closer to him and laid my head on his shoulder. I felt both of us flinch at the shock of it. It is still interesting to me just how willingly we ignored the tactile hallucination of shocking touch when it came to each other. Anyone else tried to even brush up against us, it was full on war.

The troupe had roasted a pig and some chickens. Master Boyd and I both took our portion of the chicken and ate it ravenously with our fingers. We had decided the Boswells were not in on the plot, so their food was safe to consume. It was a good thing we decided to stop by. Neither of us likely would have made it much longer without something to eat.

When Kenzia saw our obvious hunger she ordered Shady to bring us both a second plate. We didn't argue as we ate that one as voraciously as the first. She sat there smiling with pride to see that we trusted her and her family so much.

NOTE: *It is very common for schizophrenics to be naturally suspicious and distrustful. Often they will refuse to eat due to delusions of poisoning or tampering of the food stuffs. If you can get a schizo to eat for you, especially when in the prodromal or acute cycles, you have their full trust and respect. That means they have overcome hallucinations and delusions that warn the you are out to get them, hurt them or even kill them.*

Kenzia had apparently dealt with our kind before, the gypsies did wander the country and realized we would eat for her. To repay us the honor we had shown her own family, she made sure we were fed to capacity likely understanding we would starve to death otherwise.

It was a kindness I have never forgotten to this day. The poor family was happy to feed my Master and me sharing all they had without complaint, including risking one or both of us potentially being dangerous. No one there that night showed us anything less than complete human dignity and respect. Master Boyd had been right. In that camp we were just like everyone else. I can't say either he or I ever were ever treated that fairly among the Ganjos of our own town.

After eating, the fiddlers began to play and the young girls of marrying age got up to dance seductively trying to catch the eye of a potential young mate. Master Boyd and I smiled at each other as we watched the young ladies undulate, swivel and shoot moon eyes at the one she hoped would be her One and Only. The males then got up and did a stomping clapping dance trying to demonstrate their strength to the swooning girls.

The whole scene was colorful, beautiful and amazing to behold. The girls in the bright colored dresses with dozens of gold coins appeared to move as if they had no bones, and the males radiated out power with each stomp. It was hypnotic to watch. Master Boyd too seemed caught in the pulling of the fire, the hues, the rhythms. I could feel his hand tense as the courtship dancing ended and the married couples took off to join the youngsters swaying to the sounds of fiddles and spoons.

I felt the grid calling to me but this time I would not be happy with Simon as my partner. "Master, you said you would dance with me. God will forgive you. I want to join with you in the tapestry as we do in our units," I whispered in his ear.

He closed his eyes appearing very seduced. "I can't say no to you. It is calling me too. I can hear it. I am under a spell."

I nodded as I took his hand and led him away from the other dancers far from the offensive light of the campfire. I took his hand as he pulled me to him. We kissed deeply then began to spin, twirl and stomp around each other never missing a single step, nor letting each other go. Master Boyd could dance like the schizophrenic he was and is.

He said he never danced because God didn't permit him to do it. The reality was Dennis wouldn't allow it. Master Boyd was like me. He only dances when he is acute. Dennis feared him dancing or talking to God. So, Master Boyd always said he did neither, but in secret he did both. To my joy, he knew every step of the schizophrenic trance dance by heart. He turned out to be a beautifully matched partner.

Our psychotic symptom of rhythmic movements in unison almost appeared practiced and choreographed. The Boswells watched us engage in our illness with awe. Not many are witness to such a scene, as often our kind don't dare to pair up with each other. Song after song played on through the night as he and I continued our 'tango of the touched,' appearing to never tire.

The Boswells were enjoying our display of adoration for each other when suddenly a police car pulled up from the other side of the encampment. The locals had seen the fire raging into the night and heard the heathen fiddles play.

Dennis and Linda were called by Cathy to go and ask the troupe to call it a night. The town folk could only sleep better knowing the devil was no longer being hailed by that demonic music. They were all sure that is what was going on at the party on the hill with the Gypsies.

Shady motioned for the players to put down their bows while he attended the party crashing cops. When the sounds stopped Master Boyd and I were freed from our trance. He pulled me close kissing me with passion, panting and sweating from our marathon of madness. I felt my unit melt into his with wantonness.

Neither of us feared the police showing up. Why should we? We were adults on vacation and this was just a dance. There was no reason to panic or run.

Dennis and Linda were politely speaking with Shady and Kenzia about the noise complaint when Linda suddenly spotted the two Ganjos kissing just beyond the light of the fire. I heard a commotion from the troupe but ignored the noise as my Master's interest pushed into my belly promising a pleasurable moment was soon to follow. I had no plans to tell him no this time. In fact, I could assure him he would hear yes being screamed out at him more than once very shortly.

"Psycho? Boyd? Holy shit. Dennis, come here, I found them," Linda yelled out.

Her yell snapped both of us out of our lustful enchantment. My Master and I looked over to see the two police officers rushing toward us. In terror, Master Boyd grabbed my wrist and took off running with me hauled behind him to his car. We jumped inside as Linda and Dennis still on foot tried to stop us by yelling out our names.

Master Boyd backed out then spinning tires sped from the scenes full of terror and adrenaline at the very sight of the cops coming at us. I could barely breath as he tore down the hill at breakneck speed nearly running off the road several times in a blind panic. I looked behind us absolutely sure they would somehow run faster than my Master's car and haul us both away in chains before you could say how do you do.

Master Boyd flew down the back-road head back to our secret campsite still gasping for air near hyperventilation himself while I clutched my irregularly beating heart trying to convince myself we had gotten away somehow.

We made it back to our clearing in the woods without being spotted. My Master parked the car behind the bushes. We sat there in the dark cab breathing heavily while listening for what seemed like hours. Neither of us dared to say a word. Every sound made us almost jump out of our skin suits. I suppose we expected a sudden whirl of blue lights and loudspeakers with helicopters any moment no doubt.

Finally, my Master looked at me, "They almost got us Niemand. That was too close for comfort."

I nodded in the darkness. "Yeah, we had better not go back there again. They will expect us to come back I bet."

Master Boyd let out his breath appearing relieved. "I would be okay with staying here with you forever. I don't want to ever see anyone else. I could be happy here. Would you be happy?" He reached out and took my left hand.

I smiled. "Master, I never wanted to leave Darlin. They had to drag me out in chains. I only ever wanted to be left alone with Simon and maybe Zeppelin and Seine. Then you came. I would be happy if you were with us too. Bastard can keep Simon busy."

He chuckled. "You know what? I don't like Dennis always telling me what I can and can't do. I got to dance with you. He told me not to do that because it makes me sick. You don't tell me not to talk to Bastard or God either. You love me for me. You never treat me like a child. You stand up to me when I am an asshole and love me when I am weak. You even forgave me for the awful things I did and made me pay it back. You have always been fair with me. You don't threaten to send me to a hospital every time I fuck up. I want that kind of world. Let's stay here forever. That is a directive."

I giggled. "As you wish Master. Anything else?"

He pulled me into a passionate kiss. "Yes. I want you to dance with me, then make love to me like there is no tomorrow. That is a directive."

"I am happy to follow those directives Master but what about our drug habit? Won't the DTs come again soon? The script is running long. It could cause another shut down of the programming," I said feeling the urge to rut with my

Master almost overwhelming my ability to stop myself as he began to paw at my clothing.

He moaned out as he began to push back his seat then grab my unit to turn me around for his canal advance. "They won't find us here. We are safe to detox without interference. We can never go back there now. They will just make us liars and druggies again. They are bad for us. We will stay here until the earth stops and the stars fall."

He then made love to me in the front seats so magnificently I was convinced staying there with him forever was the right thing to do.

Back in Wheatly, our sudden appearance, actually our disheveled appearance, had startled both Linda and Dennis deeply. We had not appeared to recognize the pair, and we didn't due to our deep acute phase psychosis, and ran from them as if they were monsters. Dennis could no longer lie to himself. Master Boyd, his ward and responsibility, was obviously not being held hostage by his schizophrenic fiancé. The two stunned officers spoke with the Boswells who informed them of our very disturbed state, failing health (thin, hungry), and signs of severe self-injury.

Linda was confused by my Master's behavior as reported to her and by what she saw. Dennis had no choice but to fess up to my long-time friend and Goddess that my Master was afflicted by the same demon as me. She would tell me later you could have knocked her over with a feather she was so shocked to hear the truth. I will tell you all what she said in another book so let's leave this here for now.

After the initial 'holy shit creepy Boyd is a schizophrenic' wore off, she realized with great terror what this new information meant. Not only was her High Priestess in grave danger of being killed by the extreme expression of my disease, as tended to happen every so often for over eleven years now, but now there was the added terror of her co-worker and cop buddy Boyd joining her in the Summerlands. With two dangerous and violent schizophrenics running together unleashed and in full acute cycle, the chances of death (by cop, suicide, homicide from each other, starvation, exposure, or accident) of one or both of us had raised to almost certainty if not found very soon.

Linda, Dennis, and Randall made the tough decision to come clean with their fellow officers regarding Master Boyd's secret sickness. We were now suspected of being somewhere near Wheatly or so everyone hoped. The old bulls believed getting the word out to police family only with sworn promises to keep confidentiality if at all possible, would lite fires under asses of the boys in blues to find their ailing brethren before this manhunt ended in tragedy.

A schizophrenic cop murdering his insane fiancé, a towns person, or committing suicide would not look good for their department. Not a single city cop nor county deputy wanted that kind of press in those small towns. Every officer from day to night shift made the oath willingly to keep what they heard and saw with regards to my Master's delicate condition to themselves. Even the trio of bullies Mark, Will and Trenton, who now had to face the shame of having picked on a helpless mentally ill person publicly for years.

While the law dogs began to spread out looking desperately for our hideout, Master Boyd and I danced in the darkness for mother moon. We were caught in a trance of love, delusions, and hallucinations so frightening the world of the real had completely melted away. Our thought disorder had grown so deep we no longer remembered we were cops once. Neither of us could recall that we had people out there that maybe worried about us.

Our memories were scattered and our delusions had taken over. We couldn't figure out who they were. We no longer knew who we were anymore either. If something wasn't done soon, we would eventually get psychotic enough to forget who Master Boyd and Niemand were to each other too.

Uh oh, the shit just got real, didn't it? Schizophrenia is one ugly monster. Me and Master Boyd are in deep shit and worse of all we don't understand it.

Chapter 73: "That's Paranoid Boyd" Part 3
The Fall of Psycho
The Rise of Niemand and Master Boyd

Bet you are all just dying to know how the fuck I survived this latest fubar in my life. Well, the story is as complex as the reasons it happened in the first place. The funny thing about madness is there is no way to predict any real outcome. In the world behind the shattered looking glass the rapist is your lover, the killers are your friends, and your inner self is a drunkard. Nothing is ever really what it appears to be. That Christmas season in 1998 I was facing one of the most dangerous situations I had encountered in many years. I'm lost in the woods, out of own mind, sharing a cell with one more insane than myself, things looked grim. I had always believed I was expendable, unimportant and forgettable. This experience would teach me that everyone matters to someone, even a schizophrenic cemetery kid.

Sixteen days of desperate plight had led to victimizations of schizophrenic blight. To escape this hell, we would have to fight. As our madness raged on day and night. They wanted to separate us but had no right. Hand in hand the D/s couple held on tight. Master Boyd tried with all his might, but we would be prisoners of they by morning's light.

Ready to see what true schizophrenic hell looks like? Ah, sure you are. Nothing wrong with checking out the depths of hell as long as you are only visiting that is. Okay, so grab your napkins in case you want a snack, and don't forget to put that fucking turkey into the fridge. Don't mind those blue and red lights, that is just the sunrise. Bastard and Simon are back from the bars, and Master Boyd and Niemand are out to lunch. Everyone get ready to haul ass. Here THEY come.

"Because you said it was a directive Master. I came to fix all of this. I am here to bust you out. We can run away back to our secret place and live there forever like you said we should. Hurry, the nurses will be back in a minute. They will notice I have slipped out of my restraints."
--Niemand to Master Boyd, January 1999.

"Who the fuck are you. Why do you keep babbling like that? Did you see an old drunk come by here recently? He said I was supposed to meet him here. Hey, do you have something to eat? I am starving," I said to the strange vagabond sitting on the ground writing numbers in the dirt with a stick.

He narrowed his eyes. "Beat it. I am busy. Can't you see this is important? Did you say you had seen something to drink," he growled while looking up from his weird writings.

I sighed. "Why are we here Simon. This is not correct. There is an error in this program. Did you find the answer yet? I am really sick of California. I think we should go home." I looked at Simon who was pacing and wringing his hands.

Simon grimaced. "I can't remember where we are. Our location is lost," he muttered back as he rubbed his head still pacing.

The vagabond looked up at me startled. "Who the fuck are you talking to? Fucking crazy woman. You are crazy. Get the fuck out of here idiot. You are interrupting my work. I need quiet. All of you need to shut the fuck up."

I jumped at his sudden yelling. "Fuck you asshole. You are the crazy one. You had better leave before I call the cops. We don't like your kind around here," I yelled back at him.

The creature stood up growling. "I am happy to leave. Just tell me which way to the nearest expressway and I will make sure to run you over. I used to do long haul trucking, you know. I was the best. Are you saying I wasn't? You don't know. What do you know about anything? Nothing, that is what." He pushed me out of his way then walked back to the tent.

I narrowed my eyes suspiciously at the dirty, bearded, vagabond storming past me wearing nothing but boxer shorts. He didn't even have on a pair of shoes. I wondered if he wasn't cold. It seemed cold to me. I looked down at my boots and jacket realizing suddenly I was wearing only underwear under my coat.

What the fuck was happening here. Suddenly terror hit me. I couldn't recall. Where the hell was I? Who was that half naked guy over there mumbling to himself? Who am I? I looked back at the pacing railroad man. Simon would know. He always does, doesn't he?

Master Boyd and I had been missing for two weeks. The entire police force of Wheatly and the surrounding county was out looking for their lost schizophrenic brethren and his psychotic fiancé. We had been off our medication during one of the most severe acute episodes that either of us would ever face to this date.

Our disease had been ravaging our minds unhampered by aid of any kind. Thanks to Master Boyd's powerful delusion that we were being stalked by they, we had been hiding deep in the woods where no one was going to hear our screams for help.

The Queen Mother of Madness had now demented us rapidly into constant misunderstandings, forgetfulness, and pure insanity. We had no water left, no food, nothing for any of our basic needs. We didn't even seem to realize we required these things. From time to time one of us would but it never lasted. Worst of all, we had degraded to a point of not always recognizing who we were as individuals nor each other as lovers and friends.

At different times neither he nor I could even understand our own unit comforts leading to the dangers of exposure to the elements during the cold winter season. We both had stripped down to our skivvies due to problems with seizures which causes bladder release, sweating psychotic fits, and just good old-fashioned delusional process. We both believed that our clothing was shrinking.

It was very clear by this time Master Boyd and I were in real jeopardy of death by exposure, starvation, thirst or even suicide or homicide. We both were experiencing moments of intense symptoms that would cause a desire to end our life and irritation that had already led to violent attacks on the others unit. Adding peril to this desperate situation, both of us also had been engaging in self-injurious behaviors such as head and wrist banging.

Sometimes our fighting each other and ourselves was caused by delusions. At other times it was due to lack of identification of the other's relationship to us. We were covered in cuts, bruises, mild concussions and Master Boyd had broken his collar bone. It is a wonder he had not broken worse. Both of us had lost more than ten pounds and were suffering mild dehydration. Some of the weight loss likely started before our idiot run. To this day, I still wonder how we did not end up dead. This was seriously one fucked up moment in both of our lives.

"Hey, Master. We need water I think. I am thirsty," I yelled at my Master suddenly recalling his identity.

Master Boyd looked back at me wild eyed. "Oh, yeah I am thirsty too. Maybe there is some in the car?" He walked back toward me his face stiff without emotion.

I nodded. "Maybe. Did it rain? If not in the car, maybe in a puddle or something? I am happy to drink anything." I walked toward the black car still parked behind the bushes.

I opened the passenger door while Master Boyd joined me and we hunted the interior and the trunk looking for water, food, anything to calm our very upset stomachs. All we found was a roll of paper towels and a small bag of chips in the trunk. I told Master Boyd he could have the chips since I could not digest them anyway. He ate them ravenously while I continued searching for water around the vehicle.

I sat down on the ground finally giving up. I ran my hand across my forehead feeling the sweat beads. I licked the sweat off my hand while Master Boyd stared at me in a trance. It was then I noticed the ditch. It was just off the side of the road with muddy water rolling down it from a storm that night. I jumped up and ran for it dropping to my knees drinking deeply the silty, dank liquid. Master Boyd saw me tear off and came running after me. He dropped next to me also sticking his face into the foul waters to quench his extreme thirst.

When I was sure I could drink no more I ran back to the camp, leaving my still guzzling Master, to get our water jugs to fill up. For a change I had a forethought to collect some of the drainage before it dried up leaving us both without the required necessity again. When I returned Master Boyd was looking down the road appearing nervous wringing his hands.

"Hurry up Niemand. Fill the water jugs. They could be coming any second. We are exposed. Remember what happened last time. I don't want to have to bust you out of the hospital again. You run too slowly. They catch you every damned time," he said appearing irritated.

I filled up the first jug looking back at him angrily. "What are you talking about you fucking loon? You have never helped me, never. I always rot in those hospitals. You were not there. What the fuck do you even know?" I put the lid on the first jug and grabbed the second filling it as well.

Master Boyd looked at me appearing surprised. "You better start respecting me, Niemand. You can't cuss me like that or call me a liar. You want to find out what happens when you fuck with me?"

I glared at him. "I know what happens, Master. I get pregnant. Stop trying to make children with me. It is never going to happen. I am sterile. Besides, I don't need children. Where would I even put them? I don't have that kind of storage space."

My Master wrung his hands. "Not pregnant yet? I don't get it. I thought we should have kids by now. I remember we had kids. We don't?" He hit his head with the palm of his hand and began to mumble incoherently.

I shook my head. "Good thing we don't. Christ, do you want them to be like us? Monsters. They would be monsters." I got up and began to head back to the camp carrying the jugs while Master Boyd followed me still mumbling to himself.

I sat the jugs by the tent, then got the paper towels and sat down tearing off a sheet. Master Boyd came and sat down cross legged watching me still mumbling under his breath. I took the sheet and tore it into tiny pieces and began to eat them. He stopped mumbling appearing frightened.

"What are you doing? That is not food, Niemand. Stop that." He reached out with his long arms trying to snatch my lunch.

I pulled it where he could not reach it. "Leave me alone. This must do. I am hungry damn it. Master, get your own. There is plenty. This is mine," I growled.

Master Boyd glared while I continued to eat the paper towel glaring back. When I finished the first sheet, I grabbed another one. His eyes narrowed in suspiciousness.

"If you eat too much you will get fat. Then when I fuck you, I won't have to chase you so hard. You'll be easier to catch," he said while grabbing the paper towels pulling off a sheet to eat himself.

I snorted. "I will always be able to outrun you. I don't want you fucking me anymore anyway. You are too rough Master. You need to go away and leave me alone."

Master Boyd swallowed his paper towel bite. "I will fuck you how I like and when I like. You belong to me. God said so. Stop being a bitch. You may be able to make a great dinner, but you are not to speak to me like that. I am getting tired of your insolence."

I began to eat the paper faster. "Shut up. Too much fucking noise? Why are you talking? No one cares. Stop lying to me. You don't know. You don't fucking know shit." I jumped up yelling at him while he sat there staring in shock at my sudden outburst.

I began to pace and mumbled, shouting out while covering my ears. "I don't fucking know. I don't know. Too much noise. Stop pushing me. Get off of me now." The

Looper was taunting me with his hundreds of voices and sounds.

Master Boyd got up and waited till I turned back walking toward him. He reached out and grabbed me hugging me tightly to his chest.

"Let go of me. Don't touch me. Stop touching me. Let go, damn you," I yelled now panicking unable to recognize him again.

He hugged tighter. "Niemand, stop this. You are just upset. Calm down. I have got you, baby. Please calm down." He put his head on my struggling unit trying to calm my psychotic fit.

My head felt like it was going to explode. I reached up to claw at my eyes. I needed to get them out of my sockets so my brain could get some space before my skull blew up.

"Ahhhhhhhhh, help me. God help me, ahhhhhhhh," I screamed while scratching at my face.

Master Boyd pushed me to the ground on my back and grabbed my wrists pulling them off my face. "Stop this. No! You will tear that pretty face. Stop this, Niemand. Look at me. I am the Master. Stop trying to hurt yourself. That is a directive," he yelled while pinning my arms above my head and using his weight to keep me from clawing.

"God help me. Please kill me. I can't. I can't. Make it stop," I screamed out in full schizophrenic panic mode.

Master Boyd looked at me hard. "Stop this now or I will send you to the Snake Pit. Do you hear me? Stop it, that is a directive."

I heard him loud and clear. I stopped screaming and fighting him as fear froze my limbs. He was going to lock me up with the electric machine if I didn't be still. I knew he had the power to do it too. I could still hear the Looper taunting me, so I opened my mouth while tears rolled down my cheeks. I was miserable and all I wanted to do was make it stop. Death seemed like a valid and coveted state to be in at that very moment.

Master Boyd did not let up his weight or hold but sighed in relief. "That is better. Stay with me, baby. I have got you. It will stop. Just hang in there for us. We are together, remember?"

I nodded. "Yes Master, I remember but it hurts. It hurts so bad. Make it stop, lease make it stop," I begged.

He nodded his face frozen in a lack of affect like my own. "I know it hurts. Believe me I know. You can't rip out your eyes or cut off ears remember? We agreed not to do that. Is it Looper? Is he bothering you?"

I nodded. "Yes. Please, my head is going to blow. Make holes in my head so the air can get out. I can't take it anymore," I screamed while starting my struggling anew as the next wave of terror fill me.

My Master felt my half naked unit colliding against his own. He closed his eyes trying to fight the dark urges surging within. Despite his best efforts, he had suddenly become aroused by my screams and flailing. His sex drive kicked into high gear with psychotic lust filling his mind to the point of madness. He could not understand it, this was not his fault nor could he ever have hoped to resist his baser desires. His impulses were unhampered by the rational thinking process of the normal brain.

He began kissing my neck causing me to scream even louder. My desperation further set off his needs to copulate. Master Boyd let go of my arms unable to hold back any longer. He then started wildly tearing off my undergarments. I fought by pounding on his chest and then tried to push him off screaming that he let me go. I grabbed him around the neck trying to choke him demanding he get off my unit.

He easily subdued my arms before I could even apply enough pressure to cut off his airway. Once he had me pinned, he took me without hesitation or reservation nor did he hold back his full strength in his thrust. I screamed and cried begging him to stop hurting me, unable to understand or recognize who he was or even what was happening.

Master Boyd was also off on Mars somewhere while his unit reverted to that of a mindless animal rutting with its mate. Not even after his orgasm did, he return to any kind of sense for some time. He merely held my screaming unit down still coupled panting and mumbling to the voices himself.

NOTE: *While some of the stuff that happened during these sixteen days neither he nor I can recall, the constant* sex is one thing we both remembered. Our mental capacities had degraded to pure simple brain levels by the third or fourth day. After the hard-core symptoms of our disease had set in, he constantly engaged me in carnal congress simply because that is what he was biologically supposed to do when the prospect of mating became available. I can recall it like a dream, as could he, but neither of us could stop ourselves while it was going on. Not that we needed to since we were a mating pair, but at least some understanding of what we were doing would have been nice.

Therefore, what you just read nor the act in the white cell was rape though I did think so until I found out the truth of his illness. When you are psychotic, you really can't figure out what is going on, stop yourself and half the time you don't even recall what did happen at all. Sad but true.

You don't have to believe me. There is a thing called not guilty by reason of insanity. Well, both Master Boyd and I qualify for that damned verdict in many of the attacks. We were both bat shit crazy during nearly all the nasty crap we ever did to each other. Master Boyd never pulled this on anyone else. But then again, no one else was ever stupid enough to date him, now were they?

The need to procreate is not rational, it is natural. The seeking of pleasure is what drives the need for climax. Therefore, despite our deep insanity, this scene was playing out repeatedly during those weeks of our acute cycle. It is this very issue that causes most mental hospitals and psych *wards to separate men and women. If they didn't, mindless intercourse would occur non-stop. When a male and female psychotic schizophrenic are left alone, this is the shit that you can promise will happen.*

It had been ten days since the Boswell dance. Neither Master Boyd nor I had eaten anything of worth since. I had taken to eating grass, and paper. Master Boyd had a single snack size bag of chips and paper as well. Our units were weakening from the constant double burning of calories caused by psychosis. It is a lot of work to be psychotic that is why so many schizophrenics are rail thin when not on their medication. The unit works double time and eating is often forgotten. We were sleeping a lot more often now, unable to keep going at the high rate of speed that our madness kept trying to push us into.

I screamed and cried myself to sleep. When I finally went quiet, Master Boyd also fell into unconsciousness while never moving from his spot of engagement with my unit. The darkness came on while we slept. The cold night woke my Master first when at last he reached a point of extreme discomfort from the near freezing temperature.

"Niemand, where are we?" He woke me up looking around appearing frightened.

I gasped in pain from having been held under his weight for hours "I don't know Master. Please get off me. You are hurting my unit."

Master Boyd looked down realizing he was indeed laying on top me. "Oh Jesus, baby. I am so sorry. Are you hurt? Did I hurt you?" He reached out grabbing my arm to help me sit up.

I shook my head. "I don't think so. I am just stiff and cold. I am hungry Master. We need food." I got up moaning in pain while my circulation returned to my various limbs.

Master Boyd also stood still looking around trying to get his location. "How long have we been on vacation? Do you think it is time to go home yet?"

I looked around too, also lost in my location. "Uhm, a couple of days maybe? I think it has been at least five days. It had been fourteen days. We could spend our last two days off resting up in our bed if you wanted to Master."

He looked at me then started giggling spontaneously without affect. "Okay yeah, that could be nice. I think we should have turkey left over from the dinner at Dennis's Sunday. Do you think it is still good?"

I wrinkled my nose. "I love Carla, Master, but her turkey is dry as hell. Besides, five days is kind of long. I think you left it on the counter long ago too. We had better throw that out. I can make us something else."

Master Boyd nodded. "Yeah, make something else. I think we had better get dressed. It is pretty cold unless you want to fool around?"

I snorted. "Of course I want to fool around, Master. But let's go home and do it there. I hate being cold."

"I need earplugs first. God is bugging me again. Have you seen Bastard? He was supposed to pick up the big rig. I think he got lost. He should have been back by now." Master Boyd walked with me to the tent to get our soiled clothing.

I shook my head. "Use the paper towels over there for your ears, Master. That is what I am going to do. Looper is being a fucking prick. How long do you think we will have to drive to get home? How far is our house from California anyway? I don't even remember how we got here. I must have been pretty sleepy to have slept the entire trip."

Master Boyd put on his shirt while I helped him button it. "Uhm, two thousand miles maybe? Shit, we won't be home for two days, Niemand. I will be late for work. Dennis is gonna be pissed off. God damn I am such a loser," he groaned.

I paused while trying to get my whirling confused thoughts in order. "Just drive faster. Take the backroads and then we won't be late Master. Or maybe we should try taking a plane and send for the car. I think we have enough money for that."

Master Boyd put on his pants with my help. "Uhm, I don't like heights or enclosed places. Let's skip the planes. We will just have to speed and hope we don't get a ticket." I made him sit while helping him put on his boots.

I hurriedly got dressed after locating my bra that Master Boyd had thrown into the bushes during our last psychotic sexual tryst. Master Boyd paced and babbled wringing his hands while waiting on me. I watched him wondering if I

312

should call the cops on the weirdo bum wandering around my camp. I had again failed to recognize my own Master.

Once dressed I began to stomp and twirl dancing to the sound of the Earth's heartbeat while forgetting about the homeless guy that paced around me. Master Boyd saw my now clothed unit and took off for the car to drive us back from California so he could get back to work as a long-haul trucker.

He waited by the car for me, but I didn't follow him. Angrily he returned demanding to know if I was purposely trying to cause him to lose his job. He said I was just like my sister, hateful and pushy.

I stopped dancing and stared at this nut. "Huh? Who the fuck are you? Dude, seriously, get a life. I don't even have a fucking sister. Does your probation officer know you are bothering innocent citizens? I am going to call the cops pal. Beat it."

Master Boyd growled. "God damn it, I am your Master, loon. Stop calling me Dude," he stomped and yelled.

"Master? Huh? Hey, wait, don't you call me a fucking nag, asshole. Why are you bothering me? My husband is gonna show up here any second fellow. He is in the Army. He will kick your ass," I screamed back hoping to scare the homeless guy away with threats from a pretend spouse.

My Master rolled his eyes. "I am your fucking husband, idiot. Christ, you need medication Niemand. You're losing it. God damn, you know what? I think you do have schizophrenia. You are delusional."

I felt anger fill my unit and burn my ears. "Fuck off, asshole. You are the one with schizophrenia, you crazy motherfucker. I am not even named Niemand. I don't know who the fuck that is. My name is Psycho, stupid. I have never seen you in my life, creep. You come near me, I will call the law. You will be sorry." I stood my ground ready to fight this weirdo.

"God damn it. What is everyone yelling about? Why does it have to be so fucking loud all the time. Someone fucking change the channel. Where the hell am I? Help, someone help me. Help," my Master yelled into the air while rubbing his hair appearing very agitated.

I covered my ears. "Shut up. Shut up. Shut the fuck up," I yelled while falling to my knees rocking from the sudden outpouring of voices and laughter all around me.

Master Boyd started giggling while covering his mouth. "No, that is funny. What? Oh, okay." He sat down and began to write numbers into the earth with a stick he picked up while I rocked and cried.

The night raged on as did our complete breakdowns into madness and dementia. Neither of us could get our disorganized thoughts together long enough to get help. This scene replayed repeatedly for the entire ten days since the Thorazine had left our systems. Our initial several days had been much more violent due to detoxification of the heavy sedating antipsychotic medication. By day seven we both had degraded to a level of near profound, completely disabling, psychotic breaks from reality. Likely, the lack of food and basic proper care also played a significant role in our very stark crash right into the abyss of madness.

By sunrise of day fifteen we were barely able to recall our own names. We often couldn't recall where we were, how we got there, or that we could leave and go home. We didn't even remember that there was one.

NOTE: I *had been deeply psychotic for many months already. My symptoms were more severe in expression. That said, I was better equipped to handle them due to my long-term survival without medication and higher level of education about my disease. I was suffering extreme cognitive slippage (memory loss), hallucinations, impulsivity, disorganization of speech/thoughts and repetitive moment disorder. I also had mild inappropriate affect (giggling, crying for no reason).*

Master Boyd had been just entering his acute cycle when he stopped taking the medication. His symptoms were more congruent with the genetic severe expression of the disease with deep frightening delusions (they are out to get us, they are taking his wife away), heavy hallucinations, intermittent cognitive slippage, confabulations (making up wild stories to answer what he couldn't understand), impulsivity, mild repetitive moment disorder, and negative symptoms such as inappropriate behavior and lack of affect.

Even though we both appeared to the normal to be demonstrating the same symptoms, we only shared a few of them. His schizophrenia classified as Paranoid type was a bit different from my own Differentiated type. The easiest way to understand how the same disease can express symptoms that are not the same but look that way is like this: He was more delusional, with less emotional expression, and less hallucinations than me. I was confused to the point of being unable to communicate at times, and much worse hallucinations but less delusional. I believed they were out to get us, but only somewhat and didn't believe he was a trucker. He was a hobo maybe.

Meanwhile back in the world of the real Dennis, Randall and even Linda were starting to give up all hope of finding the two of us alive. Two weeks had passed and no sightings of us had been reported anywhere. Dennis now had to assume that if we were in the mountains or thousands of acres of wooded land around the county, the cold weather coupled with our obvious poor mental health would have ended our time on Earth.

If we were holed up somewhere it was now likely we had killed each other, ourselves or maybe even died of starvation or psychotic induced accidents. House to house searches were not necessary as no one assumed anyone would have taken in two very ill schizophrenics with such strikingly violent symptoms.

Daily checks of statewide jails and hospitals had not produced any John or Jane Does matching our descriptions. With heavy hearts, the police officers had begun to include all reported homicides, suicides and accident reports from around the state in their daily data searches. Still, not even a glimpse of the wayward cop and his loony girlfriend could be found.

I was told privately, much later, that the old bull cop Dennis was beside himself with worry and grief. He thought his adopted son and favored town pet had bitten the dust. He blamed himself for not locking the two of us up the second he realized Master Boyd was very ill. He also thought he may have set off my Master into this crazy run by demanding that he end his relationship with his equally disturbed fiancé. Linda told me he would get off shift and spend hours searching wooded areas, parks and staking out Master Boyd's house hoping we would return.

Dennis was correct about one assumption. His belief that our flight was caused by his continued demands that Master Boyd end his engagement. My Master had become convinced that Dennis would keep him from having what God had promised him. This errored belief strengthened an already impressively tough delusion in his cracked mind.

Eventually, Master Boyd viewed Dennis as 'they' hell bent to take away his girl. When Dennis took him off work on sick leave and threatened the Snake Pit, Master Boyd flipped out believing his worst nightmares were coming true. He and I ended up taking a vacation neither of us meant to book thanks to a series of misunderstandings and deepening psychotic process.

QUICK NOTE: I *didn't believe in his 'they' delusion at first, but thanks to my own stresses (Sheryl, job) I was easily swayed by my Master into falling for his explanation of what was wrong in our world. I quickly fell under the spell of his delusion thanks to my own already present significant schizophrenic delusion that the world was sick not me. Once off our medications, the rest was just a disaster waiting to happen and it did happen very quickly.*

As my brother the sun rose on the fifteenth day of our mental health vacation it found my Master wandering around the tent in a circle babbling to Bastard about numbers. I had danced till late in the night but was now rocking and crying once again with my back to a tree. I had been hallucinating that the shadows were trying to kill me since early that morning. I was too tired to run anymore. I gave up. In my terror I had put my back to a tree ready to be devoured by some imaginary monster that had come to finally drag me off to hell.

Master Boyd walked over to my weeping and rocking unit. "Niemand, I want to go home now. Can we go home? Do you know if seven days has passed yet? I have been counting the days, but God won't let me think straight. I keep losing my place. Has it been a week?" He kept his eyes to the ground while he rubbed his hair appearing agitated.

"I don't know Master. Please make them stop. I want to go home too, but I can't find the map from California. Oh God we are lost. They are coming. Can you hear them," I wailed out my eyes open in terror at the sounds of heavy footsteps.

My Master groaned. "I can't hear shit over God and Bastard arguing constantly. I can't even hear my own fucking thoughts. What the fuck is wrong with me. Someone please tell me if it has been seven days? Anyone, tell me? Work damn you. Why won't my brain work." He hit his mangled forehead with his hand several times.

I gasped then wailed. "Kill me. Kill me, Master. I don't want to do this anymore. Please, mercy." I fell over prostrating at his feet sobbing completely giving up.

I screamed out from the shock as he reached down lifting me back to my feet. "Niemand, I don't want to live anymore either. Let's go back to the house and get my gun. It will hurt less if we just put a bullet in our heads. I am ready if you are. We can go together baby. No more voices, no more pain. Just think we can make it stop." My Master looked deep into my wet goopy eyes.

I nodded. "Yes Master. Let's go get the gun. That will make it go away. Thank you for your mercy." We kissed deeply while ignoring the horrid shocking sensations of our units being touched.

He pulled me along behind him running for the black car. We both knew we had to hurry before we forgot our mission like we tended to do. I got into the passenger's seat while he got behind the wheel. My Master pulled onto the dirt road headed for the back roads that led to our house. We both were ready to end our battle with schizophrenia once and for all. If we couldn't win, then we decided we would not be taken alive, not this time.

We popped out of the little-known dirt road again on the road in front of the house. The black car sped along with two very weary psychotics sitting quietly ready to take our boat trip to the Summerlands at last. When…

Master Boyd saw him first. Parked in our driveway was Dennis's squad car. We saw the bull cop standing on the porch talking to Linda. They looked up and Linda pointed while both took off running for their vehicle.

"Fuck, they are here. They saw us Niemand. Hold on honey. I will outrun them. They won't separate us. I won't let them," he screamed out while making a wild U-turn in the middle of the road.

I gasped. "Christ, Master, they are coming. Hurry, they are going to catch us. Oh no, help, someone help," I yelled as the squad car started speeding after us blue lights rolling.

Master Boyd pushed the peddle to the metal. We sped wildly down the dirt road sometimes in the ditches sometimes on the road throwing dust for miles. I sat backward in my seat watching in horror as Dennis kept pace with our car bobbing and weaving. The siren was wailing making me grab my ears.

"Make it stop. Make it stop. Too much noise," I screamed out.

My Master winced. "Christ, shut them up. Why are they screaming? They will hear us. Niemand please, my ears. Stop the noise," he yelled out.

I turned and looked at him frightened while he rushed down the old dirt road like the madman he was/is. I reached onto the floor grabbing gum wrappers then reached over forcing the discarded silver papers into his ear holes while he yelled out from the shock of my touch.

"God damn it. Shit fuck, where the hell are we. We have to hide now," he spit out yelling in anger.

I wailed out. "They are going to take us to the Snake Pit, Master. No more. Please no more. Drive off the mountain. Drive into a tree. I can't go back. Please kill us now with mercy."

Master Boyd moaned, "Okay, okay, I will go to the mountain. Calm down, baby. I can get away. I know the way. Hold on, just hold on."

He sped up even faster then turned so suddenly I was thrown into the door as the black car fishtailed but made the sudden left into a small single laned dirt road. The car continued to slip and slide, but my Master turned the wheel in the opposite direction with each slip of the tires managing to keep us from sliding off into the muddy ditches or the trees. I watched as Dennis tried to follow but his fishtail sent him into the ditch.

To my excitement his vehicle tires were spinning but he wasn't getting back onto the road. "Master, they are stuck. We got away. WE GOT AWAY," I yelled laughing and covering my mouth as the high centered squad car shrunk in the distance.

Master Boyd looked at me appearing stern. "Sit down, Niemand. We must get off this road now. I must make another turn then double back or they will call others to wait at the exit of this one. They know where this road lets out."

I whimpered. "We have to go back? Go back by they? But Master, they are stuck, they will catch us."

He shook his head. "No, they are stuck in the mud. We will just drive past them and grab another road this one only comes out in one place. We will get boxed in. Sit down. We have to hurry before they get unstuck."

I did as he commanded while he made another wild U turn in the center of the road and tromped his gas pedal headed back toward, gulp, they. We were flying like the wind when the stalled squad car came back into our view. Master Boyd sped even faster as we approached Dennis and Linda who had now gotten out and were looking over the situation. Dennis had his CB in his hand when he saw Linda pointing at our rapid approach looking stunned.

The officer threw himself into our path causing Master Boyd to turn his wheel with cat-like reflexes. We immediately hit the ditch to miss killing the well-meaning officer. Unlike his own car, we were going so fast we bounced back onto the road without getting stuck. Dennis stood in the road looking as Master Boyd turned right wildly fishtailing down the dirt road never hitting a brake or looking back.

I sat in the seat stunned. "Uhm Master, that looked like Dennis. We almost just killed Dennis. Master?" My heart was beating like a hummingbird's wings in my chest.

He shook his head. "No, that was not Dennis. It was they. They are fucking with our heads. They are going to get us if we allow them to fool us. Stop being crazy. You know that was not Dennis. Why would he be chasing us? Think Niemand, huh? Why would he be chasing us," he yelled out angrily.

I shook my head. "You are right Master. He wouldn't be. They must have stolen his skin suit. I think they killed Dennis Master. Oh my God, they killed Dennis." I began to cry feeling despaired that our dear friend was no more.

Master Boyd stole a glance at me. "It is okay baby. When we get to the other side Dennis will be there too now. See it will all work out. Stop crying. Think, do you really want to live in a world full of they? They will put us on drugs and lock us up in cells or put us into chains. I won't go back. I want to be with you. I want to be with Dennis. We will go to the mountain and drive off. That is easy. It won't even hurt much."

I sniffed looking down at the floorboard understanding he was right. "You are right Master. I have people on the other side too. We can all be happy on the other side. I don't care if it hurts. Just hurry please. The pain in my head is starting again. I don't want to go back, don't let me go back."

He reached out and took my left hand then kissed his engagement ring. "When we get to the other side, I will take you dancing right in front of Dennis. We will be married and have kids too. Then no more, wait, something is wrong. Was it always like this?" He looked at me while slowing down our wild pace down the dirt road.

I shook my head. "I don't know what you mean Master. Can you make it stop?"

Master Boyd nodded then pulled over to the side of the road. "I seem to remember, I am not sure what is wrong. I need to walk for a minute to clear my head." He got out of the car pacing alongside it wringing his hands talking to himself and hitting his temples.

In a few moments he jumped back into the car appearing upset. "They are coming again. We have to get out of here." He tore off down the road at high speed.

I looked behind us to see blue and red flashes in the distance. "They know where we are Master. Can we outrun them?"

He shook his head. "Not forever. We will have to hide out till dark. Then we can sneak out to the mountain. I know a place where they won't see the car. We can stay there till the coast is clear. It's going to be okay. I won't let them get you. Protect and defend remember?" He reached out and stroked my cheek.

I nodded. "I love you Master. Thank you for not letting they get us. I will always take care of you too. Protect and defend." I grabbed his hand and kissed his now infected knuckles while he winced from the pain and shock of my touch.

I coughed deeply feeling very weak. My Master was coughing too. His color was paler than usual and both of us were dizzy as he kept the police far enough behind for his exit into a small thickly wooded logging trail. It was not a real road, but more of a rutted foot path barely big enough for his small black car to fit into. He drove down the trail parking behind a large group of bushes. We got out of the car and peeked around the brush watching several squad cars with sirens and rolling lights speed past us.

My Master let out his breath. "They didn't see us. We are safe for now. No one remembers this place anymore. Just relax baby. Let's sleep for a while. I am feeling bad." He rubbed his hair appearing to be panting.

I coughed deeply "My head hurts Master, and my chest too. I think I caught the flu." I watched him sit down using the car to brace his back.

He nodded. "Me too. It feels like the flu. We should have washed our hands after hanging out with the Boswells. Shady said some of the kids had the flu." He appeared sleepy.

I walked over and sat in his lap both of us flinching at the shock. "Yeah, we have it then. Sucks to be us. We need to just rest a while. Then drive off the mountain. At least we won't have the flu anymore." I chuckled at that.

Master Boyd nodded. "If I survive the crash, finish me off, that is a directive." He closed his eyes already drifting off.

I snuggled into his chest and fell deep into sleep wondering how he expected me to finish him without a weapon. We didn't know it but both of us were indeed sick with the flu virus. It was quickly infecting our lungs becoming a respiratory ailment of significance with every passing hour.

Due to the many days of depravation and exposure to the elements, a usual nasty bug was slowing us down substantially now. This common ailment, along with low sugar issues, caused both of us to sleep the rest of the day and the night without stirring. It was midday of the sixteenth day of our vacation before either of us would finally awaken from our illness driven sleep. Master Boyd and I came back to consciousness fevered, disoriented, and coughing like elderly smokers.

"God damn, I think I may die Niemand," coughed out Master Boyd while moaning as he tried to stand up holding on to the car from dizziness.

I was staggering around myself nodding. "Jesus, I hope I do die Master. What the fuck is going on. Where are we?"

He shook his head. "Beats the shit out of me. I think Vegas? I didn't mean to stop so long. We will never make it back home in time for my shift now. Fuck, we didn't even get two states closer." He was rubbing his head while coughing hard.

I nodded. "Well I think getting off the road was smart Master. You were driving like a maniac. We could have killed someone. Never drive tired. It gets people killed. Hey, can we stop at a restaurant and get some pancakes? I am starving." I coughed then stretched and yawned.

My Master looked up at me. "Yeah, that sounds good. Some eggs too, maybe even some coffee? I could use some coffee. Come here and let me kiss you good morning beautiful."

I snorted. "Beautiful? Huh? Wow, you must have a fever Master." I walked over while he hugged me tightly kissing my mouth until we both started coughing again.

Master Boyd looked at me without affect. "Sorry baby, that was not very romantic. Hey, let's get into the back seat and have some fun before heading back home. I mean we have this private room and all."

I looked at him in surprise. "What Master, even sick? You are as tough as you look. Though I think the beard needs to go. Okay, I am happy to provide special services, but I get a double stack of pancakes for my performance."

He kissed me deeply. "Equal service for equal service, my love. I promise to shave the second we are home. I kind of personally thought it made me look more like a mountain man. Oh well. You don't like it, off it goes. Let me show you my etchings. They are just over here in the back seat. Oh, and you have to eat all the pancakes on your plate this time, that is a directive." He took my hand opening the back door allowing me to go inside first.

We took our time making love slow and lovingly. I am very glad that we did take that last trip to the back seat no matter the desperation surrounding that amazing sexual session with Master Boyd. This last time ever being with him medication free is likely why I recall it as well as I do despite his and my very deep psychotic state and failing physical health.

The orgasms we shared that afternoon were beautiful and worth remembering. Sadly, from that moment on our disease would prevent us from ever knowing each other this way, the way a normal does. The numbing effects of our cursed anti-psychotic medication was just about to come down right on our shattered heads. In all our time together for the next six years we never had it this perfect in carnal congress again. Not that we didn't give it our all many times in the future to try to beat it.

We had no concept of the trouble we were in or had caused. We believed we were traveling back from our vacation in California. We had convinced each other we were merely enjoying one final tryst unencumbered by the bonds of employment, responsibility or adulting. We were just two lovers at a rest stop, engaging in the one thing that can make life worth living: love infused intimacy, albeit ours was psychotic as hell.

Once we were completely satisfied from our couplings, he and I ate another paper towel in sheer desperation and hunger. We seemed to recall that no traveling was to be done until my father the darkness covered us with his inky blanket.

Neither of us could recall why that restriction existed, only that it did. We sat in the back seat giggling, wringing out hands and mumbling to each other about things that likely made no sense. Our flu bugs had caused a great fatigue.

Usually, we would have been too irritable to dare to even try to talk to each other for very long without it coming to blows. With our violent psychology dampened by failing physical difficulty the mood was peaceful for a change. But our discussions were very weird and disorganized.

At last my brother went to bed in his western house. The night made the shadows kings of the living realm once more. Master Boyd kissed me deeply trying to ignore the growing shocking sensations overcoming both of us. Our irritation was starting to overshoot even our weakened units from the hours of being unable to walk off our constant inner restlessness.

"Time to go home, Niemand. I have really enjoyed this vacation. I never knew it could be so wonderful. I am only sorry we didn't start doing these trips sooner. We will do this every year from now on, that is a directive." He pulled up my hand kissing his ring.

I giggled. "As you wish Master, but next time I am doing the driving. You are a wildman behind the wheel. You know all my friends said you should join a Nascar team."

Master Boyd nodded. "Well, driving is all I have ever done since I was a kid. It is always Boyd, you drive, wait,

Dennis says that. He always makes me drive. I thought I was a long-haul trucker?" He appeared suddenly confused.

I got out of the back seat to get back into the front, "You are the best long-haul trucker but you will be an unemployed one if we don't get back home soon." Did you say Bastard parked the truck at the house?"

Master Boyd got in taking the wheel once more. "Uhm, yeah that is what he told me. Bastard lies all the time. Can't trust the fool as far as you can throw him. He was telling me the other day, uhm, wait, do you hear that?" He strained in the dark cab appearing to be listening to something.

I rolled my eyes. "I hear the fucking radio waves like I always do. I hear fucking Looper, You have to be more specific Master."

He shook his head. "It sounds like thunder. It likely is a storm. I can even hear it over God. Maybe God is pissed off?" He started the car shrugging as we backed up then headed back for the main road.

I listened hard. "No, wait I hear it too. A baby crying? A panther? What the fuck is that noise?" I looked at my Master confused as he took a right turn headed back for his house.

We both heard the whining sound in the distance, both unsure of the origin. We shot each other discombobulated looks and shrugged as my Master cruised lazily along the dirt road. I looked out the window at the dark forest on each side trying to see if maybe someone left a baby in the forest. What the hell was that noise?

We went around a hairpin curve and Master Boyd slammed on the brakes nearly sending us both through the windshield. Up ahead were the bright lights of two cars rushing toward us. On the tops were the flashing red and blue colors that they used. Sirens were blaring. My Master swore loudly while making a wild U turn then speeding off almost flying off the curve we had just cleared as he scrambled to stay ahead of the squad cars.

Once back on the straight stretch he stomped the gas speeding without restraint making a rush to outrun our pursuers. I sat there silent in horrific panic attack hell while Master Boyd swore and cursed They under his breath and promised not to let them get us. I looked behind and saw more police cars than before. I couldn't breathe from the terror pouring into my chest.

"Master, there are more of them," I said almost in a whisper.

Master Boyd growled. "Fuck, just fuck. Okay, let me think. There has to be another way out of this God damned box," he yelled out.

It was then we both saw headlights with rolling lights now coming at us just ahead. We were now sandwiched between they behind and they in front. We were screwed. We watched in horror as they in front pulled side by side blocking the road almost half a mile ahead. They behind us did the same formation.

"Son of a bitch. Will you look at that horse shit. What the fuck are they doing," he screamed out angrily.

"Catching us Master. They got us. It is over. Electricity city here we come. Fuck!" I felt the tears start to fill my eyes.

Master Boyd looked at me in horror. "Oh hell no. Not that again. Fuck this shit." He turned his wheel harshly to make another U turn but this time we were going far too fast.

The black car began to spin wildly fishtailing all over the dirt road finally flying off the road smacking right into a tree on my side crushing the door shut and throwing me into Master Boyd's lap. He tried hitting the gas to head back for the road but the car was hooked onto the trees and a barbed wire fence held us still while our pursuers surrounded us parking and getting out of the squad cars hiding behind them like shields.

I felt Master Boyd trembling while the police shined spotlights into our eyes. We heard Dennis's voice over a loudspeaker demanding we come out with our hands on our heads.

"Boyd, come on out nice and slow. We are not here to hurt either of you. Listen to me boy, we don't want any trouble. We are here to help you both. Come out peacefully and we can work this all out," said Dennis sounding stern but kind.

I looked at my terrified Master who was looking back at my own frightened face still practically in his lap from the crash. "Okay, we are going to have to run for it. Are you hurt? Can you run?"

I shook my head. "Dennis will catch me, Master, he always does. No way I can outrun him. They are going to get us." I began to cry.

Master Boyd reached out and stroked my face lovingly. "I can distract them while you make a getaway. Then you can come and bust me out, that is a directive."

I really began to cry at that. "No, I am coming with you Master. They get you then they get me too. I won't leave you. Not now, not ever." I grabbed his wrist while both of us were shaking like newborn colts from the inner terror at the thought of being taken back to the Snake Pit and the ECT machines.

Master Boyd kissed my left hand then smiled. "I do love you Niemand. Okay stay behind me. I will fight them off long as I can. We may be taken down but not without taking a few to hell with us."

I nodded "I am with you Master. I love you too, see you in the Summerlands." I braced my nerves really believing that we were about to be shot down and sent to our graves by the police just as I always expected to be.

The cops had started to fan out moving around the disabled car to block any possible escape exits even if we did try to run. I noticed they were careful to keep trees or hide with a hill on one side. I realized they thought we were armed. That made electrical fright jump down my spine as

Master Boyd opened the door to get out. I wanted to warn him they were likely going to shoot but I said nothing as he got out reached in and pulled me along with him. I winced the second we were both in the open waiting for the bullets to start to rip through my chest.

Master Boyd reached over pulling me to the car while he shielded me with his own unit. He was wringing his hands and looking at the ground but stood his fiercely against the army of police. I shuddered trying to peek around his tall frame to see when I could expect the gunfire to begin.

Dennis shined the bright spotlight on us causing both of us to groan and cover our faces blinded by its horrid glare.

"Boyd, put your hands on your head, son. Niemand, you too. Come out where we can see you sweetheart. No one wants to hurt either of you, but you have to do what I tell you," said Dennis through the speaker.

"Leave us alone. We didn't do anything. You are not taking her from me. I will not let you," yelled back my Master while he pushed me back behind him when I tried to do as Dennis told me to do.

Dennis put down the loudspeaker and nodded to Randall who apparently was riding with him. The two old bulls started to walk toward us slowly each flanking our right and left side. My Master was starting to tremble harshly. I could tell he was about to lose it if those officers tried to get to me.

They both stopped within talking without shouting distance. Dennis looked at Boyd appearing very concerned.

"Boyd, you have to let us take you for some help, son. You and Niemand are very sick. Don't you want to feel better? You are both off your medications, your thin, and I bet hungry as hell. Boyd listen to me. No one is going to hurt either of you but you have to put your hands on your head and be still okay?"

Master Boyd shook his head wildly. "I am not stupid, Dennis. You are going to take us to the Snake Pit. You want to take Niemand away too. You know what, start shooting motherfucker because I will die before I let you take her and hurt her anymore. No more. You hear me. You always hurt her. I won't let you hurt her anymore."

The two old bulls back up a step or two as Master Boyd began to growl and glare at them agitated and ready to fight. I wrapped my arms around his waist and hugged his back feeling him flinch at my touch. No one had ever tried to make the normals stop hurting me before until my Master Boyd. He was ready to die to keep them from sending me back to the Pit, and him too. I felt the tears pouring down my face from the love, no matter how insanely delusional it may have been, he was showing me that night. For real he was ready to die to protect and defend me.

Dennis must have determined my Master was not armed at this point. I saw him nod at Randall then the two old bulls came charging at me and Master Boyd. My Master pulled forward blocking them from grabbing me not realizing it was him they had come to take him down. He was the one everyone feared would be an issue to capture, not the slight, frail female Niemand. He was the Dominant of us, so it made perfect sense if you think about it.

Randall caught a punch to the face while Dennis jumped my Master from behind. I immediately jumped on Dennis hitting him with all I had screaming for him to let us alone. Linda came running to pull me off Dennis. I struggled with all I had but more than two weeks of starvation, sickness, and constant fighting made me weaker than a kitten. All I could do is kick out and yell while Linda pushed me to the ground and rapidly cuffed my unit.

Master Boyd heard my distress calls and went ballistic blowing his very last gasket. In pure Hebephrenic hell he let out a blood curdling howl and hit Dennis in the sternum knocking the cop to his knees while Randall managed to deliver a blow to Master Boyd's knees knocking him to the ground.

In seconds, the old bull jumped on my Master's back yelling for help while he struggled to keep the cursing, yelling, fighting schizophrenic pinned to the ground. Dennis had recovered though he was still gasping for air and red faced. He ran over and jumped on Master Boyd's back too. It took both of the tough old cops to finally get my Master's wrists into the cuffs.

Despite the cuffs, my Master was still giving them much difficulty as was I. Linda was having to use all her strength to drag me to her squad car while I yelled out leave Boyd alone repeatedly.

Both old cops were dragging my Master to Dennis's squad car while he kicked at them dug his feet into the ground and cursed yelling out incoherently at them with the only word that made any sense being 'Niemand.'

He and I were stuffed into squad cars that were parked side by side. Dennis shut the door on my Master as Linda shut me into her own rolling cage. I watched my Master who was glaring at Dennis then looking at me with panic. I felt forlorn that despite our best efforts they had gotten us.

I truly believed my Master and I were going to be sent away to the Snake Pit where our brains would be fried out for daring to be schizophrenics. When that was done, Dennis would make sure Master Boyd and I were spilt up forever and I would never get to see him again. It wasn't fair. We had not done anything wrong. We took a vacation and we even had permission to be off work. Why were they doing this to us?

Somehow my Master read my mind. He looked at me with tears as he began to kick the door of the squad car wildly. Dennis was speaking to his officers and to Randall catching his breath when the loud pounding began. I too began to beat on the door with my legs trying to kick the door open or the front seat out. Dennis walked over to our doors demanding we settle down or else.

Master Boyd started to scream out my name upon hearing or else and bashed his head into the glass with as much strength as he could muster. Blood went splattering all over the door as he bashed it repeatedly. He then kicked the doors basically went 'berserker' in the back seat alternating between the two loud, and self-injuring behaviors.

My Master's and my own sudden violent behaviors scared Dennis. He called in the ambulance to bring sedative immediately. Blood was everywhere in both squad cars as the psychotic pair tried in desperation to get back to each other. Master Boyd was wailing and kicking wildly completely gone from his last bit of sense. I still understood what was happening but the cries of my Master in pain sent me into a frantic need to defend him from his pain.

The ambulance arrived at the scene quickly. Linda hauled me out of her backseat kicking, fighting and cursing but she easily got me to the ground on my face pinning me with her knee. She yelled at me to settle down.

I ignored her but watched, as best as I could, while Dennis and Randall hauled my raging Master from the back of the squad car. His face was unrecognizable from all the blood. He was wailing and mad with anger. It took both old bulls to get him thrown to the ground despite his unit being cuffed and near helpless.

The emergency crew worked rapidly injecting a powerful sedative into my Master's backside while Dennis and Randall held him down with all the strength they had. He let out guttural screams while they got the medication into him at last.

Within only moments my Master's voice went silent and his unit went limp. They had knocked him out. The crew then brought out the stretcher as Randall and Dennis rolled the now unconscious Master Boyd to his back. The crew began working on closing the gashes on his forehead while one of them loaded another syringe coming for me.

I stopped fighting while the man in the blue scrub shirt approached me. I no longer cared what they did to me. My Master was hurt and they were going to separate us forever. I had only just begun to start to adore him and now he would be gone. Just like all the others, no one ever keeps my collar for long.

I felt sadness fill me at the thought of losing Master Boyd. He had been the best Master I had ever known and he loved me. Worst of all, I suddenly discovered I loved him too. I wanted to stay with him for good, but I knew our sickness and the world would never allow such an unholy union to exist. Hell, they could barely stand us as individuals. As partners, they had hunted us down like animals and were sending us to prison cells for daring to try to pair.

I felt the needle going into my backside while Linda tried to sooth me by saying Master Boyd was going to be okay. My last memory of that horrible night before the sedative took me to the nothingness was seeing Dennis watching the emergency team work on Master Boyd and me with a look of pity and sadness.

Ah well that didn't end the way we hoped it would. We intended to end this wild ride by testing our power to fly. Luckily, old Dennis was a clever old bird. He got the nutballs wrapped up tighter than leftover Thanksgiving turkey. All the King's horses and All the King's men can put the Humpty Dumpty and his insane fiancé back together again.

**To be continued in "A Harbor with a View"
of the "27 Masters" series**

About the Author: Alexandria May Ausman

Alexandria May Ausman in her 16th year was diagnosed with Schizophrenia. She was quickly abandoned by her foster parents. While still only a teen, she was forced to battle this devastating illness alone.

Alexandria has struggled with lack of a support system, numerous psychotic episodes, exploitation, homelessness, and an uncaring mental health system.

Alexandria raised two healthy children. After obtaining her bachelor's degree in psychology she worked as a child abuse investigator and became a diagnostic psychologist while acquiring her Master's in psychology. Alexandria never forgot the experience of 'slipping through the cracks.' Her life's goal is to help people suffering abuse and/or mental illness have access to necessary services. By accident, she became a model of 'gothic attire' and the World Goth Queen.

She began writing a fictionalized account of her life experiences after a catastrophic return of psychotic symptoms. Today, Alexandria is retired, and homebound due to crippling symptoms of schizophrenia. She currently lives in Tallahassee, Florida, with her loving husband and loyal support dogs.

www.ingramcontent.com/pod-product-compliance
Lightning Source LLC
Chambersburg PA
CBHW071518260626
4717OCB0000ZB/421